"A first novel that is so arresting, so immediately involving you want to start talking up a storm about it."
—*Publishers Weekly*

"The Bexleys' lives of unquiet desperation are grotesquely comic; Vincent Shepherd's season of discontent is quietly moving. Bausch is a writer worth watching and, more important, worth reading."
—*Library Journal*

"[An] excellently crafted first novel."
—*The Critic*

"[Bausch writes] simply and sensitively about the power of love's example to transform pain, suffering, and isolation into occasions for rebirth and redemption."
—*America*

VOICES OF THE SOUTH

REAL PRESENCE

REAL
PRESENCE

RICHARD BAUSCH

LOUISIANA STATE UNIVERSITY PRESS
BATON ROUGE

Library of Congress Cataloging-in-Publication Data
Bausch, Richard, 1945–
    Real presence / Richard Bausch.
        p.   cm.
    ISBN 0-8071-2477-X (alk. paper)
    I. Title.
    PS3552.A846R39   1999
    813'.54—dc21
                                                    99-15679
                                                    CIP

The paper in this book meets the guidelines for permanence and durabil-
ity of the Committee on Production Guidelines for Book Longevity of the
Council on Library Resources. ∞

Of course,
for Karen, with all my love

. . . you know, Hopkins once said that if he couldn't believe in the real presence of Christ in the consecrated host, he'd be an atheist the very next day. . . .

James Dickey, in conversation

🙟🙟🙟

Then, in prayer, all sweetness becomes a sickness. Consolation repels you. . . . All light brings pain to the mind by its insufficiency. Your will no longer seems able to dare to act. The slightest movement reminds it of its uselessness, and it dies of shame. . . . And yet, strangely, it is in this helplessness that we come upon the beginning of joy. We discover that as long as we stand still, the pain is not so bad, and there is even a certain peace, a certain strength, a certain companionship that makes itself present to us when we are beaten down . . . hoping for hope.

Thomas Merton, "Inward Destitution,"
New Seeds of Contemplation

🙟🙟🙟

Oh, former renter,
I know it all, all . . .
Down to the very cold
you felt.

Issa

I

1

Demera had never grown much beyond its Civil War bound-
aries. It was, and presumably always would be, an outpost of
sorts for the patchwork quilt of farm and forest one saw from
the Shenandoahs, looking west. There had been no reason for
it to expand because there were no coal mines nor any indus-
try, and farms held most of the land. A man named Townsend—or a business concern called Townsend & Son: no one
had ever seen anybody named Townsend—had bought a
large tract of woodland not far from Demera, and had put
signs up everywhere about what was forthcoming in terms
of development. The signs were on telephone poles, fence
posts, bridge abutments, trees, like the marks of sudden mi-
gration or a trail left by a passing army. Three years ago
ground had been broken for a man-made lake, and thousands
of leaflets went out all over Virginia advertising vacation
lots—cottages, camp grounds, swimming, golf: hunting and
fishing in the heart of the Old Dominion. The people of
Demera, many of them having never been more than twenty
miles away in their lives, were unenthusiastic. Some were
even a little frightened: growth meant change, and change
is, of course, universally disconcerting. But there had been
nothing, finally, to fear. There was a hiatus in progress on the

lake these two years, and the signs were fading on the trees, curled and peeling away.

Townsend & Son still maintained an office above the drugstore on Jefferson Street; two middle-aged women, whose dispirited and lackluster appearance seemed to exemplify the company's failing health, went there to open it up every morning, and to sit behind desks cluttered with crossword puzzles, newspapers, and paperback books, ostensibly busy with the firm's mail and with whatever else the firm could find for them to do. Occasionally they had the unhappy task of sending away some poor soul who had come to Demera thinking there were vacation cottages to be bought, or work to be had—Townsend & Son having also advertised a plenitude of positions available for self-starters in a new, expanding company. The last one they had turned away—this was in late July or early August, neither could remember exactly—was a man whose children, five of them, had followed him into the office. He had walked in without knocking, the children crowding around him, had stepped to the first woman's desk, reached into the sweat-stained pocket of his shirt, and brought out one of the Townsend ads.

"When do I begin," he said. "I'll do anything you got for me to do."

"I'm sorry," the first woman said. "I don't understand."

"I come here to work," the man said, putting the ad down on top of her crossword puzzle and pinning it there with a finger. "Right there. I'm a self-starter. When do I start?"

"I'm afraid," the second woman said, rising from a folded crown of waxed paper in which a limp cheese sandwich lay, "you are out of luck, sir."

"Who're you?" the man asked. "Where's this Townsend?"

"I'm Martha and this is Louise. We're the only ones here, sir."

"I'm terribly sorry," Louise said, "but the company stopped

hiring quite a while ago." She took the ad up and handed it back to the man, then she walked around her desk and tickled the chin of the smallest child. Every one of the children needed a bath, and they all looked cowed, afraid, slightly driven, sleepless. They were very quiet, standing in a row behind their father.

"We've had to send a few others away," Martha was saying, "like yourself. But there just isn't a thing going now."

"It says right here," the man said, his voice rising, almost quavering with exasperation and disappointment and puzzlement. He held the ad out. "Right here. 'Self-starters, immediate openings. Construction work.'"

"We're terribly sorry." The two women had spoken almost in unison.

There was a long pause, and then the man said, "Yeah. You're sorry." His lips barely moved. "I got a pregnant woman out there—" He stopped; his hand went out and settled, as though of its own accord, on the tousled head of one of a pair of boys whose features just now revealed themselves to both women as identical.

"Why, you have twins," Louise said.

"Yeah."

The two little boys looked at each other and smiled.

"Oh, this is just something," said Martha. "You have a beautiful family, sir." She thought for a moment. "There must be something—"

"How about your Father McManus?" Louise said. "Out at Saint Jude's?"

"No," said Martha. "He was transferred. Remember? There's a new man out there, an older man. An odd one. I mean he's odd—he wouldn't—nothing against my church, now, but he's just not very friendly."

"Look," the man said—his voice was angry—"I don't want no damn church charity."

"Of course not," Louise said. "It's just that Father Mc-Manus got on so well with everybody—he might've been able to find something for you."

The man turned, as though to leave, but then he crumpled the ad up with a furious motion and threw it down. Slowly his head went back, and he looked at the ceiling. Martha touched the edge of the waxed paper on her desk, as though to re-assure herself of its presence. Then she looked at Louise. "You don't suppose Torgeson—"

"Yes!" Louise said. "Why didn't I think of him? Try Torgeson. The Torgeson Farm. It's right next to Saint Jude's." She told him how to get there, hurrying the words because he had already started for the door.

"Please," said one of the children—a girl perhaps twelve or thirteen—"Daddy, I don't want to look anymore."

"Torgeson has a lot of money," Louise said. "See him. He might have something for you to do."

"Aw, Christ," the man said. He was speaking to the children. "Come on."

They all filed out. The two women went to the air conditioner in the window, stood leaning over its cool column of air, and looked out at the hot street below. A gray, rust-spotted truck was parked along the curb, its wooden railed bed piled high with belongings, over which and under which the children crawled, arranging themselves until they seemed part of the tangled configuration. The truck coughed and sputtered as though exhausted by the heat, and the two women watched with a species of proprietary fear as it tottered away from the curb, gathering momentum. It faltered into a slow turn, stopped, backed up, came past them in the other direction, toward the Torgeson place and St. Jude's. Through the shifting sun and shadow of the windshield and in part of the open side-window, they caught the shape of a woman, a pink rumpled summer dress, lean hands folded on a generous lap.

As the truck went on up the street, a thin arm went out of that window, and a piece of cloth—it was a handkerchief, no doubt—waved from the closed fingers of the hand like a small white flag.

"Imagine," Louise said, "coming here with everything you own and with your children and your husband—imagine that, pregnant to boot, in this heat—only to be disappointed?"

They were to think about this moment during the months ahead—especially as events concerning these people who had so briefly walked into their lives unfolded and became known in the town—a town that had always prided itself on its order and its peace and its tolerance of the frailty of its individual citizens; but which, somehow, had never properly understood misfortune, failure, tragedy. For Demera was a quiet place, a place where nothing serious ever seemed to happen; people lived out their lives quietly and died quietly, and grieved the dead just as quietly. And if there were people in the hills who spoke a dialect no one could understand, who grew beards as long as wedding trains, making their whiskey in little homemade stills and chancing an occasional foray into Demera to undersell the A.B.C. store, Demera accepted these people as one might accept an embarrassing cousin or an uninvited guest at a barbecue, accepted them as it did the eccentricities of the new pastor of St. Jude's or the vulgarity of Torgeson's talk of the money he had made and how he might spend it all; accepted even the idea that two generations of children had grown up believing a witch lived above the feed store, the rain-gray, boarded place that had been closed as long as just about anyone could remember, and whose occupant everyone knew merely as Miss Jane, a harmless old woman, lover of cats, possessor of a fortune many believed to be greater than the new fortune Torgeson had made. Talk about these things never became general: people discussed them in their various separate associations, and then only to the point of remarking that it was nobody's business. Demera considered itself fortunate enough to be so insulated, so set in its ways, like an old bachelor whose orderly habits had not changed, even if everything around him had changed. The world could have its passions and its ambitions and its will, but Demera would boast proudly that there hadn't been a murder in the town for more than thirty-five years.

2

One morning in October the odd old man who had replaced the pastor of St. Jude's awoke to a phone call. This was not particularly unusual, since he had awakened to the telephone many times in his almost forty years as a priest. The caller was Mrs. Jane Trevinos, and it was the seventh time she had called him that week, each time at an ungodly hour. The experience now was the same: he awoke with what had become the familiar sense of weightlessness, as though he might drift up to a corner of the ceiling and dissolve, and then he heard the faint metallic bleat of the telephone, the little bell turned down as low as it was possible to turn it. It rang and he lay listening to it, trying not to think about his heartbeat. (His heartbeat was the first thing he thought about every morning—or rather, every waking—as if his brief sleep had been a cold dip into death.) When he lifted his hand to wipe the sweat from above his lips, the hand dropped to his face, heavy and numb. Each ring of the phone made him wince, as if each were a blow, something that narrowly missed him. He opened his eyes, saw that the window was dark; the lamp on the night table still burned.

Gradually he worked himself to a sitting position, the blanket bunched at his hips. His pocket breviary lay under the blanket—its pages creased, pleated, torn. He had fallen asleep reading, probably just at the moment he had convinced himself that he would not sleep. Now he set the breviary on the night table, where the telephone still rang; in one motion he was standing, the cold wood waking the soles of his feet. He knelt, picked up the receiver, put his face an inch from the clock, the receiver held over his chest.

Four thirty.

"Four thirty," he said into the receiver.

"I know," said Mrs. Trevinos. "I can't sleep."

"All right," he said. "What is it this time?"

"I had to talk to somebody, Father."

"Well, talk then."

"I can't sleep."

"Yes, yes, yes, yes."

"My heart. It's my heart now."

He sat back against the bed and let his head fall forward, breathed a long sigh. Out of the moon-colored nail of each toe on his exposed left foot a face looked at him; he tucked the foot under the blanket.

"Father, I have tempted a man."

"Mrs. Trevinos—"

"You don't believe me?"

"No, I don't."

She began to cry.

"Mrs. Trevinos, please, let me explain."

"Okay for you," she mumbled. "You're a priest. You don't have to worry."

"Mrs. Trevinos, I only meant that you imagine you have sinned. Try to remember you're in the hands of a merciful God."

"I did tempt him, Father—I'm so low, right now. If it's my heart—if I go with a heart attack, I won't be in a state of grace."

"Mrs. Trevinos, I said a *merciful* God."

"You can't imagine, Father, how I feel."

"Yes," he said, "I think I can."

"Will you come see me today?"

"I'll see what—"

She interrupted. "You never go anywhere, do you?"

"All right."

"People need help all over—"

"All right, Mrs. Trevinos. I'll stop in on you today."

He heard the line snap shut. Echoes and reverberations licked toward him, pulses that traveled along his nerves like a signal. He put the receiver down and as if trying to follow a complicated set of instructions, got to his feet, the blanket like a towel around his middle.

"Foolish old woman," he muttered. "Witch."

She might tempt a man with money; she might tempt him to mayhem.

He threw the blanket off and padded into the bathroom, looked at himself in the mirror. He had never been a vain man, had never even felt comfortable looking at himself— his face was angular and ruddy, and faintly suggested some ferreting creature to him: a raccoon, perhaps: the droop of the eyes, the shadows under them. The chin was pointed, a little weak; the nose stretched over the plane of the lower lip. And the eyes . . . well, the eyes always just looked back at him, simple and opaque, neither blue nor green, never very moist, never bright, short-lashed and surrounded by a net of wrinkles and the small filaments of the broken capillaries that lined his forehead as well. At the center of the forehead was a vein, a forked bulge in the skin, that stretched from just above the eyes to the hairline, or what would have been the hairline twenty years ago. It was not an ugly face, but it was one that others often mistook: to the eye of the layman it was monkish, pleasant, almost sweet. Now he checked its coloring, examined the vein in his forehead. He believed he could tell, by the color of this face, whether the vein was receiving its proper amount of oxygen-rich blood, all valves and ventricles contracting and expanding as they should.

The habit of each morning. An unhappy way to begin the day.

Now he shaved. The tap water was ice cold, and always took a long time to warm up. Age had not brought him patience as it had not brought him wisdom or peace, so he lathered himself and brought the cold razor across his face too quickly. Two cuts on his neck let out two trickles of blood that ran together and were diluted in the stream of water and shaving cream. He daubed the blood with a piece of toilet paper and tore the paper into tiny triangular pieces, which he wet with his tongue and stuck to the cuts. Then he bathed and dressed, and walked the floor of his room with the breviary, reading his Office aloud.

Monsignor Vincent Shepherd had been a heart attack victim. Now he walked rooms at night. He watched hour upon hour of television—Sundays in the fall, the NFL, doubleheaders, AFC, NFC; old movies at all hours, the night-owl shows; sitcom reruns all day when he could steal the time: Andy Griffith playing a guitar on the quietest porch in America, with Barney and Thelma Lou and Aunt Bea, while Opie slumbered peacefully in the house; oh, that peace, that order of a television summer day circa 1958. There were no heart attacks in that town: even the drunk had his own key to the jail. Television had become a matter of ultimate concern at those hours, the stolen hours for the old priest, who was afraid of groups, noise, conflict, confusion—the needs of others. He could not even read his Office anymore without an excruciating and exhausting effort. The monsignor had once been pastor of St. Paul's in New York City. Now he was visiting pastor of St. Jude's, whose parish numbers, on the busiest Sunday morning, would not fill the left side of the nave of St. Paul's.

Four miles south of Demera, tucked between two rolling fields, with the Shenandoahs as a long, low, blue background, St. Jude's offered the peace and tranquillity of a postcard. Except that there were real people in the hills and on the farms and in the uniformly white clapboard houses, people who had troubles—the thousand minor aches of existence. And there were people like Mrs. Trevinos, who was so scrupulous, so certain of her own damnation, that she lived like a horrified passenger in a diving airliner. Everybody wanted to talk to the priest: everybody knew the phone number and the address. Everybody wanted to give him dinner, or doughnuts, or tea, or talk, talk, talk. A regular group of Sunday goers, devoted, troubled; weekly confessionals who thought he remembered from one confession to the next their crimes, their little moments of passion or fear or doubt or envy, their eatings and drinkings. Oh, what a mistake it had been to come here: he missed the anonymity of St. Paul's.

Shortly after full light, he fixed himself some warm tea.

The kitchen was a mess. He had once prided himself on his ability to keep a house, cook a meal, but now the sink, full of gray water and pads of grease, offered a mute accusation. Having armed himself for the call on Mrs. Trevinos (he would tell her definitely not to call him at odd hours anymore), he gathered all of his determination to himself and aimed it at the sink. He rolled one sleeve up, reached into the water, and pulled the plug. Particles of food floated against his wrist, and something adhered to the back of his hand. He shuddered, reaching for a towel. The water sucked backward out of the sink and pushed an odor up. Turning the taps on full, hot and cold, he stood there watching the flayed end of a noodle come away from the porcelain and dance in the water.

Then he took a break and drank the tea.

It was very quiet: just his breathing and sipping, the cup clinking against the saucer when he put it down, the occasional knock of the wind. It was going to be a bright, blustery day, like a loud argument, and the leaves would fly out of the turning trees.

His eyes grew heavy from the hot steam that rose from the cup. The tea upset his stomach, so he got up, poured the remainder of it down the drain, put the plug back, and began to wash the dishes, squirting detergent on each one and rinsing it under the running tap. And here, at the door, a shape through the frost-flowers on the window, was his neighbor, Torgeson.

"Torgeson," the monsignor said, holding the door open an inch.

"Hello—let me in?"

"What do you want—it's early."

Torgeson made his way inside anyway. He wore a blue flannel shirt, jeans, cowboy boots. A new style of dress every time the monsignor saw him: a brown conservative suit on one day and a fringed Indian jacket on another. Torgeson, newly wealthy, had not decided who he wanted to be yet, now that he had the money to be anyone he wanted. It was not enough to be rich, he said. He had recently bought the property adjacent to the church, had operated, for a while, a stable of four tired horses for people from nearby towns to come in and ride for three dollars an hour, and now he was interested in opening a tree farm. Or rather, that was in his talk. As was his friendship with the departed pastor. Father McManus, he said, would do almost anything for him, they were such good friends, even though it was through Torgeson's wife, who had been a fanatically devout woman, that he had met the priest. The wife had gone back to California to continue to be devout, and had taken the two children with her. But this was not Torgeson's problem (he had learned to accept things that were beyond his control): the problem, as he had told the monsignor often enough for the monsignor to recite the whole thing like a litany, was the Bexleys. Torgeson had taken them on this past summer, had let them live in an old abandoned house on the northern end of his property, and now he needed the house. He had already rented the house to another party. The Bexleys had not worked out, but Torgeson was not hardhearted; the Bexley woman was pregnant, it was wrong to just throw them out in the cold—couldn't the monsignor allow them to use the social hall of St. Jude's as a temporary shelter until they could find something better? It was indeed an awkward situation, but he needed the house, and what was he to do?

No, no, no. It was out of the question.

Just for a few days. Seven people. The Bexleys and their five children. The man had quit a job in Richmond and come all the way to Demera, thinking he would have work at Townsend & Son. The monsignor must imagine how sad that was.

No. It was utterly out of the question—the monsignor was in no condition.

Torgeson was persistent, had come back twice in the past week. Father McManus would've done it for him; there were ways that Torgeson could be helpful to the parish.

Father McManus was a younger man—no. No. The Bexleys could go somewhere else; in any case they would have to, and the monsignor was very sorry, but that must be the end of the discussion.

"You look industrious this morning," Torgeson said now. He sat at the table and smiled, as though nothing could be more entertaining than to watch the dishes being done. The monsignor stood at the sink; he had turned the water back to a trickle. He wanted to be sure he could hear what the other man said, believing that clear understanding was the surest way to be rid of him quickly. But Torgeson said no more. For an unnerving time he just sat there watching the dishes get done.

"You've not come to ask about the social hall again," the monsignor said.

"Not a chance," said Torgeson. "Just visiting—although I do have news."

"About the—"

"The Bexleys, yes."

"I hadn't forgotten the name."

"You just didn't want to bring it up."

"Precisely," the monsignor said.

"Well, it is about the Bexleys."

"If it's all the same to you, I'd rather not discuss your tenant problem this morning."

"Would you mind if I had a little tea?"

The priest put the fire on under the teapot. Then he washed the cup he had used earlier, dried it, set it on the counter. Through the window above the sink he saw three fat birds sitting on the wire that led from the social hall to the telephone poles along the road; they huddled there while the wire swayed in the wind.

"I hope I'm not putting you to any trouble," Torgeson said.

"You've been some trouble to me, Torgeson—but making tea is no trouble."

"You know, you do need a housekeeper."

"I neither need, nor can I support one."

"The church wouldn't pay for it? Parish accounts wouldn't cover it?"

"That's not the point." The monsignor put the cup on a saucer, and the box of tea bags in front of his visitor. "The point is that *I* can't have anything of the sort."

"I know, you haven't been well," said Torgeson.

"No, as a matter of fact, I've been relatively well lately—I don't want to ruin it. I asked for this assignment because I wanted a little peace. This parish seemed to offer the right combination of priestly activity and—peace. It's been a deadly disappointment, but it's manageable, anyway."

"You don't look well, to tell you the truth."

The monsignor did not respond to this. The water boiled. He carried the pot over and filled Torgeson's cup.

"You look tired."

"I was on the phone with Mrs. Trevinos at four thirty this morning."

Torgeson made a clucking sound with his lips, dipping a tea bag into the steaming cup.

"I promised her I'd go see her today."

"You know," Torgeson said, "my news has to do with her."

"I thought you said it was about the Bexleys."

"Them too."

Presently Torgeson said, "You're not going to have any tea?"

"Go on and tell me your news."

"Well, I've decided to evict them."

"You have. I thought you already *had*." The monsignor sat down across from his guest, watched him take the first sip of tea.

"Well, I'd been looking for a way out," said Torgeson, swallowing. "Of course I had no real grounds except that I wanted the house for other—for another tenant. A preferred tenant. It's stupid, and it was stupid of me to take the Bexleys on in the first place. I just didn't think he'd stay around anywhere very long—he didn't like what he was doing for me. But they did clean the place up and make it livable."

"So now you're going to evict them. And you have grounds?"

"Now I do—you bet."

"What about the wife—the pregnant—" Torgeson sipped his tea. "—the children."

"You know, I could pay you to let them use the hall," said Torgeson.

"Torgeson, I just can't do it. I would not have the physical strength to handle a family that large."

"Well, see, that's the sad thing—I've already fired him. And they're to be out of the house by tomorrow morning. I know it's tough but I had to, finally. You knew I'd been paying him to be a sort of chauffeur for Mrs. Trevinos, trying to soften her up about selling me some of her land. She never had a driver's license, you know—all she has is land."

"I'm afraid I know more than I want to about Mrs. Trevinos."

"I can imagine—but anyway I found out this week that Bexley hadn't been showing up at her place. He'd been taking my car every Friday and driving it all over the countryside instead of going to her—she hadn't seen him in four weeks."

The monsignor watched him plumb one ear with the little finger as though he had just surfaced from a deep dive in water. Torgeson's hair was soft as a baby's, thin, uncut, sandy.

"I am worried about his wife, though. She's what I'd call a—well, a strapped woman. Pregnant, tied up with a man like that."

"A man like that."

"Bexley's a no-account—he's ignorant, older than she is. He has no real skill at anything and he's bitter on top of everything else. He's like a volcano waiting to erupt."

"And you want me, in my—with my—feeling the way I do. . . . You want me to take them on."

The other man made a motion in the air as if he were writing on an invisible chalkboard. "Touché." Then he sipped his tea, swallowed noisily, smiled. "It would—as I've said—only have been temporary."

"I assume they haven't found a place—or that *you* haven't found one for them," said the monsignor, "since you're the one who's been looking."

"Nobody wants them."

After a moment Torgeson said, "Listen—I'm curious. What would your bishop have to say about your—your position here."

"I don't understand what you mean. My bishop knows what my position is here."

"No, I mean about the Bexleys."

"Why don't you say what you have to say." The monsignor did not try to suppress the anger in his voice.

"No offense—but isn't it a sort of priestly obligation—you know, charity?"

"I was unaware that as a priest I was required to shoulder the burden of responsibility for an entire community."

"Now don't be angry, Father. I was just curious."

"I fulfill my obligations as a priest, Mr. Torgeson."

"I never said you didn't."

When Torgeson had finished the tea, the monsignor took the cup and saucer away, hoping to make a point of not offering more. But his visitor, apparently, didn't notice. "You have to understand, I'm alone here. I can't do anything to jeopar-

dize my ability to serve the members of the congregation, such
as it is."

"I concede, Father."

"And what about *your* sense of charity?" the monsignor
asked.

"You're perfectly right," said Torgeson. "I never should've
mentioned charity."

"Are you being ironical now?"

"Not in the least."

"Why don't you just give them the money you've offered
to give me?"

Torgeson had gotten out of the chair and held a napkin up
to his nose. He blew, wiped the wings of his nostrils, frowned.
"If I gave money to everybody who needed it, I wouldn't
have any. Besides, there's something wrong with that—to
just hand it over. Especially to a man like Bexley."

"Well then—there you are," the monsignor said.

3

Sleep hunted him when he needed to stay awake. It pursued
and ambushed him. Listening to confessions, he missed
whole paragraphs; saying mass, he bent down over the Host
and felt a rush of sea sounds in his ears, as if his head were
a conch shell; the altar before him slid toward shapelessness.
Driving the old Ford, he woke up with the tires cracking
gravel and the trunks of trees veering at him. But when he
lay down, undressed, a groom of sleep, prepared for it, it fled,
and Vincent Shepherd became the pursuer, the wooer—he
dressed, as if to go out, lying across the bed in his shoes,

wrapped in an overcoat or a sweater, trying to trick sleep into believing he was not on the hunt: sometimes this worked, sometimes nothing worked. He lay reading, perhaps, having given up, waiting for sunrise like Caligula, who wandered Rome while the city slept and searched the sky for the beginning of dawn. And at last, when it couldn't matter, couldn't give the rest he needed, sleep came, and left him the next day feeling as if he had been drugged, beaten, hauled a great distance through mud. Immediately sleep became the pursuer again.

On the way into town to call on Mrs. Trevinos he struck the guardrail along the road. It was just a bump, because he had been slowing down behind a pickup truck, a gray, rusting, dented old thing with one wobbly tire. The truck had gone on and Vincent had drifted slowly into the guardrail. The sudden bump shocked him, and for a bad moment he sat quite still, waiting for the signs of heart attack—as always upon waking, even from such a brief sleep, his nerves were all lit up; they generated heat along the bones of his face. Outside there was bright sun and wind, trees shaking and dropping leaves brilliant and colorful as tropical birds. The mountains looked like smoldering mounds along the curve of the road ahead. He got out of the car and paced a little, calming down, breathing deeply, thinking of the quiet afternoon he would spend alone, after he had paid his call on Mrs. Trevinos.

All the important buildings of Demera were on Highway Sixteen, bunched together: the banks, the stores, the funeral home (Walker & Edison, Est. 1889), and one or two small houses with neat squared lawns and white trellises on the porches, where a few clerks took care of the town's business. There were sidewalks on either side of the street, and young maples, evenly spaced, decorous enough, but looking like skinny afterthoughts, since the buildings were so clearly of another century. The monsignor parked the Ford on the corner of Sixteen and the first crossing street, which was Byrd Avenue. The feed store, closed and boarded long ago, was across the street, facing west. There were curtains in the windows above the store, and an unhealthy-looking stairway led up the side of the building to a private entrance. On his infrequent forays into town Vincent had always marked the closed curtains, the abandoned look of the place. Now he climbed the stairs—loose, rusting nails; splinters of peeling paint; gouges; a rickety shaking of each board. Above him a cat walked the pitted rail, pacing with a quickness and certainty that was as incongruous as the fact that anyone lived in such a place. The cat walked down, past him, its tail up as if to gauge the wind.

Mrs. Trevinos opened the door. She wore a housecoat, sleeves rolled up. Her hair was a bungle, a mistake, a gray profusion of wires. The housecoat was like a cloth bell, out of the bottom edge of which, like two blue things peeking out, her feet jutted, full of veins.

"You," she said.

"I said I'd call on you today—"

"I didn't think you'd come." A cat with pink eyes and a bluish tongue looked at him from behind the housecoat.

He followed her through a large, cluttered room to a hallway. He saw prints on the walls, a threadbare sofa, a few books folded and torn in a metal stand. Then the hallway, which was dim, musty, papered with calendars going back decades, all of them with pictures—of men in hunting gear, or of wild birds and blue skies, or of deer standing on outcroppings of rock overlooking bodies of water. The hallway let out into the kitchen, where five or six cats paced and sat. One primed its claws on a piece of canvas Mrs. Trevinos had hung from the counter on a nail. Another cat cleaned itself on the counter, which was cluttered with bread crumbs.

Cabbage boiled on the stove, a cloud of steam rising and forming a thick nimbus around the room light. It was a dim room, the color of rainy windows.

"Wasn't expecting company," she said, offering him a chair at the table. He took it. The table was relatively clean: one dish across from him with food calcifying on it and two crushed cigarettes in the food. His nostrils stung.

"I was mad at you this morning, Father," she said. She stood at the stove, speaking over her shoulder. She rattled a metal spoon in the pot, her hand made invisible by the rising steam. Her arms were bulbous, the elbows large and white as softballs.

"I know I had promised to come see you, Mrs. Trevinos— but I had promised others too. And there just hasn't been time."

"You never go out—everybody talks about it."

"I've not been . . . feeling well."

"Father McManus was always going around to the houses— even the non-Catholics got to know him. Like that Torgeson that just got divorced."

"Yes, I know him."

She stepped away from the stove, into some slippers that lay near the radiator. Then she came to the table, the slippers brushing like a broom across the floor. The cats parted in front of her.

"You want a cigarette?"

"No, thank you."

"Something to eat?"

"Perhaps a glass of water."

"What did you come for if you're not going to eat?"

"I'm not very hungry, really."

She lighted a cigarette.

"You asked me to come, Mrs. Trevinos."

"I didn't think you would."

In a moment she said through smoke, "That Father Mc-Manus used to come around all the time, just to talk, or eat. He never minded when I called him."

"Well," said the monsignor, "I try not to mind, but—"

She interrupted him. "He was good. He gave good sermons."

"Yes."

"I like a priest that gives good sermons."

"Yes—I haven't—"

"That's easy to listen to, and believes what he says."

The monsignor kept his silence at this. It was true that he had never been what Father McManus had so clearly shown himself to be during his last mass at St. Jude's, at which Vincent had been introduced as the visiting pastor, the replacement: the younger man was a spellbinder, no doubt about it—a master at the art of the pause and the slowly rising inflection. The monsignor had never been able to bring himself to such artifice, though when he was young, he may have lurched toward it once or twice. His voice simply wouldn't permit it: he was birdlike, high-pitched, unresonant, halting. These days, in this tiny parish with these incommunicative people—these people whose ignorance of the ways of the church reminded him of his mother (who had talked about the saints as though they were big, stupid children she knew how to get around, about God as if he were a celestial bell-hop at her beck and call for a thing so small as a second heart in a bridge game; who had died bitterly cursing over and over, all the disappointments and hatreds of her life surfacing like some dead thing thrown up out of a river in a flood)—these days he was nervous and shaky during the homily; he held his hands low because they trembled, or he continually wiped his forehead with a handkerchief sour and starchy with his sweat. The alb, the surplice, his underwear, clung to him, full of static electricity; his teeth throbbed, were knocked loose, it seemed, by every word. The parishioners, mostly farmers—leather-faced, with eyes permanently squinting as if into some perpetual sun—or workers in some way connected to the farms (machinery salesmen, truck drivers, foremen, wives) yawned, looked out the windows, traded recognitions of each other and their children. And the monsignor, woefully ill-fitted to his task, talked, downhearted, through it all.

Now Mrs. Trevinos said, "I didn't mean anything about you, Father."

"That's quite all right," said Vincent.

"But I miss Father McManus."

"That's natural."

The old woman got to her feet, walked to the stove again, stirred the cabbage. "Father McManus went to Rome," she said. "Do you suppose he'll see the Pope?"

"He may."

She kept her back to him, stirring. "He won't be in the Vatican, though." She bent over to touch the head of one of the cats—a small, striped one that ignored her utterly. "There, Charlie, good little cat. Good cat. Come to see Mom-Mom?"

"You have a lot of cats," said Vincent.

"Used to have nineteen of them—when George was alive and we lived in the big house. Only have five now." She sighed, returned to the table, and crushed her cigarette out in the hardened food on the plate. "Can't keep more than that."

"How long—uh—how long have you been alone?"

"I told you that before."

Vincent said nothing.

"Past twenty years now. George was just sixty-one. He never had any warning. An active man like that. Made all his money himself, you know. When he was a kid, he didn't have a thing—nothing."

"You lived in the big house?"

"He already owned that when I met him—we married late. I was thirty-three and he was forty-five. He kept these rooms above the feed store so he could have some privacy when he wanted it—he was a very private man, George was. He'd come here and spend the weekends sometimes, he was so used to being alone, you see, when we married. When he died I just—well, I moved in here. Too much room up at the house. I stay here most of the time."

Two of the cats began a skirmish by the sink. She quieted them, cooing at them as though they were her children. She could never have been an attractive woman—her features were too bulky, too cumbersome to quite fit the oval of her face, which was eyebrowless and coarse, like a man's face, perhaps—yet her voice was pleasing, warm, almost sensuous, as she spoke to the cats. She called them by name: Charlie and Eddie and Bob and Billy. Human names, male names. The cats ignored her.

"Ever own cats?" she asked, stirring the cabbage again.

"No," said Vincent.

"George hated them—but he let me have them. No, that's not right. He hated cats, but he loved kittens. That's why I could have them. He was always a pushover for the kittens."

"Mr. Torgeson tells me you had a chauffeur for a while."

She made no answer.

"Must've been nice."

"No, it was not *nice*." Mrs. Trevinos put the metal spoon down hard, turned, reached for her pack of cigarettes, found it empty, crushed it, and let it fall on the counter. "It was not one bit nice. Did he tell you I thought it was nice?"

"No—he—"

"The nerve of him to say anything about it."

"Well," said the monsignor, "he's fired the man, if that's any consolation."

"Did you come here to talk to me about that?"

"I came here because I said I would when you called me at four thirty this morning."

"I didn't look at the time, Father. I had to talk to somebody."

There was a completely unsatisfying moment of silence, during which the priest began to summon up the words to excuse himself and leave her there. She had found another pack of cigarettes, had lighted one and now stood glaring at him from the center of the floor, under the room light. The radiator made a little whispering sound and then clanked once.

"You're going to tell me not to call you anymore," she said at last.

"Not at all."

"I miss Father McManus."

"Yes, well, as I said before, that's natural. I *am* here, though."

She squinted at him. The curve of her scalp was visible through the wild blue-gray tangles of her hair. "I'm sorry, Father. I'm seventy-six years old and I haven't got anybody. I got a son in New York who has a boyfriend."

"I don't have any family at all," Vincent said, "so I know how you feel."

She walked in a tight circle about the room, not looking at him now. "Don't talk about yourself—what does that matter to me? I need you to be a priest—give me something to go on. You come in here and all you want to talk about is how many cats I have."

The monsignor cleared his throat, and his voice came weakly.

"Perhaps I shouldn't have come, then."

"Listen to me," she went on. "That's all I want. I want you to listen to me when I call because I'm trying to tell you something. I've been crawling around in this body for more than seventy years, and nobody listens to me. You were very rude to me this morning."

"I certainly meant—there was no rudeness intended. Would I have come here if I'd meant to be rude?" Now he was angry. He tried to swallow, as though he could gulp it all down before it came forth in a stream of bitter words.

"I tempted that man." She had stopped before him. "That Bexley. I tried to get him to do something to me."

The monsignor drew himself up, thinking to rise. The odor of the cabbage, or his thwarted anger, had begun to nauseate him a little. The steam tumbled downward from the ceiling, and he thought he could feel it on his face. "Do you," he said as evenly as he could, "wish to ask absolution for it?"

"No," she said, moving back to the table. "I don't want to do anything now. I don't even want to eat." She leaned over and turned the gas off under the cabbage. "You don't want to eat?"

"I'm sorry," he muttered. "Perhaps a glass of water—"

"Let me tell you about George. George was a one-of-a-kind. He never bothered me if I didn't feel like it and I never bothered him and we had a good marriage. A good marriage. He did the cooking, the washing, the cleaning—just like we had a maid. But he never liked people in the house, and he did it all himself. I was a woman of leisure, rich; I had everything. But I wasn't happy. I've never been happy, as my son could tell you if he was here. 'Be happy,' he says to me when I call him. 'I'm happy, Mama, you be happy.' Be happy. Like you could decide about it. I wasn't happy because I wanted a baby and couldn't have one, then I had the baby and George didn't want it, and didn't want people in the house, but let me tell you, no matter what else I thought about George, or how it hurt me, I loved him. I loved him, Father, because he took me and I'd never figured I was much worth the taking.

But I hated him when he started on me about the baby. I guess I hated the baby too, because of what had happened to us. And then it just all settled that way. He stayed here all the time, and the baby was growing up—we almost never saw George. To this day that boy doesn't know what his father was like. And the day George died, my son acted like he'd been set free, like he'd won a contest or something. 'I don't care,' he said to me, 'I don't care and I'm glad. I'm happy.' He was twelve years old. And as soon as he was old enough, he left me alone and went to New York and took up with this—friend. Friend. That boy will be forty years old next month and he's been living with the same man since he first left home. Imagine that. That's all just what happened. And through it all I kept telling myself, God had a reason, God had a reason. But I hated and I hated and I still hate, and I can't see any way out of it and no matter how many times I confess it, it's still there."

Vincent had folded his hands on the table, had tried merely to listen, had almost succeeded, though phrases of leave-taking swam through his mind. The result was that when she stopped, he had nothing at hand to say or do. He watched her put out the second cigarette and light a third. She sat down wearily across from him.

"And then here's this man Torgeson sent me—this Bexley with his five kids and his pregnant wife. He didn't fool me. There's violence in him. I saw it right away, like I saw it in George. Both of them loners, carrying it around. All coiled up inside and ready to hit. George got rid of his by hunting. Hunted all the time, every season."

"So you tempted him. Is that what's bothering you— bothered you—this morning? Are you bothered by that . . . ?" Now he really wanted to know.

"Hell," she said impatiently. "Everything. Can't you under-

stand? Everything." Then, after a long drag on the cigarette,
she said, "I'm fighting despair. Do you understand now?"

"Yes, I do," he answered, and he believed he did understand
that.

"Do you really understand everything?"

"As much as I can," said Vincent, "given what you've
told me." He was aware of the priestly tone in his voice and
cleared his throat again. "I still can't help but feel you're being
too harsh on yourself."

"No," she said, crushing the third cigarette out. "You
don't get it. And I can't find a way to tell you."

"You wanted this man to—have relations with you. Isn't
that it?"

"No—forget it." She sat staring at the table, and something happened to her face; one eye drooped a little, the lips
tightened. The monsignor thought he saw his mother. He
wanted to ask for water again, but the old woman had gone
into herself, watching her own fingers twirl the fur of yet
another cat, which had leapt up onto her lap, and gave off a
purring loud as the idling of an engine.

"I must go," he said. "I have to get back. . . ."

She said nothing.

"I hope you'll forgive me." He went into the hall, toward
the living room and the door. At the door he turned, looked
back at the watery rectangle at the end of the hall. A cat
wandered toward him, its sleek shadow on the linoleum like
another cat.

"Good-bye," he said. Oh, but what had he wanted to tell
her? He walked a little ways back. "Mrs. Trevinos?"

"I hear you," came from the kitchen.

He took a breath. "Could you—"

"I won't call you anymore, if that's what you want."

Clairvoyance.

"I'm sorry," he said. "It's just that I've been having a little trouble going to sleep."

Silence.

"I'm up late all the time," he said.

"I said I wouldn't call you anymore," said Mrs. Trevinos. "Now leave me be, will you?"

He let himself out, shut the door quietly, sneaking away. He saw a man coming up the stairs, looking back over one shoulder as though anxious about being followed. The man had black, grease-combed hair. When he was almost to Vincent, he looked up. "You scared me."

"Sorry," said Vincent.

"Who're you, anyway?"

The monsignor told him.

"You scared me, old man."

"You didn't see me." Vincent went down, carefully stepping by him. He thought the man seemed queerly agitated; the priest looked back at him. "Are you waiting for someone?"

"No."

"Is something wrong?"

"Nothing I know of."

"You aren't the son, are you . . . ? Who are you?"

"I'm nobody you'd know—friend of the old lady's." The man turned, went on up the stairs.

"You wouldn't be Bexley, would you?" the priest asked.

The man did not respond.

Vincent walked to the Ford in the wind. Paper and dust swirled in little funnels in the street. When he turned to look back, he saw the man watching him. He got into the car, conscious of being watched, but when he looked again, the man was peering through the window in the door, hands up to his face to shut out light.

4

His dreams, since the heart attack, were generally frightening. The morning after his visit with Mrs. Trevinos, he was awakened by a dream of her shape, her face and trunk at the top of a white whorl, like a soul. He had no idea what it meant, nor did he want to know. It was not yet light out. He sat in the easy chair in his living room—or rather, Father McManus's living room, the largest room in the house. A crushed velvet sofa, two hardback chairs (walnut, polished, and forbidding), the easy chair, and the television. The front door was blocked by a floor-to-ceiling bookcase crowded with magazines and paperback books; just the frame of the door was visible, but it was enough to give him the sense of a closed passage, and so he never looked at it without feeling barricaded in. The explanation for the blocked door was simple: The front stoop had fallen apart and the flagstone walk had long ago been buried by wild grass and running mud; beyond the broken stoop, on a small wild-grown knoll, was a cemetery more than a hundred years old. He did not mind the barricade. Especially this morning. The room was warm, comfortable, fairly neat (he had worked on it the night before), and quiet. He fell asleep with his head back on the soft cushion and his finger keeping his place in the book, the words of matins bumping through his mind like figures groping for each other in the dark. When he came to, it was light out, and the book was clamped on his finger like a metal trap; the circulation was cut off, and the bone ached.

It was past nine o'clock in the morning.

He shaved quickly, without cutting himself this time, changed into a sweater and slacks, and walked over to the church to try to pray. The air outside was cold and clean and the lines of the world looked sharper, clearer. There was no wind, the sky empty but for a few clothlike strips of cirrus over the mountains. It was the kind of morning he had always loved: brisk and sweet-smelling, with the promise of snow and woodsmoke and burning leaves. The idea buoyed him up as he crossed to the church, which was made of white clapboard and looked, in this autumnal air, newly washed.

The church, the social hall, and the rectory were set like the points of a triangle around an area of macadam and crabgrass no larger than a baseball diamond. Highway Sixteen ran along the northern side, and beyond the highway—all around, really—were farms, fields of bluegrass, scrub pine and oak. To the west were miles of corn, row upon row upon row. At night yellow windows shone at the end of the corn, far off, fragile as tissue laid on the dark, and separated by it; they made him think how land must look from the sea. The land to the east, Torgeson's property, bounded by a strip-log fence, was overgrown with knife grass and timothy. Torgeson did not know what he wanted to grow. The old priest smiled, thinking of Torgeson, and he smiled all the way to the Communion rail in the church, walking through falling sunlight. He knelt, gazed at his own shadow on the polished floor before the altar. Then he cast his eyes up at the tabernacle as though he might speak aloud to it.

The altar, set behind the plain wooden table that was the church's surrender to modernism, always faintly depressed him. It was carved marble, gleaming as if from centuries of polishing. Far too ornate for a church of this size—St. Jude's was really no more than a chapel—the altar had become for Vincent an emblem of misplaced grandeur, abandoned tradition, lost beauty. Above the altar was a wooden crucifix, a wooden Christ with square, unsuffering eyes—eyes slightly out of line, browless, dispassionate, almost deranged—an athletic Christ whose cross was only an afterthought, an addendum, a necessary but meaningless prop. There was no historical moment of that suffering anymore, no idea of the spiritual value of a suffering Christ, a wounded God. It was as if Christ had never really suffered and died, but had only had the Last Supper, with twelve smiling men of social commitment and three folk guitarists, and then knocked the stone away from the tomb. The cross was gone—or rather, it had become a throne. And the religion whose mystery and pageantry had been the monsignor's life was now a sort of half-baked, neo-Protestant celebration that refused to *look*, that searched out an idea of God only for the reassurance that the search would mean an uncomplicated life, a life free of doubt, question, fear. His parishioners talked about God as if they had found him under a stone, talked about salvation as if there were no uncertainty in it, as if they didn't have to do anything once they had made their minds up that they were saved.

Here was the church, his church, stumbling through the twentieth century; and it had lurched away from him, had left him quite alone in the shadow of itself, like the shadow of a ruin.

Now men and women who were supposed to understand the mystical separation of the spirit from the world had become obsessed with life spans, surest sign of the belief in the ultimate victory of death—an extra minute here, an added year there, everyone saving himself for that last pull, that last inch . . . and Vincent—Vincent had become infected with a form of the same disease, holding on, worrying excessively about himself, his heart, his poor, tired spirit. Yet, fearful as he was of a second heart attack, he was not exactly afraid of dying: in fact, sometimes, he longed to die, wanted some final answer to his trouble. "Do you understand," he had said to someone (who? A confessor? Father McManus? No, Grayson. Father Grayson of the simple smile and the round eyes, eyes so round, they looked drawn by some unkind caricaturist. The monsignor had found, upon his release from the hospital, that he could not bring himself to do most of the things required of him as a pastor, and so he had spent a year on retreat, at a monastery in eastern California, where priests went to heal themselves of the numberless shocks of life. Poor Grayson had, in his age, developed a sad kleptomania: he had been caught stealing a pair of black lace panties from a department store in Point Royal—it was the mention of Point Royal, in fact, that had given the monsignor the idea of seeking assignment in Virginia, where he hoped he might find the pre-heart attack version of himself—Father Grayson, caught once, had confessed to other thefts, and now could no longer say his own name or utter one word of the Paternoster. Father Grayson, to whom Vincent had spoken as if speaking to an icon, because those round eyes understood, the way a saint must understand: the simple, harmed man, so humble in his fall from grace, so strangely holy in his madness). . . . He had said to Father Grayson, "Do you understand that I am afraid of death. Not of dying. I mind the idea of a public dying, of course. I don't want to tumble over during a homily, or a wedding, or at the moment of consecration. But it's death itself, the principle, that freezes me." And yes, he remembered, Father Grayson had nodded, his movements quick and clumsy, folding his hands and nodding more deeply, looking back at him, until the monsignor understood what he wanted to communicate. *Pray.* "I know," Vincent said. "But I can't pray." Father Grayson only repeated the pantomime. *Pray.* "I have tried," said Vincent. "I have tried so hard." *Pray.* Poor, sad Father Grayson. Reduced to a child-mime, a reasonless smile.

And now he thought he heard a child's cough. He stood, turned, saw only the beams of sun from the windows.

Had he imagined it?

"Hello?" he said.

"Hello," came the answer. A little to the left of the door, under the balcony where, on holidays, St. Jude's pathetic choir sang, someone was settling into the last pew.

He did not know how much time passed before he thought to fold his hands over his belt buckle and begin the walk back. As he did so, he kept his eyes trained to the floor, feeling the eyes of the other on him. He did not believe he had ever seen anyone in St. Jude's on a weekday.

"Hello," came the voice again.

A woman gazed at him with her head cocked slightly to the side, a quizzical yet pleased expression on her face. Her eyes were dark, brilliant, like drops of wet ink. The lashes were brown, long, not fitted to the face, which was bony and too white, with colorless lips thin as a drawn line—or the vestige of a line. The face dipped slightly, the sharp chin disturbing a red bow beneath it. She wore a scarf, a heavy and frayed woolen coat. The scarf was wrapped tightly about her head.

"Nice morning," she said.

As she spoke, something moved on the other side of her, and another white face, a boy's, peeked from a fold of her coat. The boy smiled.

"Sit back, sit back," the woman whispered.

And yet another face appeared. Another boy, or rather, the same boy: a copy, an exact duplicate.

"I said sit back."

"Twins?" the monsignor said.

"Identical."

He put one hand on the back of the pew, shifted his weight so that he might lean wide and look at them.

"You the pastor?"

"I'm Monsignor Shepherd."

"You the pastor?" she said again.

"Yes." Perhaps she was hard of hearing. He said louder, "Yes, I am—just visiting pastor."

She nodded. She had confirmed something for herself. She sat back on the seat and gathered her coat around her. The two boys lolled forward, at angles that suggested fallen objects. They could have been her younger brothers: she was certainly not past thirty. The monsignor sat down at the end of the pew and looked at his hands for a moment; then he looked at her to ask her name, watched her pull the coat more tightly about her. The coat stretched over a bulge, round and firm as a ball.

"You're expecting."

"Oh," she smiled, not at all self-conscious, not at all embarrassed, "I'm always expecting." This was given merely as a fact. "This your church?"

"No."

There was a pause. She gazed straight ahead. The two boys were paging through a mass book as if searching for a familiar passage of the liturgy. "This isn't your church?"

"You're Mrs. Bexley, aren't you?" said the monsignor.

She smiled again.

"Did Torgeson send you here?"

"No, sir."

"Why did you come?"

"I came to pray, sir."

"You needn't call me *sir*," the monsignor said. "And please —don't let me disturb you."

"This place is kind of run-down—"

"Good day," said Vincent.

But she was gathering herself to rise, even as he stepped to the door and out.

The rest of them waited in the lot, gathered around the same rusty and wobbly-tired pickup truck he had followed yesterday just before he had bumped the guardrail. It was overloaded now with every imaginable thing: mattresses, lamps, boxes, clothes dummies, bags, wires, brass posts, brooms; the pages of a magazine fluttered in the breeze, turning as if from an invisible hand, at the very top of the pile. Mr. Bexley pulled a red baseball cap out of his jeans and put it on, spitting through his forearms into the gravel as he adjusted it.

"So now I have your name," Vincent said, "as well as who you are."

"Yeah?" The dry, cracked lips parted in a smile.

"This is my husband," said Mrs. Bexley. "His name is Duck."

"Yes," the monsignor said. "We've met."

"You never met me, old man."

"Of course I did."

"I was telling him how the place looked run-down," said Mrs. Bexley. Her children stood quiet, like people waiting in a lunch line.

"I saw you yesterday," Vincent said.

"Place needs a lot of work," Bexley said.

"I have no authority to have work done, Mr. Bexley."

"Could use painting, I bet—inside and out."

"I told Torgeson this. I couldn't pay anyone to—"

"Oh, but you wouldn't have to pay us," said Mrs. Bexley.

Her husband said, "We'd do it in exchange for a place to stay. Just a while." He spit again, wiped his mouth.

"Don't spit, Duck."

"I'm sorry," Vincent said. "But as I told Torgeson—"

"Torgeson's got nothing to do with anything, old man."

"Don't call him that, Duck."

The monsignor watched one of the children, a boy almost as tall as his father, take something from the tip of a white tongue. The boy looked at it carefully, then wiped the back of his jeans. Now each child eyed the priest—patient, with the innocent rudeness of babies.

"I'm terribly sorry, but you've wasted your time coming here."

Bexley, who had been standing alongside the truck, now pushed away from it and stood very close to Vincent. He had a lean, hawklike face, stubbled and gray. He was at least forty. There were sharp lines in the skin from the wings of his nostrils downward, past his lips; and his eyes, which were under the shadow of the cap, looked like two blue marbles.

"You're the last stop, old man," he said. "I come looking for work. I got to put these people somewhere."

"Duck," the woman said, taking her husband's arm.

"Leave it."

"Look," said the monsignor, "I just don't have—I can't take you. I'll gladly see if one of the parishioners—"

"We got no place else."

"As I was saying to you—I'll gladly ask one of my parishioners to lend a hand here—with your problem. I'm sure we can find someone who . . ."

Mrs. Bexley looked at him with an intensity that made him falter inwardly, as if what he had planned to say had become suddenly irrelevant.

He turned to her. "Mrs. Bexley, you must understand. It simply is impossible for me right now."

She walked toward her children, who made a little circle around her. They all stood there in the sun, their shadows making one shadow. Bexley had faced the road and stood there as though trying to remember the name of it, his hands on his hips, his face pinched in a frown.

"I'm certain we can find someone to help you, Mr. Bexley."

The other man shook his head. "Never asked for charity. I don't want charity."

"No, of course not," Vincent said. "Someone who needs work—needs someone to work."

Bexley spit again, this time as if to remove something distasteful from his mouth. "Been all over this damn place looking for work."

"But you'll find something with my help."

"Yeah." He turned to Vincent, a sardonic smile on his face. "Live in the truck until I do. Right?"

The monsignor was silent.

"Yeah."

Now one of the children, apparently the youngest, began to whimper a little, and they were all—Bexley, too, hands in his pockets, feet kicking gravel as if to say there would be no whimpering from him—moving toward the truck. The older boy and a girl, not quite as tall, climbed onto the mountain of possessions in back. Quite suddenly there was confusion, one door of the truck open and Bexley crouching in, bent over, dust rising and feet quickening in the gravel there. The boy jumped down from the back and rushed to his father.

"What is it—what's happened?" Vincent asked, moving to the truck, putting one hand on the open door and gazing over the boy's shoulder. At first all he saw was Bexley's back, but then Bexley stood up, hands on hips, and through the crook of one skinny arm Mrs. Bexley was visible. She was sitting in the lower part of the door frame against the seat, eyes shut, head back; her skin was almost blue. She let her head fall forward, down between her knees.

"Is she all right?" Vincent said. Something pressed against

his back. He turned, saw the older boy looking at him, the rest of the children crowding in. "What's happened? Is she faint?"

"Bleeding," said Bexley.

"My God, *bleeding.*"

"That's all right. Everybody around here's so helpful. Don't worry yourself."

"Shouldn't we get her to a doctor?"

"We?"

"Mr. Bexley, for God's sake."

"Leave it, old man. You had your say."

"No, wait—wait."

Bexley looked at him. They all looked at him.

"If she's bleeding, she ought to see a doctor."

"All she needs," Bexley said, "is a place to lay down for a while."

"Yes—oh, of course. Bring her inside—let's bring her inside."

"I can walk," Mrs. Bexley said, "if it's to a bed."

"Right in here—can you manage a stairway? I have a sofa."

"Sofa's fine," said Bexley. He smiled at the monsignor out of the sharp shadow of the baseball cap. The children had already begun to move toward the house, gazing at it like prospective renters. *My God,* the old priest thought, *you have not sent me this, not this.*

II

1

"You'll only stay until I can find you a place?" said the monsignor.

"We'll only stay that long," Bexley said. "And I'll paint the church for you."

"He does good work," said his wife. She lay on the sofa, hands folded over the ball of her belly. She had not mentioned the bleeding, nor had she seemed affected by it, since she had lain down. They all seemed to have forgotten that anything had happened. She lay there unministered to; now and again she looked at the monsignor and smiled, each time the same smile, like a signal, an agreement; it was unnerving.

"We're proud people," Bexley said. He sat in one of the hardback chairs, had arranged himself directly across from Vincent, legs crossed, arms folded.

Vincent saw dirt in the wrinkles of his neck. He said: "Well, I can't have the church painted, Mr. Bexley—I haven't the funds. I couldn't afford to buy the paint."

"Then I'll keep house for you," said Mrs. Bexley.

"I'm sure that won't be necessary," Vincent said quickly. He breathed the odor of stale sweat, felt crowded, outnumbered.

Bexley leaned forward. "Priscilla can help her."

"You'll be staying in the social hall," said Vincent.

"The social hall."

"It'll be quite comfortable, Mr. Bexley—you can see how little room there is here in the house."

"Looks roomy enough to me."

"I'm sure the social hall is the best arrangement—you'll grant me that, won't you?"

"Duck," said Mrs. Bexley.

"Grant you," Bexley said. "What do you mean—'grant you.'" The skin around his lips was white.

"I didn't mean it the way it sounded," Vincent said.

There was a silence. The children were out under the windows, running and shouting; the noise seemed to rake at the house.

"The social hall is all I can do, I'm afraid."

"Yeah." Bexley's mouth gave forth the word as it had given forth spit earlier.

Vincent looked away. "Mrs. Bexley, are you—is there anything we should be doing?"

"Not a thing," she said, sitting up. "We're very grateful to you, sir."

"You needn't call me *sir*."

"Yeah, you said that." She moved the hair away from her eyes. "I keep forgetting myself."

"What do we call you?" asked Bexley.

"Father."

"*Father*."

"It's just a form of address, Mr. Bexley."

"Yeah, I remember."

"Duck was a Catholic when he was a boy."

"You were Catholic, Mr. Bexley?"

"My mother was. Never knew her."

"Duck lost his father this past summer," Mrs. Bexley said.

"I'm sorry to hear that."

"Lived long enough," said Bexley. "Eighty-one years."

"A good, long life."

"How old are you—*Father*."

"If it's uncomfortable for you, Mr. Bexley—"

"How old are you."

"I'm sixty-two."

"You look older."

"I've not been well—which is one of the reasons I was reluctant—"

"What's the matter with you?" Mrs. Bexley asked.

"I've been—convalescing. From a heart attack."

"Lately," Bexley said, "everybody goes with a heart attack—or cancer."

"Yes."

Now Mrs. Bexley arose, one hand on her hip, as if it hurt there. She moved through the entrance to the dining room. "Got some aspirin in the truck," she said.

"I have some here," said the monsignor.

"This is baby aspirin—can't take the regular stuff."

"How far along are you—if you don't mind my asking."

"She's about six months."

"Be six this week," she said. "Sometime this week."

"Have you been to a doctor?"

"*Doctor*," said Bexley. His wife had gone through to the kitchen and out. There was the sound of the door opening and closing.

"You should get her to a doctor," Vincent said.

"Yeah."

After a moment Bexley said, "Look, don't say you saw me at the old woman's place."

Vincent waited.

"It won't look right. So shut up about it."

"Are you asking me to lie, Mr. Bexley?"

"Asking you to shut up about it. It's got nothing to do with anything."

"Mr. Bexley, if there's something going on here—and if I'm going to be taking you in, I have to—" Bexley's cold eyes glared at him. "Well, I have to know about it, sir."

"I'm sick," said Bexley. He spoke so casually that for a moment the monsignor did not understand the words; they went through him like a breath.

"I'm probably going to be dead."

"Mr. Bexley, will you please just say it."

"Just said it, old man."

"Dead of what?"

But now they heard the door again, voices. Mrs. Bexley and the eldest girl came in, the girl talking about the social hall; she did not want to stay there: she wanted to know why she could not live in a house like everyone else.

"Leave it," Bexley said, and she stopped cold, though her lower lip quivered.

"This is Priscilla," said Mrs. Bexley.

The girl looked at Vincent, then looked away.

"Say hello to the nice man, Priscilla," her mother said.

"H'lo."

"Hello, Priscilla."

"May I be excused?" she asked.

"Sit down and shut up," said Bexley.

2

He introduced each of the children. It was like a ritual. He called them all inside, and they came as if they knew what he wanted; were subdued and shy, gathering themselves according to age, their eyes trained to the floor. The eldest boy was

Harvey. Then came Priscilla, the twins—Mackinley and Wallace—and the littlest, the baby, Sandra June. Harvey, said Bexley, was mute, and when he said the word his voice took on an edge of defiance; it was as though Bexley held a grudge against the unmute world. The monsignor nodded apologetically, feeling the blame, somehow. Priscilla had her mother's dark eyes, but her face was a small model of her father's. The twins looked so much like each other that it was hard to see any other likeness in them, and Sandra June's small, fat features gave no hint of what her appearance would be—she was blond as the others were dark, and while she had her mother's fair skin, there was in her movements a more general reflection of Harvey, who seemed to combine his parents in himself, and was for this an ungainly child with a body he did not know how to use.

"Harv and Priscilla won't have to leave school now," Bexley said to the room. There was no reaction from the children.

"What do you want for lunch?" Mrs. Bexley asked Vincent.

"Lunch—"

"I'll cook the meals. I'm a good cook when I have something to cook with—so's Priscilla."

"Oh, that won't be necessary—"

"You going to cook for all these kids?" Bexley said and smiled incredulously.

"You won't be here that long," said Vincent. "You can't be here—you can't spend the winter here, Mr. Bexley."

There was a long quiet.

"I'm going to find you some—circumstance. Something."

"Suppose you can't?"

"Leave it, Duck," Mrs. Bexley said. She started toward the dining room again. "Priscilla?"

"You going to kick us out," Bexley said. "Right? If you can't find somebody to dump us on."

"Oh, can we not talk about this," said the monsignor. "I promise you I'll find something. And I won't kick you out, or dump you, as you put it."

Mrs. Bexley looked at him and said, with extraordinary dignity, as if he were to derive from her tone rather than from her words that she would not be considered less than what she was, merely because she now had less than what she'd had, "We will cause you no trouble, nor will we take from you a thing we can't pay for with work, sir. We'll stay out of your way and we'll keep the children out of your way. But people have got to eat. . . ."

"Yes," said the monsignor. "Of course. Help yourself. Please. If you could just understand how impossible it is for me to maintain anyone other than myself—"

"You made yourself clear," she said. "Come, children."

One of the twins put his hand over his mouth and said, "Tee-hee. Mommy sounds like *him*." He pointed at the monsignor.

They all followed their mother out of the room, the last, Sandra June, stamping down hard with little shoes on the rug, apparently disappointed each time the nap softened what she thought should be a loud noise. When they were in the kitchen —cabinets opening and closing, shoes making the loud noise now—Bexley got out of his chair and stood over Vincent.

"Look," he said, "let's just forget what I told you."

"Mr. Bexley—"

"We didn't come here to cause you no trouble. . . . We're thankful. Believe it." He extended his hand. The monsignor took it. "Be out of here before you know it," Bexley said.

3

It took all afternoon to get them moved into the hall. Five long
tables and about fifty metal folding chairs had to be stacked
along one wall; Priscilla mopped the floor while Bexley,
Harvey, and Vincent began unloading the truck. Mrs. Bexley stayed in the house—she had already begun to clean, and
could be glimpsed in the upstairs windows, rag in hand, dust-
ing and arranging. The younger children played in the lot,
running and calling names, throwing gravel or making little
mounds out of it to kick or run through. Bexley and the monsignor put two bed frames up and lay mattresses down where
the floor had dried from Priscilla's mopping. Boxes of dishes,
clothes, books, and magazines were stacked against the opposite wall. One of the boxes was made of cedar and was marked
and pitted, having obviously been dropped a few times.
Priscilla said this was Harvey's own cedar box, and she opened
it to show the monsignor what was inside. Costume jewelry,
parts of clocks, crayons, scraps of paper with hundreds of animals drawn into every available space—it was these she
wanted him to see. The animals, mostly horses, drawn darkly
as if by a hand that was heavy and feverish, were perfectly
rendered, every muscle given its right amount of tension;
every line, really, carrying the authority of training, of a
genuine skill that had been refined. It was quite extraordinary,
Vincent said.

"Harvey's a real artist," said Priscilla.

"I should say so."

They stood alone in the hall, though now one of the twins
ambled in and wandered over to the only closet—a storage
room, really, where Bexley would put many of the boxes.

"How is it that he can't—" Vincent began.

"That he's mute?"

"Yes."

"Something about his brain. He's not a retard, you know."

"Yes, I can see—"

"He reads magazines and books." Priscilla seemed proud, and for the first time now, she smiled.

"Well, these are excellent—he should go to art school."

"He don't need that. Lookit. Why does he need that?" She held one drawing close to his face. Her thumbnail on the edge of the page was delicately painted.

"Perhaps you're right," he said.

And now they saw, at the same instant, the twin letting a can of white paint over, the paint flowing out on the floor and spreading.

"Where did you get that, Wallace?" Priscilla said.

The boy stood up, holding the can.

"Wallace," said the monsignor, "put it down, now."

"Fuck you," the boy said.

"I'm going to tell Daddy." Priscilla bolted out of the room.

"Going to paint this place," the boy said, pouring.

"Don't—stop that."

"Fuck you," said Wallace, eyebrows up, watching the paint flow. "Going to paint."

Vincent went to him and reached for the can, but the pool of spreading paint had made a border around Wallace, who knew this and stood there smiling, the can emptying out.

"You little—malicious—"

"Fuck you."

"Mr. Bexley," said Vincent, turning, calling, "Mr. Bexley." He rushed out into the bright, cold sun. Bexley was sitting on the running board of the truck, the red cap pulled low across his eyes, his hands on his knees. Priscilla was nowhere in sight, nor were any of the others.

"Mr. Bexley," Vincent said, approaching him.

"I already know about it."

"Do you know what that boy is saying?"

"No." The eyes were not visible from the shadow of the cap.

"Where are the rest of them?" Vincent whirled around, as though guarding himself from a sudden attack.

"Around somewhere." The voice was calm behind him. "Priscilla's in the house with her mother."

Vincent looked at him. "What're you going to do?"

"About what," Bexley said.

"About that boy in there. We can start with that."

"We'll clean the paint up." The blue marble eyes seemed amused. It was enraging.

"And that's all?"

"What do you want me to do," said Bexley, and now he grimaced. "You tell me and I'll do it." He put his arms around himself and rocked forward a little.

"What is it?" Vincent asked. "What's the matter?"

"Nothing—I get tired."

"Mr. Bexley, this illness of yours—"

"Forget about that. I should live to be fifty at least. It ain't anything that'll kill me now."

"Then why did you tell me about it—why that way? If you would just be straightforward with me—"

"Maybe I thought you might be able to tell me—forget it. Leave it."

"Mr. Bexley, for God's sake."

"Look," Bexley said, "you're a damn minister. I never believed in any God. I'm in trouble—Jesus. What do you want, a damn written statement?"

A cloud sailed past the sun; its shadow went across the field like the shadow of an aircraft. After a moment Vincent said, "All right. What about this—what about that boy in there and his language."

"Worried about language are you?" Again the other man smiled.

"Yes, I am when it's offensive—when it's obscene and it comes from a child who's not even in school yet."

Bexley leaned back, put one leg up, and crossed it over his knee. "You tell me what you want me to do and I'll do it. Want me to beat hell out of him?"

"He's your child, for God's sake."

"That's right."

Presently Bexley said, "We'll clean it up, old man. We got trouble enough—can't seem to get all worked up over a word. You want us to leave you alone, and we'd like it if you did the same for us right now. You're looking at a man with deeper troubles than anything you ever saw or dreamed about. So just—we'll get the paint off the damn floor. Let's just get through this afternoon."

They both watched the boy wander out of the hall, still carrying the can, paint spattered all over him and over his shoes, which picked up dust with each step—dust and stones. He was crying.

"Got to get Priscilla to mop the floor again," Bexley said.

4

The house was cleaned, the possessions were arranged in the hall, and the Bexleys had settled in far too well: they already seemed to feel at home. Mrs. Bexley made a dinner and they ate quietly, the children whispering when they wanted to talk, their parents and the monsignor encased in an awkward silence that would not easily be broken. Now and again the twin—the one twin, Wallace, though of course Vincent could not be sure—made a sly face at him. He tried to ignore it by not looking at the child, but his eyes were drawn continually back, and each time the boy made that face at him. Perhaps ten minutes passed in which there was nothing but this quiet game—if that was what one could call it. The forks sounded against the plates, and Sandra June whined or sang, according to her mood and whether or not her corn would stay on her spoon.

Finally Mrs. Bexley said, "We got a little money left over from Torgeson—we can buy some food."

"Never mind," said Vincent. "You keep the money—you'll need it later."

"Hate the early dark," Bexley said, chewing.

Perhaps another minute passed.

"Are you all from Demera?" Vincent asked.

"Treetop," Bexley said. "Near Richmond."

"We left Treetop in August," said Mrs. Bexley.

"Why did you leave?"

"Wants to know why we left, Elizabeth."

"Leave it, Duck."

Vincent waited a moment. Then he looked at Mr. Bexley. "Is that going to be a mystery too?"

"What do you mean—mystery?" Mrs. Bexley asked.

"He don't mean a thing by it," said Bexley. Then he glared at the monsignor. "Do you?"

"We left," Mrs. Bexley said, "because we thought there'd be a better job for Duck than the one he had in Treetop."

"What did you do in Treetop, Mr. Bexley?"

"Drove a milk truck—a milkman. Can't have a thing made from milk or cream, but I carried it around for thirteen years. Well—how old's Harv, Elizabeth?"

"Harv'll be fourteen."

"Almost fourteen years."

"You can't have dairy products?" Vincent asked.

"Makes him sick," Mrs. Bexley said. "He's got a sickness that means he can't have milk or cream."

"Sickness?"

"You got it," Bexley said. "You hit it right on the nose." There was a look from him that told Vincent to say no more. He went on: "You come from here?"

"No," Vincent said. "I've been—well, I grew up in Point Royal."

"They send you guys around a lot."

"Yes . . . well."

"You been overseas?"

"No."

"Duck was in Korea," Mrs. Bexley said.

They had all finished eating, and now Priscilla was clearing the dishes away. Sandra June kept saying "Where's cake, cake. Where's cake, cake."

Mrs. Bexley went on: "Duck was a hero in the war."

"Wasn't a war," Bexley said. "Police action." He smiled bitterly.

"Bronze Star," said his wife.

"Yeah."

There was a pause. Bexley stretched his arms out, yawning. "Valor beyond the call."

"Don't make light of it, Duck," said Mrs. Bexley.

"Maybe," Bexley said, leaning toward her, "maybe I ought to run for president or something."

"Were you in the infantry?" Vincent asked.

"Sure—that's where they put all us educated types."

"You could've gone to college after the war, couldn't you?" Vincent asked.

"Yeah—right on the nose again, old man. Had a little detour."

"How so?"

"He—" Mrs. Bexley said, too loud. "He stayed in the army."

"That's right," said Bexley. "I stayed in the army."

The monsignor looked at each of them, decided that he did not want to know any more. He got up from the table and quietly excused himself.

"You going upstairs?" Bexley asked.

"Yes."

"Then you want us to leave. Go over to the hall."

"If you don't mind—"

"I have to make breakfast for the children," Mrs. Bexley said.

"I'll be up early," said Vincent.

"You got another television?" Bexley asked.

"No."

"We got a little portable but it's busted—it's in one of the boxes we hauled in. Picture tube's gone."

"I only have the one," said the monsignor.

Bexley extended his hand again and, when the monsignor took it, gave a bone-cracking grip. His eyes were narrow and serious, and his voice shook. "I hope you don't mind my ways —I'll hope you'll excuse everything. I mean no dis-respect, sir."

"Of course."

"We'll do right by you."

"Yes—well, thank you," Vincent said. "I'm sure we'll find a way to"—Bexley had let go of his hand—"to uh—yes, well, good night."

"Good night," said Bexley. And then they all, in unison, said good night.

5

In his sleep he had the second heart attack, and died. He hovered above his own body and said, "I'm dead now." Then he sat up quick, awake in the bed, feeling the pulse of the dream all over him, breathing like a man who has run, has sprinted uphill. The window was dark, with one star shining through it. He did not remember having turned out the light. He did not quite remember where he was—and then his eyes caught the shape of his own feet pushing up the blanket. "Oh," he said, getting out of the bed, "oh." He went into the bathroom and realized after a few moments that he was combing and combing the hair over his ears. He washed his face and washed it again, splashing the cold, clean water all over, and then he went back into the bedroom and turned on the light. There was his breviary; there was the chalice his father had given him when he left for the seminary, so long ago—it lay locked in a blue-velvet case because he had never used it; it was too valuable to use, had cost his father too much for it to be used. Aside from his clothes it was the only thing he had brought with him to St. Jude's. He opened the lid, touched the silver place where his own elongated shape was given back to him. "I'm all right," he said aloud. "I'm all right." Breathing deeply, slowly; he had learned that it was impossible to think straight when he was afraid, so he would try not to think.

And he remembered the Bexleys.

"Oh," he said, moving to the night table, where the breviary lay. He had fallen asleep with such ease tonight; now there would be no sleep. And he had to face the Bexleys early: he would not be able to nap during the late morning hours.

He picked up the breviary, the habit of thirty-seven years. He would read until dawn.

6
🙰🙰🙰

He had had the heart attack two years ago in July. It had come, oddly enough, without the usual signs: there had been no chest pain to speak of, and no pain at all in the left arm. He had experienced the slightest feeling of indigestion, just enough to make him aware of his stomach. He paid no attention to it, except to make a comment to the two men who were taking him out to dinner about how people were never really aware of any part of their bodies that did not hurt, and so the best thing was not to know you had a stomach, or a backbone, or a skull. It was a joke, and it had been treated as such. He went with them, and he ate a large meal, though before he was finished he was thinking to himself that it might be a touch of the stomach virus—or perhaps the beginning of an ulcer. It was not quite like the normal disturbances of his stomach. The two men were friends of his curates, so there was some pressure for him to be entertaining (his curates had insisted that he go with them—he had been working too hard, they said, and he ought to go out and take his ease for once). But he had enjoyed a pleasant evening, had discovered that he liked French cuisine. He had two helpings of spiced chicken and half a bottle of Beaujolais, and with a full stomach the pain had ceased. It came back, with sudden force, as if he had received a blow, as he stepped out into the parking lot. He saw thousands of moths in the lights above the lot, and believed somehow that they were taking all the air out of the night—a burning, humid night anyway.

"Those damn moths," he said. "I'm suffocating."

"Hot." One of the men spoke. "Hot," they both said.

"Heartburn," the monsignor said.

They got into the car, the monsignor in the backseat, and drove toward St. Paul's, past Washington Square and on through the lighted streets of the Village. There was music in the cafés on either side, and the monsignor put his head out the window as if to hear it better, but he was trying to get air, fearing now that he might lose his dinner. The hot air rushed into his face, and other faces spun by, while the two men talked about how good the food had been and about how hot it was.

They stopped at a light. Vincent looked at the patterns in the bright, circular glass eye. There were sirens in the distance. The sirens grew louder, or another siren began. The night seemed to be shrieking. He sat back against the seat, watching two fire engines roll through the intersection, horns blaring. A fireman in a white helmet with the number six on it looked right at him. Everything had grown furious and deafening—even the two polite voices, asking him if he was all right, if he wanted a doctor.

"A doctor," he said. "A doctor, please." Gasping. The sirens died away like hope and he shivered, looking at the shadowy outline of the two men in front: had he spoken to them? Had they spoken to him? Had he told them? "Please," he tried to scream, but it was a gasp: "Please." "Hold on," one said, or seemed to say. "Hold on." He thought they went too fast. He thought it was dangerous of them to go so fast. "Slow down," he said. They hadn't heard him. He began to say the Act of Contrition, but couldn't remember the words.

"God," he said, "help me."

Then there was yellow light, a canopy, a roof, a ceiling spinning by like the surface of a road, something rubbery on his face, a white gleaming something extending upward from it to a white shape. He saw teeth, fingers, hair; a voice said, "Hurry," but he could not be sure if it had come from above him or in front of him. Then the shape spoke. The teeth, fingers, hair, belonged to it.

"Breathe easy now, easy."

Later, he lay in a white bed in a blue room. Or that was what he thought about: how white the bed was and how blue the room was. He lay there and the doctor, Dr. Drew, a middle-aged man with bluish white hair and tufts of gray whisker on his chin, sat before him in a metal chair with a padded seat. Dr. Drew had kind eyes, round and Spanish-dark, a gold tooth when he smiled. The faint odor of cigars clung to him, and when he touched the side of his nose, Vincent saw that his fingers were elegantly manicured. Dr. Drew told him he would survive. There was no reason to think that he could not return to a reasonably normal pattern of life for a man his age. Indeed, the monsignor had suffered something like a heart attack: the symptoms, the EKG, all indicated heart attack, but the problem was something quite rare, and really rather simple to treat. "We believe you have a flaw in the ventricle wall of your heart, Father," Dr. Drew said. "It's something you had since birth. A very mild VSD— ventral-septal defect."

"Defect," Vincent said. "You mean—birth defect?"

"Yes. There's a small leakage, very small, in the ventricle— a shunt. And what happened is that a tiny clot formed in your blood and passed through this minute shunt, this little opening. There's a little enlargement on the ventricle side, Father, which would indicate that you've had the condition all along."

"It wasn't a heart attack."

"No, not in the strict sense. I mean this is a distinction that's only important in the aftermath, really. You can't correct the damage of a heart attack. But we can correct your condition, you see. We can head off any further trouble of this specific kind."

"Surgery?" Vincent said, beginning to tremble.

"That's in the offing, of course, Father. But the condition— it's very slight in your case, and of course we'd rather not operate right away—we have medicines to thin out your blood a little, and we can think about our options when you really get back on your feet."

"My father died of a heart attack," Vincent said.

"We'll watch it closely."

"I thought I was dying."

"Well," said Dr. Drew, "I don't think there's any danger now."

There had followed many tests—what seemed an endless series of tests. Dr. Drew was thorough, and he wanted to be certain. Nurses put needles into the monsignor, and concoctions that tasted like bile. He had contracted an infection, lost some weight. And as he at last began to recover, Dr. Drew decided to go ahead with surgery. The condition was corrected: Vincent lay in a drugged half-sleep thinking himself corrected at the center. He heard his blood moving, he thought. Yet when he was awake, there was no relief, no feeling of having been made well, fixed; the thought of his body trying to heal itself made him breathe as though he were straining up a long hill. When people came to see him, they were so carefully cheerful (he began to think of his mother's irritability when she had lain in just such a room, and he had come smiling, nearly singing as he spoke, as though there were no such thing as Death); no one seemed willing to admit that Death was in the room, if only this time, to watch, to measure. Perhaps two days after surgery another infection set in. It was slight, but it delayed his release.

"I'm not getting better, am I?" he said to Dr. Drew.

"This little infection set you back a little."

"I've been here almost five weeks and I feel like a pile of rags."

"Don't worry so much—we have to strengthen ourselves."

"Doctor Drew, I'm sixty years old and, if you don't mind, I'd like to be addressed as an adult."

Dr. Drew's lips barely moved: "Certainly."

Waking alone at night—stars at the window and the brittle sound of summer insects (even there, in Manhattan, amid all those miles of concrete and asphalt, the insects sang) coming to him like a dust, since he seemed to hear them with his whole body—he tried to pray. One of his curates quoted Psalms at him each visit: "I will lift up mine eyes unto the hills, from whence cometh my help." But the monsignor, at these words, saw only eyes and hills. The world had broken down into *things*, from which no idea could be easily extracted: oak was not tree anymore without an effort to make it so; it was just oak, as pine was pine and maple was maple, and no similarity wanted to connect them. It was absurd; it was queer. It terrified him.

And while he had, at last, gotten well enough to return to St. Paul's, a mended body in robes that fit loosely now, the demands of his position quickly demoralized him, not one fragment naturally fitting another, every face he spoke to broken into a disturbing aggregate of marks, bumps, gaps, bulges, sores, warts—his inability to hold the words of a prayer in his mind growing worse daily—there was nothing to do but admit defeat, ask for help. But, having decided to do so, he kept putting it off in the hope that it would all pass from him. At the end of that year he had a sort of breakdown, was back in the hospital with exhaustion, and from there he was sent to the retreat in California. He had learned, during that time, that he was not spiritual enough to live like a monk, and not strong enough to find his way back to prayer in an atmosphere of such severe attention to prayer. He told nobody. He made a beautiful recovery, according to everyone —he asked for a small parish, preferably in Virginia, because that was home and to go home, now, would certainly strengthen him further. And to his delight his request had been granted far beyond any expectation.

Demera, Virginia.

Only three hours from Point Royal over mountain roads. Familiar country, sweet, green country he had loved so much —he had never realized how much—all the years.

7

Mrs. Bexley was at the door with Priscilla early, as she had said she would be. Vincent heard them coming from the hall —their talk—and went down to meet them. It was a cold morning, and the first snow had fallen—crescents of it lay everywhere on the grounds, like white shadows at the edges of things.

"Where I grew up," Mrs. Bexley said, "we never had much snow."

"Where did you grow up?" Vincent asked, watching them remove their coats.

"Louisiana and Texas. I don't remember much about Louisiana, except my uncle Bobby losing his arm by a window frame —blew loose in a hurricane and he got hit, so it took the arm right off."

"I've never been to Louisiana," said Vincent. He hoped this

would end the conversation. He was having an attack of nerves, a lasting one, from his long night.

"All I remember are those hurricanes," Mrs. Bexley said. "Clouds like mountains, and the peace when it all rolled over and we were in the center. I bet I only saw two of them like that in my life, but I could swear I saw twenty. We moved from there when I was six years old."

Priscilla brought a frying pan out of the cabinet beneath the sink.

"Never had any like that in Texas—just a lot of rain, usually. And tornados, but I never saw one."

"No eggs," Priscilla said. She stood bent over into the refrigerator. "He ain't got any eggs."

"I don't eat them," said Vincent.

"Duck won't—I mean he can't—of course."

"You got bacon?" Priscilla asked.

"Priscilla, don't be rude, now."

"I'm afraid I don't eat bacon, either."

"We'll just have toast this morning—will you eat some toast, sir?"

"No, thank you—I don't eat breakfast as a rule."

"You drink whiskey," said Priscilla.

"Priscilla, mind your business."

"I.W. Harper—you said so."

"Priscilla."

"In fact," said Vincent, "that belongs to the man I replaced."

"*He* drank it," Priscilla said.

"Mrs. Bexley, when you have this baby—"

"Yes?" Mrs. Bexley had begun to put napkins down on the table; she already knew where everything was, and her motions were as natural as if she had lived in the house for years. This troubled him.

"Never mind—I've forgotten what I was going to ask."

"We got caught this time," she said.

"We're having an accident," said Priscilla.

"Torgeson sent you all here, didn't he?" Vincent said. He had taken a place near the sink, and was leaning against the counter. The table was between him and them—the smooth Formica top and the light fall of the napkins. Mrs. Bexley's hands were chafed and rough, but slender.

"Torgeson?" she said.

"Yes."

"He did suggest you, but I used to like to ride by here— we been by here a lot since we arrived. It's a nice little church. Sort of puts me back to—" She stopped as if she had caught herself. "No, that isn't exactly true—"

"What isn't exactly true?"

"That this place puts me back to anything. It's just a nice little church in the country, and I never really lived in the country. I lived in the suburbs. New Orleans and then Galveston."

"We're not country bumpkins," said Priscilla, who had put two slices of bread in the toaster, and now stood with knife in hand over an open package of margarine and a jar of jelly.

"So Torgeson put you up to it."

Mrs. Bexley frowned. "You make it sound like we played a trick on you or something."

"No, I didn't mean that."

The toast popped up and Priscilla gave a little cry.

"You see I had told him—Torgeson—I had told Torgeson that I couldn't take you on. I mean he had come to me about it before."

"You're not going to eat anything?" Mrs. Bexley said.

"No."

She gave a quick, prim smile. "Then will you please get out of our way?"

He left the room, feeling vaguely like a scolded boy. He was almost to the stairs when something touched his arm; it was like a breath of air. He turned.

"You're not angry?"

"No, Mrs. Bexley."

"You're not changing your mind?" She stood there clicking her thumbnail against her index fingernail.

"Look, I'm only temporary here myself. I tried to explain that to Torgeson."

"Then you *have* changed your mind." She was incredulous. The clicking sound was distracting. Noise. Noise and confusion, and they had already made themselves at home.

"Have you?" she said.

"I'm going to find something for you."

"Yes, you said that."

"But this is very difficult for me."

"It is for us all," she said simply.

"Well then, if we can just accommodate each other—"

"I don't know what that means." She had set her black eyes on him.

"Just please," he said, "leave me alone. Eat what you want, use the hall, but leave me alone."

"That's fine with us." Her lips were now more pale; her whole face had tightened. "We wouldn't think of dirtying you with the likes of us."

"No, you don't understand—" But she had turned, and was walking away. He thought of following, of calling her back, but then he lacked the energy to say anything else to her. At the top of the stairs he spoke to himself. "I'm supposed to be *overjoyed* by it all," he said.

There were two rooms upstairs: the bathroom, which was at the end of the hall, and the bedroom. A simple place, the bed-

room: night table, small writing desk and chair, the bed. The
floor was hardwood, much polished, and, like the walls, bare.
The one window let in a hard trapezoid of light. It was a
room not so much *of* the house as *surrounded* by it. The window was curtained, but only to shut out light—this with dark
blue cotton cloth too heavily starched. Indeed, everything
here suggested austerity, stiffness; it was as if the absent
priest, the true pastor, had concealed some inner severity of
spirit by furnishing the downstairs rooms in such contrast to
this room.

Now Vincent sat at the writing desk, next to the window,
and watched the rest of the Bexleys trail over from the hall—
Duck Bexley, carrying Sandra June on his shoulder, leading
the way. The twins made quick snowballs and threw them
at each other or at Harvey, who responded in kind. Bexley
seemed oblivious.

The monsignor took a pencil and paper out of the desk
and wrote: HOMILY: FEAST OF CHRIST THE KING. He waited a
moment, the pencil lying in his fingers, like a memory.

> Today, I took a family into my social hall because
> they could find no one else in this community who
> would give them the simple kindness of a shelter
> until they might find their own way. As Christians,
> I believe we are responsible to each other in a spe-
> cial way, an individual way, beyond the charity of
> institutions. Christ is King, but He knocks at your
> door every day, hungry, ill-fed, needing your help

He read what he had written, made a wide circle through the
whole thing, and crumpled the piece of paper in his fist. It
was too obviously his own desire to rid himself of the Bexleys.
Oh, could you all please take these people off my hands so

I can have what little peace there is left to me? He might as well fall on his knees and beg.

"I'm overjoyed," he said.

"What?" came from behind him. It was one of the twins. "What?" A bright, cheerful little voice, and neatly combed hair the color of dishwater.

"What do you want?" Vincent asked.

The boy walked to the desk, touched it, moved to the night table, and picked up the blue-velvet case where the chalice was. He touched the lid, humming softly to himself.

"Young man, will you please tell me what you are doing up here?"

"Daddy sent me."

"Yes—*and?*"

"What's in here?"

"Nothing that would interest you."

The boy frowned, sighed. "Daddy says to tell you—" He put one hand to his mouth, the frown deepening. "To—" he stammered. "To—"

"Oh, come on, please. What?" said Vincent. Then he called: "Mr. Bexley!"

"Says to say I'm sorry."

"You're sorry."

"Yeah."

There were footsteps on the stairs. Another emissary. "You're the one with the paint, is that it?"

"Yeah." The boy looked down at his shoes. There was no shyness in this; it was as if his shoes had spoken to him.

Vincent took him by the arm and escorted him to the door. There he met Bexley, who wore the red baseball cap, and who took the boy by the shoulder and guided him out of the room, saying, "Did you tell him? Did you tell him what I told you?"

"He told me, Mr. Bexley."

"Get on downstairs," Bexley said to the boy. Then he swung around and faced the monsignor, looking beyond him at the room. "Little room," he muttered.

"Would you care to come in and satisfy your curiosity?" Vincent asked, intending to be sarcastic.

"Never saw a priest's room before," said Bexley, and he entered, hands in his pockets, going past Vincent as people walk past the silent guard in a museum.

"Look, we are going to have to arrive at an understanding—"

But the other man, standing at the window, gazing out, had said something.

"What?"

"Said you can see the hall real good from here. Didn't remember a window looking out on this side. Real good view here."

"Yes."

"What're the other windows?"

"The bathroom."

"That's a nice big bathroom in the social hall."

"This one's big, too."

"Yeah," Bexley said. "Odd. Such a small room you got. What's this?" He touched the velvet case, as the boy had— the same careful motion, as if it were something dropped from another planet.

"It's a chalice."

"Oh, yeah. Like a victory cup. Been a long time since I've seen one."

"Mr. Bexley," the monsignor said with as much patience as he could muster, "if you don't mind, I have some work to do."

"Where'd you get it?"

"My father gave it to me." Vincent ran his hand over his mouth. "My father. It's a gift from my father."

Bexley opened the case, slowly, as if he expected to hear music. "A regular trophy. Your father still with us?"

"If you mean is he alive—no."

"It's what I mean."

"He died my first year in seminary."

"Long time ago, hunh."

Vincent walked over and closed the lid. "Yes."

The other put his hands back into his pockets, turning slowly, looking at the room. "You and your father were close."

"As a matter of fact, no—we weren't particularly close."

"Did you know your mother? I don't have much memory of mine."

"My mother lived a long time, Mr. Bexley—yes, I did know her."

"Never knew mine."

"Now, if you'll excuse me." Vincent moved to the door and held it, waiting.

"You have any brothers or sisters?"

"Mr. Bexley, please—"

"Never had any brothers or sisters."

"I had a brother," Vincent sighed, "when I was nineteen. He only lived a year."

"That's rough," Bexley said. "Must've been hard on your mother."

"Yes. Yes, it was."

"When did she pass away?"

"About four years ago—look, Mr. Bexley, I really must ask you to leave me alone now. I spoke to your wife about this—"

"Yeah, I know," Bexley said, lifting the cap with finger and thumb, and scratching the dark, matted hair beneath. "Kind of hurt her feelings. What I wanted to know was what you got in mind for today."

"I have work to do."

"Yeah, but I mean about helping us get out of here—it's what you want, id'n it?" The cap dropped back down on his head.

"I had thought I'd talk to Torgeson first—this morning."

Bexley was shaking his head. "No use looking there."

"Well, I have to speak to him all the same."

"Yeah."

"Are you going to go out and look for work?"

"Been all over this town," said Bexley, still shaking his head. "All over."

"Well, you've got to find something. There must be something."

Now the cap came off, and the other hand traveled through the hair. "There's five cans of paint in that storage closet in the hall—you want me to paint the inside of the church? Needs it pretty bad."

Vincent held the door open in what he hoped was a final gesture. "I'd rather you looked for work."

Bexley looked down, holding the cap. "Should've stayed in the army," he muttered.

8

The mailbox, set like an ornate hat on a plain metal post, was a miniature of the house; iron letters on the little roof spelled out the name *Torgeson*. The driveway was lined with spruce trees, the lower branches nearly touching the ground as if from the weight of their white-green color. The driveway angled down to the right, back toward St. Jude's. Vincent could see the clapboard steeple in the spaces between the heavy spruce branches; it looked like a monument stuck up out of the hill. There was thin, brilliant sun now; the little wedges of snow that in the morning had lain everywhere were gone.

He parked the Ford behind Torgeson's Lincoln, got out, looked at the house: all redwood, with curtainless windows like the windows of a real estate office. There were flagstone steps leading up to it, and on the northern side a flagstone patio with redwood furniture and a brick barbecue. It was a depressing place, finally, like so many of the newer houses, which always called to his mind those split-level homes where the dentist or the ear, nose, and throat man had downstairs offices.

Torgeson came out and walked down to him, his face twisted into a smile so broad, it looked like a wound. He wore the jeans, the leather boots, a lumberjack shirt rolled up to the elbows. "This is indeed a surprise," he said, reaching down to take Vincent's hand.

"This is not a social visit, Torgeson."

The smile changed, but persisted. "Certainly I can talk you into an afternoon drink."

They walked up to the house. The air smelled of leaves; was still and warm.

"Can I make you a drink?"

"No."

"Not anything? I have tea." Torgeson led the way in. A big room, with a high, beamed ceiling slanting down to the right, an enormous flagstone mantel, an aquarium, a red shag rug, a sofa and two chairs—it was all like the most expensive suite in a Holiday Inn.

"Let me make you something."

"Make yourself something, if you like."

There was another room to the left, from which the muted sound of a television issued forth—a chorus of frantic voices

singing the praises of Bell & Howell. A stairway along that
wall led up to a loft, a hallway, closed doors. Beneath the loft
was another hallway, down which Torgeson had gone.

"You've come to talk about the Bexleys," he called. There
was the sound of ice cubes tumbling into a glass. "Am I
right?"

Vincent did not respond. He did not want to have to shout.

Torgeson came back, his drink poured, rattling the ice and
smiling. "Am I right?"

Vincent nodded.

"Sit down." His host took the sofa, fell into the sofa, it
seemed, holding the drink out as if to make a toast. He
brought the glass to his lips and licked the edge, sipped, said,
"Ah. You don't know what you're missing. Sit down."

Vincent said, "No, thank you."

"So—shoot."

"I think you know what I'm going to say."

"I have a pretty good idea. I drove by yesterday and saw
them carting stuff into the hall."

"You planned the whole thing, Torgeson—you sent them to
me after I told you I couldn't take them."

"Sit down, why don't you? You might as well sit down."

Vincent sat at the edge of one of the chairs, his arms folded
over his knees. Behind Torgeson the fish dangled in the green
light of the aquarium—long, plumelike fins, mouths that
seemed to utter some vowel over and over.

"How could you presume—"

Torgeson cut him off, sitting forward. "I didn't presume
anything except that you'd refuse."

"But why send them? You know I thought you were rather
amusing, Torgeson, with your tenant family and your already
rented house; but now you've involved me—"

"All right," said Torgeson. "Let's not start lecturing until we get one thing straight. Taking the Bexleys in was your choice, not mine. I don't see why you have to blame me."

"Well, you've got to do something—and soon. I can't have those people in my social hall."

Torgeson drank—a slow sip, as if he were thinking.

"You've got to take them back, Torgeson."

"Out of the question."

"Well then, you've got to find another place for them."

"I already have."

The monsignor waited.

"I tried everywhere—and I'm afraid you're it," the other said, and put the drink down on the coffee table. "You could've sent them away."

"Yes," Vincent said. "And so I will."

The other man shrugged. "Well then, there's no problem anymore, is there?"

"Except that you've put the moral problem of throwing them out onto *me*."

"If Father McManus had been here—"

"I am *not* Father McManus."

"No, but you're a priest, and that isn't your home down there, it's a church."

Vincent got up and walked toward the door, his face burning, his hands balled up into fists. The door wouldn't open, or he was too angry to make his hands work the knob. "Damn it," he muttered. "Damn it."

"If you leave now, Father, you won't have one lick of help from me."

Vincent whirled. "*Help*. I should say you've done quite enough."

"You don't want any help—look, I'm not trying to stick you with anything. I had to fire the man—all right, I'll admit that I was glad to have to fire him. I don't like him, to tell you the truth—he makes me nervous. But he has a family and I wanted to see them provided for. God knows *he* can't—or won't. So I suggested you to *her*. And you took them in. Now, if you let them stay, and if we can cooperate instead of accusing each other, I'll do everything I can monetarily to help. If not—well, that's up to you."

"Do you know, he told me he was dying," Vincent said.

"Did he?"

"Yes, he did. He said he had a sickness that would kill him. Now what am I to do, Torgeson?"

Torgeson frowned, picked up his drink. "I wouldn't know about that—he never said anything about it to me."

"He's also still stopping to see Mrs. Trevinos. Did you know *that*?"

"Did he tell you that?"

"No, I saw him over there when I went to call on her."

"Well, maybe he'll get some money from her and that'll solve your problem."

"It would solve my problem if you gave him some money— say, what you'd give me to help support them."

Torgeson finished his drink, rattled the ice cubes in the glass. He seemed to be thinking about the monsignor's suggestion. "No," he said, shaking his head. "As I told you before, that just goes against my grain. Besides, I don't know that he'd take it from me—and even if he would, I don't know that he'd use it properly."

"That wouldn't be anybody's business, would it?"

"No. I just can't dole it out like that—not to Bexley. And there's something more, Father. A guy was here yesterday afternoon, looking for Bexley. A fat guy named Wick. Mr. Wick seemed very interested in locating the Bexleys, and he didn't seem to have friendly intentions. I don't know what he wanted because I couldn't get anything out of him. I thought he might be some sort of a detective—he showed me a circular about the Townsend company project. Said he knew it had belonged to the Bexleys, that one of them had torn the address part of it off, and that was how he'd known to come looking for them. He was very elaborate about all of that, but when I asked him what he wanted, he just claimed he had some unfinished business with them. I don't know—he might never turn up again. But you ought to know about it."

"What did you tell him?" Vincent asked.

"What could I tell him? I said Bexley was no longer working for me, and I didn't know where he was—as a matter of fact, I really *didn't* know where he was then."

"But you had a damned good idea."

"I suppose you could say that, yes."

"So now I'm to know that Bexley is being hunted. Wonderful."

"It might not be anything."

Vincent opened the door; it did not resist him now.

"She'll have the baby and they'll move on in that damn truck and that'll be the end of that, Father."

"You say."

Torgeson did not respond to this.

"Wonderful," Vincent said.

9

He kept to his room as much as he could. He carried the portable television up there and put it on the writing table, facing the bed, trying the antenna at every angle—the reception was much poorer in that part of the house. He put aluminum foil on the tip of the antenna, but this did not help. So he watched a double image when he watched—when he could manage the solitude. There was no avoiding the Bexleys, who had nothing really to do in the hall, and so found excuses to come over to the house: Bexley wanted to paint the church, or polish the pews, or trim the trees in the little cemetery; the children wanted the television, and when they couldn't have it, lamented the broken one, their own, and played noisily in the lot, just below the window; Mrs. Bexley acted as if she wanted nothing more than to let Vincent alone, yet she, too, found ways to rob him of what little privacy he could manage (she had to arrange the meals—would he eat? When would he eat?). And on top of everything there were the phone calls. Torgeson phoned, or Mrs. Trevinos, who had said she would not call anymore, but had called four times since. The first time, three days after the arrival of the Bexleys, the monsignor had worked up enough courage to sweeten his voice and ask about the Trevinos house, the big, empty Trevinos house; before he could go on to link the Bexleys to it, she huffed at him that the Bexleys could go back where they belonged, and had refused to speak further about it. Anyone and everyone called, jangled the phone and his nerves. With the coming of the Bexleys his need for peace and order had grown out of all measure.

So at last he went out; he flew into the face of it all, visiting parishioners and the friends of parishioners: there was a family in need of help; there was a good man in need of work. No one had anything to give. There were no openings anywhere. He had known, after the conversation with Torgeson, that this was the way it would be. Yet each time he failed, he was newly disappointed; his hopes were freshly cut down.

Everybody was terribly sorry.

And the Bexleys, God help him, were settling in. Duck Bexley no longer seemed to feel the need to converse, or exchange politenesses, or help in the search.

"I ain't cut out for begging," he said. "I had enough."

"You can't stay here through the winter, Mr. Bexley—you just *can't*."

"I won't beg here either," said Bexley. "You want us out?"

Oh, God, yes. But Bexley never waited for an answer, even if the monsignor could've found the way to say it without using the words of eviction. There was growing desperation in Bexley; that was obvious. Vincent would never find a way to deal him the last blow.

"You have to understand what he's going through," Mrs. Bexley said. "You have to try to do that a little."

"Yes," said Vincent. "Yes. But I just don't know what I can do if he won't even come with me."

"He's a loner. You have to know that—he always was. Even in a family this big, he's a loner, in a way. He never mixed well."

"I know just how he feels, Mrs. Bexley."

Mrs. Bexley missed the irony.

"He always kept to himself," she went on. "Even with us he always keeps something back."

The monsignor walked the rooms of his invaded house at night and wished for the return of what he knew now had been days of unappreciated peace.

At the end of the second week, in a driving morning rain—shortly after Bexley and the older children had left for town to get supplies—Mr. Wick arrived.

III

1

Here is Elizabeth Bexley, peering through the almost closed door of the social hall at Mr. Wick, who struggles toward the house, hunched forward as though he carries something secret under his clothes. She had opened the door to look for a pause in the rain, had seen the car pulling into the lot, and, recognizing it immediately, had backed quickly out of sight. Now she watches the fat man enter the house. The rain comes down like a thin sheet of gray light, and the sky is not visible.

"Mine," Sandra June says. "Mine." She is on the bed, wrapped in a woolen shawl, pulling a corner of it away from Mackinley, who knows quite well that what he is doing will cause Sandra June to cry.

"Mine."

Wallace is under the bed. Elizabeth can see his legs and feet —one toe jutting out of a hole in the left sock. He lies very still.

"My blanket."

Mackinley pulls the corner of the shawl, stretching it, his face impassive, as though he is a small animal performing some instinctual task.

"Mackin*ee*," Sandra June cries.

Elizabeth closes the door behind her, leaning on it, watching

Sandra June throw her head back and begin to shriek. "Let her alone, Mackinley."

"Mine, mine."

"Stop it," Elizabeth whispers, hisses. "Stop it, stop it."

"Mackin*ee*."

"I want it quiet now."

"She's such a crybaby."

"I'm dead."

Wallace remembers what he saw through the window, when Alphonse Bexley, Sr., died. He wants to pretend he is dead all the time now. Elizabeth comes away from the door and stands over his jutting feet.

"Get out from under there," she says.

"The dead can't move. I'm dead."

She leaves him there, walks back to the door, looks out again. The car is a gleaming shape in the rain. She leans out a little, looks toward the road, past the old Ford. If Duck comes now, he'll kill Wick; Duck blames it all on Wick.

"Mackin*ee*."

Elizabeth shuts the door. "Mackinley, I'm going to beat you good."

Mackinley lets go of the shawl, and her children now are quiet, looking like three dolls in a pile of junk. Oh, how she hates it that Wick is here, and that he will know they are caught this way, stuck in this place, in this clutter of their belongings, living off the uncertain charity of a man whose disdain for Elizabeth and her family is on him like an odor. "Wallace, get out from under that bed."

"Okay," says Wallace. "But I'm supposed to be dead."

Sometimes Elizabeth believes she can smell a person's feelings. Part of her still believes in the charms of her childhood: ghosts; visions of the dead; substances from trees and the roots of plants that could drive a person mad, or make a virgin conceive, or cure a hopeless disease. Because she can't sleep well (this latest pregnancy is causing some discomfort), she often walks out toward the field beyond the church at night, her scarf pulled tight under her chin, her coat collar up: there is always the idea, just under the flow of her mind, that she might go on into the tall, dying grass of Torgeson's land, and search out the mysterious substances she had learned about as a child, listening to her mother and her mother's aunts—those women who had grown up in the deep country, old women with queer eyes and stained teeth—telling their odd tales in the night. Jimsonweed, dandelion dust, wild mushrooms, the bark of certain shrubs. Devilry and witchcraft and spirits wandering the dark. Tales that never belonged there, where there was always the sound of a sprinkler throwing water out on the lawn, and the occasional whisper of a passing car, the far-off sirens of Galveston; her father saying good night to a neighbor, crossing the lawns, a cigarette in his mouth, the little aureole of red light showing his face.

Now she pulls Wallace from beneath the bed, her hands locked around his skinny ankles. His eyes are open at her, but unfocused. "I'm dead."

"Get up."

"Mommy," Sandra June cries. "Stop it, Mackinee. Mackinee's doing it again."

"Get up."

"I'm dead. The dead can't move."

Elizabeth kneels down, takes him by the ear, and pulls. He does not cry, nor does he show any sign that what she has done is painful, though she had pulled quite hard. When he stands, she holds his chin between her thumb and index finger.

"You don't know what dead is, boy."

"The dead can't talk."

She reaches for the ear again, but he shies away, and now Sandra June is screaming. Elizabeth puts one knee on the bed and covers the girl's mouth. The sound, muffled, comes through her fingers. She wants to hide—if Wick is out there, he'll hear. It seems to her that the light is far too bright, the room itself too large and bright. She releases Sandra June and moves to the door again, opening it an inch. Nothing has changed; the car is where it was, and Duck has not arrived. Muddy red puddles near the door grow wider and wider; farther out in the lot, pools of water make maps in the gravel —and the rain, hitting those pools, makes it appear that the stones are jumping beneath the surface. Elizabeth has a moment of extraordinary clarity, as if the vision of the rainy lot had broken some gauzy membrane behind her eyes and shown her the world with harm in it, a great harm that waits to happen—a flood, perhaps, or a tornado. She has an eerie sense of the very machinery of wind and cloud and air that will produce it; it is not human; it is violent, insensate force and it controls the little sudden craters of water in the expanding pools as well as it controls the branches of the trees beyond the church, which are bending now—one, at the top of the sky it seems, cracking as if by some inner explosion and dropping to the ground. And now she realizes that she is standing full in the door, the children staring at the scene from behind her dress—the door wide open, as though she had crowded toward whatever it was that was about to happen. The rain, carried by the rising wind, veers at her, and when she steps back into the hall, closing the door with more force than she needs, another pool of water forms at her feet. Everything drops from her.

2

She herds the children into the bathroom—a large, cement-smelling place; two stalls without doors, three sinks, dirty mirrors, and a high window, the only window.

"Where's Daddy?" Wallace asks.

"Silly," says Mackinley. "They went to the store."

"I want Daddy."

"Why do we have to stay in here?"

"Be quiet, all of you—I'll tell you a story."

"That was Candle's car," Mackinley says.

"No," says Elizabeth. "There are a lot of cars like that."

"Tell about Granddaddy Alphonse," says Wallace. "When we was naked."

"You never mind about that, boy."

"That was Candle's car."

"Here," Elizabeth says. "Just stand here. We're going to play hide-and-seek." Sandra June is on her hip, sliding down; Elizabeth is not strong enough to hold her any longer. She bends; the little girl's feet touch the floor. "Stand," Elizabeth says. "Stand."

Sandra June goes down on her knees and begins to cry.

"Be quiet. We're going to play now."

"I don't want to play."

"Be still. Just be still."

"We're hiding from Candle," says Mackinley.

"No."

"We're hiding from Daddy and Harvey and Priscilla."

"I want to go out," says Sandra June, still kneeling, the little white balls of her knees out of her dress. Now Wallace, too, is crying.

It won't work.

The priest will tell Candle she is here, anyway. "Oh," she says, "leave us alone."

Mackinley pushes the door open and is out, that fast. She thinks to stop him, but doesn't—and watches Wallace go next. Sandra June is still crying, face down on the floor. Elizabeth takes her under either arm, lifts gently, carries her out to the bed. Wallace and Mackinley are peeking out at the lot.

"Close that door," Elizabeth says.

"He's gone," says Wallace.

She comes up behind them, peers out, sees the empty place. "Now get away from this door," she says, "before you catch cold."

Mackinley says, "Candle made Granddaddy die."

"No. Get."

He sidles across the room behind Wallace, who climbs up onto the bed next to Sandra June and lies on his back, thumb in mouth. Mackinley kneels at the foot of the bed, worries the lid of Harvey's cedar box. Away from the lamp, he is mostly shadow, and she thinks how small and fragile he is. Sandra June lies with her face half into the pillow as if thrown there by grief. Wallace has burrowed under the blanket. These three, her smallest children, by their sudden retreat into themselves, give her a quick, proprietary feeling; this saddens her and she is unprepared for it. The blankness of the room, its metal chairs stacked in a long escarpment against the back wall—her own belongings strewn everywhere as though fallen, as though dropped by someone in flight—this all seems to press scornfully, cruelly, into her eyes. Oh, she had learned to deal with everything, but she knows she will not be able to deal with this, whatever it will be. She walks to the door— an old faith in movement, in activity as a defense against the tricks of the mind. She touches the knob, thinks again of the

about-to-happen something outside, hesitates. Then she seems
to feel another hand on the knob, from the other side. She
stands absolutely still, every nerve awake. Wick stands, as if
in a hundred mirrors, in every corner of her brain; the child
inside her gropes, as though trying to hide deeper in her
bones. She lifts her hand away from the knob, her fingers
trembling away from it, and then the door swings open wide.

"Here you are," Wick says.

3

"Your priest friend sent me away." He is sitting on the bed,
holding Sandra June in his lap. Sandra June sucks her thumb
and watches his face.

"Sandra June, come here," says Elizabeth.

"No, no. This little girl likes her Uncle Candle."

"Sandra June."

Sandra June smiles from the heavy crook of his arm.

"Where's your car?" Mackinley asks.

"Oh, I parked it down the road a little."

After a moment he looks at Elizabeth. "Your priest friend
told me you were staying here, but he said you were all gone
into town."

"Duck is coming back—you better not be here when he
gets back."

"Oh, but I want to talk to Duck."

Elizabeth says nothing.

"There's a little matter of some back rent. Some property
damage."

"That was not Duck," Elizabeth says. "That was Alphonse Bexley. He told you about it—I was there."

"Alphonse Bexley wasn't in any shape to burn down a place I'd already agreed to rent him—besides, why would he? He wanted to move in—was going to move in."

"He hated you."

"No, no—now there's where you're wrong."

Elizabeth won't sit down, but she can't find anything to do with herself.

"Everybody always hates the landlord."

Mackinley is toying with Harvey's cedar box. Elizabeth walks over to him and takes his arm. "Don't play with Harvey's things, you know better than to play with Harvey's things."

"Rented that place to Alphonse Bexley—or my father did—in 1952. The Wicks and the Bexleys had a long-standing relationship."

"You tried to cheat him—he was slipping and you tried to take advantage of him."

"I know that's what your husband thought."

"That's what I thought too."

"Yes, but you were wrong, and I don't see why I should have to pay for the fact that you were wrong."

"We don't have any money," Elizabeth says.

"I figure you owe me about three, four hundred dollars."

"You say that to Duck. He'll kill you."

Wick puts Sandra June down, gently, still smiling. "You're perfectly welcome to pay by installment. As long as I get what's coming to me."

"Four hundred dollars—"

"Last month's rent, and some cleaning up I had to do after you'd vacated. The lease did say one month's notice, Elizabeth."

"Candle," Wallace says, "did you make Granddaddy die?"

"Shut up," says Elizabeth. "Wallace, you shut up."

"Did you?"

Candle reaches out as if to tousle the boy's hair; but Wallace shrinks away, eyeing him suspiciously. "What're you teaching these kids about me?"

"You were there—you had that argument with him on the porch the day he died. You told us you wanted us out of there—"

"I was a little upset, wasn't I? I never had to argue with a naked man before. Elizabeth"—he hesitates—"you know that was all crazy."

"You told us you wanted us out."

"And I gave you a month's notice."

"Well, it doesn't matter—we don't have any money."

"I'll talk to Duck about installments."

"I'm telling you," Elizabeth says, "Duck'll kill you if he finds you here." She is trying very hard not to cry.

"Elizabeth," says Wick, "everything just sort of fell apart for you, didn't it?"

"Get out," Elizabeth says, crying. "Why can't you leave us alone?"

"Here I thought I was one of the family."

Now the children are just watching. Elizabeth moves to the door, opens it on the rain. "I'll send you something when I can—please, just get out."

"What about the property damage?" asks Wick.

"That was not Duck."

"Oh, come on—of course it was."

"You can't prove it," Elizabeth says.

"You been worrying about me coming here because you knew damn well I never believed Alphonse. That's what's got you so upset now—you're worried that I'll have your husband put away again. You see, I found out a few things about Duck Bexley."

"Please," Elizabeth says. "Leave us alone."

Wick rises slowly, pulls the yellow raincoat he'd been wearing up from the floor: it drips, wets his forehead as he swings it over his heavy shoulders. "Just don't make raincoats like they used to," he says. Then he crosses to Elizabeth, edging the children out of his wake, the flat, fat fingers in their hair, as if he owns them—this is the way he has always been, as if the Bexleys rented their very lives from him, and he had rights, privileges in the family. "I knew if I could just talk to you, Elizabeth, I'd find out for sure."

"No," Elizabeth says. "No."

"Don't worry, I'm not going to do anything—just send me what you owe me. That's all I want. I have a habit of going after what's owed me. I'm like the shepherd with his flock, Elizabeth," he says, putting one hand out, a grand gesture. "I go after the ones that are lost, so to speak—and you people cost me some money."

"Just go," Elizabeth says.

"Duck still blames me, does he, for what happened with the old man?"

"If you hadn't—" Elizabeth begins. He stops her. Puts his hand on her shoulder.

"If I hadn't tried to give an old man what he wanted."

"You make it sound like—like you were just being generous."

"In a way, I was."

"Just get out."

"The money, remember—installments. I hope I don't have to come looking again."

"All right—please."

"I don't care how large or small the installment is—but I

want something from you every month. Get it from the priest if you have to. He'll understand."

"All right," Elizabeth says. "All right, all right."

"I really am trying to be fair, Elizabeth."

She thinks if she does not speak, he'll go; but he stands there looking at her, his eyes trailing down to where the baby is.

"Lord," he says finally, moving past her. "Another Bexley."

4

"He's gone," Mackinley says. "Fat Candle is gone."

"You say Mr. Wick," Elizabeth tells him, but she can manage no forcefulness of tone. He is playing with Harvey's cedar box again, has it open, his little fists in the paper there. She reaches for him, but he evades her.

"I'm not hurting it," he says.

"You come here."

"Mommy," says Wallace, "what did he mean about putting Daddy away again?"

"Nothing. You never mind. Mackinley, come here."

Mackinley stands defiantly out of her reach.

"Mackinee," Sandra June says.

Elizabeth takes a quick step, has him, holds him against her hip, her hand over his ear. "You are not to play with Harvey's things."

"You crying?" asks Wallace.

"No."

"She's crying."

"You go on and take a nap now. Mackinley," she moves him around to face her, "I want you all to take a nap."

"I don't want to," Mackinley says. "I hate this place."

"I hate this place," says Wallace.

Sandra June has begun to cry. She wanders in a little circle among the fallen clothes, thumb in mouth, crying.

"I'm not going to take no nap," Mackinley says.

"We're all going to take a nap," says Elizabeth. "All of us. Mommy too."

"Well, I'm not. We don't nap until after lunch. I'm not napping until after lunch, dammit."

She takes his face in her hands, and his lips bunch up, moist and dark as the skin of a cherry. "You do not speak like that in this—" She had almost said house. And now her discouragement is complete. "You do not—" she begins, but her throat closes. "You do not—"

"Dammit," he says. "Dammit, dammit, dammit."

She takes one breath, and strikes.

She had not meant to hurt him, but immediately there is blood. It seems to burst from his mouth and to reflect every particle of light in the room. It makes three wicked blots on the floor and it stains his fingers. For a moment he seems about to shriek at her, but then he is just standing there looking at his fingers with a horror and fascination that are more an indictment of her than his crying would have been. When she kneels to wipe his face with the edge of her dress, he only glares at her, wide-eyed and accusing; she feels the trembling of his knees, and as though to defend herself for what she has done she speaks to him in a petulant, unsympathetic way. "See what you get for your mis-behaving? See what you made Mommy do? You have no one to blame but yourself." He is motionless. Every brush of the stained cloth makes his flesh whiter, the blood darker. He waits passively for her to finish, and then he seems to wait for her to strike him again.

"Oh," she says, putting her arms around him, her palm to the back of his head. "Oh, Mac." She feels his hand patting her shoulder, and then she feels the others pressing close. "Oh, Mac. Oh, Mac. Mac."

They all wait for her now.

She lifts Mackinley, carries him to the bed, sets him down as though he is a baby. They are all on the bed now, and Mackinley is gingerly touching his lip. Wallace is fascinated; Sandra June is a little envious of the attention Mackinley has received, and moans, complaining about some vague pain in her arm. Elizabeth kisses the arm. "All right," she says. "We're going to be all right."

"All wight," Sandra June says. "All wight."

When they are all asleep, Elizabeth quietly wraps herself in her coat and steps out into the rain. There is a drifting fog now over the field beyond the church, but the top of the sky is clearing; she sees broken clouds there. Still, the rain comes down steadily and slowly as if it will go on for days, and Elizabeth, having forgotten her scarf, holds her coat over her head, is bent low and only sees gravel and water for a few steps. It is as if she has entered the storm and will not find her way to the other side, the house. She skirts the border of a puddle that seems to want to take her all the way to Torgeson's fence; then it curves, and she follows to the stoop, makes her way up to the door. She feels as if she has traveled here, over a long period of time, as if this is an appointed place somehow. For a moment her life stops here; she cannot imagine the next moment.

5

When Elizabeth was almost eighteen, she had run away with Duck Bexley. Last summer, after fourteen years and five children, she had begun to think about running in the other direction, back home. Mostly she was tired. She had never really liked Virginia. The house she had to keep was a rented house, and in it, along with her and the five children and Duck Bexley, lived Duck Bexley's father, Alphonse. In fact it was Alphonse who had originally rented the house, though now the old man was retired, and for years Duck had been paying the rent.

And Alphonse had taken to calling her Alva.

"Who is Alva?" she asked Duck, after it had happened the first time.

He gave her an incredulous look. "My mother—you know that."

"Yes," she said. "But there's no one else he might—is there somebody else named Alva?"

"Ask him."

Later she did so. "Alva?" said the old man. "I don't know anybody—" he looked puzzled. "Alva died forty-one years ago."

An odd combination of names. Alphonse, Alva, Alphonse junior—Duck. Alphonse had not liked the name Junior, so he had made up the nickname for his son. As a boy, trouble rolled off the son like water off a duck. "You never saw a more easygoing kid," Alphonse said. Elizabeth insisted on ordinary names for her children: no nicknames, no Als. Alphonse talked about her nerves. "You got to take things more easy, Elizabeth." He made her feel constantly *visited*. She longed for privacy. An old man was in the house who called her Alva now and then and whose habits made her ache with frustration and anger. He was eighty-one, tall, wiry; he had been old as long as she had known him. A former sheriff of Albermarle County, he liked to tell stories of whiskey runners, of wild chases down country roads, and of the men and women of those days. Often he spoke about going back to Charlottesville and looking some of them up. Elizabeth wished that he would, and she begged Duck to find her a place—something she could really call her own. Alphonse could visit and she would not mind at all. The old man never put the toilet seat back down and he left beer bottles in his room, or walked through the house carrying racy magazines and paperbacks, as if there were no children around. Oh, there had been times when she hated him, hated his voice and his presence and his odor, which was always a little like the odor of rotting fruit. That summer he had begun to drink whiskey more than beer, and the whiskey made him sick.

"Why do you drink it if it makes you sick?" she asked, irritated.

"Alva," he said, "I want out of here. I want a little privacy."

Elizabeth answered to the name. "Speak to Duck about it. This is your house. Your name is on the lease. Kick us out."

"Let me be," he muttered.

Later she said to Duck, "He wants a place of his own."

"No," Duck said. "This is where he belongs."

But the old man spoke to Mr. Wick, the landlord. Mr. Wick was the son of the man Alphonse had originally rented the house from. The son began to stop by in the evenings to drink Duck's beer or Alphonse's whiskey, sitting with the old man on the porch, sometimes all night.

"I'm a night owl," Wick said to Elizabeth. "Candle is the perfect name for me."

After the first visit, Duck wanted to know why he had been

there. Duck did not like company and he particularly did not like Candle. Candle was fat, and he had money. "What the hell does he want with us?" Duck asked.

"I've been talking to him," Alphonse said, "about renting me another place."

"You don't need a place, old man, and I want you to tell that fat son of a bitch I said so."

"Suppose you let me decide that," Alphonse said.

"Why don't you please let him have what he wants?" Elizabeth asked.

"I don't want him talking to Wick," Duck said. "I take care of my own."

But Wick/Candle kept coming over anyway. He learned the children's names and he called Elizabeth "Little Mama." The old man sat with him on the porch. Duck would come home and pass between the two of them, entering the house in a cold anger because Wick/Candle was the landlord, and a stranger, and would know the old man was slipping—or that was what Duck told Elizabeth. "Of course he's slipping. You know he is too, dammit. He's been calling you Alva, hasn't he? I've heard him. He really thinks you're my mother when he does that."

"Your father can decide a thing like where he wants to live," Elizabeth said.

"You never gave a damn about him," Duck said.

"Alva," the old man said one morning, "don't you love the trees in summer? Don't you love the full, green trees everywhere?"

"I'm not your Alva," Elizabeth said. "Damn you. Wake up."

Then she was pregnant again, and knew it. It was the Fourth of July. People already gave her looks in the stores when she took the children shopping with her: as if she had *killed* five children. Now there would be a sixth. When she told Duck, he stiffened, the corner of his mouth turned up, but he said nothing. The television was on. Priscilla, the eldest daughter, lay on the floor in front of it, holding a hand mirror up and gazing at the screen in reverse, or watching her own face smile, then frown, then smile again.

"Did you hear what I said?" Elizabeth asked. She spoke to both of them.

"What do *you* think?" Priscilla said.

"Duck?"

"I heard you," Duck said.

"And?"

"I figured."

"That's all?"

"Can't think of a thing," he said. The muscles of his jaw were moving.

Alphonse had been in his room, and now he came out, passed through in front of the portable, stood at the front door, and said, "Candle has got a place for me to rent."

"You ain't leaving," Duck said. "So you might as well sit down and shut up."

The old man walked out onto the porch, but he was not out there long. He came back through, went into the kitchen, and rattled glasses. Then he crossed to his room, brought out a bottle of whiskey.

"You going to pout now?" Duck asked.

The old man made no response. He let the screen door slam, and when Elizabeth went out to him, he was sitting on the top step of the porch, pouring the whiskey. It was a hot twilight, gray and still, and already there were fireworks sounding in the distance. "Don't take that from him," Elizabeth said. "Tell him you'll do what you damn well please."

He touched her elbow, reaching up. "Sit here, honey."

She sighed, was about to tell him again that she was not Alva. But he smiled.

"Come on, Elizabeth. Sit here next to a tired old man."

She arranged herself next to him. "I'm going to have a baby," she said, fighting back tears.

He patted her knee. "That's just wonderful. That's"—he gazed out at the lawn—"that's just holy."

Harvey had been out in the witchgrass behind the garage. There was always something he could find to bring to Elizabeth from the wild green places he roamed back there. He came around the house now with a bird in his palm. The bird had a broken wing; it pulsed, beak open, one glazed eye looking everywhere.

"What in God's name is happening to us," Elizabeth said.

A little later Candle came over, and sat where Elizabeth had. Elizabeth started to go inside, but Alphonse made her get a glass for Candle and then insisted that she stay. She sat down in one of the metal chairs and waited for the fireworks with them. The fireworks would come high over the trees to the east, where the Richmond fairgrounds were.

"Come on and sit down, Little Mama," Candle said.

"My name is Elizabeth, Mr. Wick."

"Well," said Candle, "I'll make a deal with you. You call me Candle and I'll call you Elizabeth." Then he turned to Alphonse and said, "I got a place if you want it, Al. It's a little risky for us, but I think it might work out."

"You hear that?" Alphonse said to Elizabeth.

She did not respond.

"Elizabeth," said Candle. "What a pretty name." Then he let out a stream of talk—someone he had known, an Elizabeth. A beautiful woman, but hard of heart. He went on. Alphonse Bexley sat swirling the whiskey in his glass, staring east.

Candle spoke about this woman, this cruel Elizabeth; and then he spoke about his father and about being fat—as if his own obesity were a skill he had acquired—and about growing up in New York, where his mother had taken him when she divorced his father. There was about him a willingness, almost an eagerness to spell out all the stored up bitternesses and embarrassments of his life, as if by doing so, he could ward off some natural force that would turn everybody against him.

The old man interrupted him. "She's going to have another baby."

"You're fooling."

"No." The old man smiled at Elizabeth.

"He telling the truth, Little Mama?" Candle put his hand on her knee. She removed it.

"I'm real proud," the old man said.

"This calls for a celebration," said Candle. He worked himself to this feet. "Duck. Where's Duck Bexley."

"You better leave him alone," Elizabeth said.

Candle paid no attention. He pulled the screen door open, leaned into the house. "Hey, old boy, I hear you're going to be a father again."

Elizabeth could not hear Duck's response, if there had been any.

Candle went inside.

"Alphonse," Elizabeth said, "you better get him."

But her father-in-law merely gazed out at the sky, which was now the color of dark water.

The door swung open, and Candle came backing out; he had Duck's wrists, and was pulling him. "Come on now," he said. "You have to drink a whiskey with us and celebrate."

Duck's face was pinched, white, narrow-lipped. His eyes were down, and Candle kept bending to look into them.

"Come on, come on, now."

"There goes the first rocket," Alphonse said.

They all stopped to watch. The children all rushed out, down the steps, out to the willow tree at the end of the clay driveway, where they would sit in a small circle and watch, as they had done every Fourth of July for years. The rocket burst in a red bloom, which opened three others of white, blue, and yellow.

"That is a sight," Candle said. Then he turned to Duck again. Duck had worked his hands loose, and stood there against the doorjamb. He would not look at anyone or anything. "Well, are you going to give this little lady a kiss and make a toast to her or not?"

Duck said nothing.

"Come on, boy."

Elizabeth got out of her chair just as the second rocket went up. In a white glare she edged between Candle and her husband.

"Damn you for this," Duck whispered.

She kissed him lightly on the cheek, put her mouth to his ear. "I'm leaving you."

"Get me a beer."

Candle heard this. "All right. Now we'll celebrate."

"Kiss me," Elizabeth said to Duck.

"Damn you."

She leaned toward him again, hearing another rocket; blue light on his face made her hesitate. Then she kissed his mouth, closing her teeth on his lower lip, biting down hard.

"Now that's more like it," Candle said behind them.

Duck's hands took her shoulders and moved her, tightening. She saw blood on his lip. The rockets were booming out over the fairgrounds, and they shook the air. Candle was watching the lighted sky now, and Elizabeth opened the door and went inside, feeling Duck behind her, though she would not turn to look at him. He was at her shoulder as she walked down the hall toward the bedroom. "I'll kill you," he hissed. "I'll kill you." She went into the bedroom and closed the door, almost running the last few steps. But when the door was closed, the latch clicked—like the conclusion of something—he kicked once, hard, and the wood in the lower panel cracked. Elizabeth opened quickly. "You want him to hear you kicking the door?"

"I hope he does." Duck walked toward her, chest out; for a moment she was almost afraid of him. But then he put his arms out. "Goddamn, honey," he said. "Goddamn." His arms went around her and he cried down into her shoulder, like a boy, muffling it there, so that no one would hear. When the rockets burst, he shook, and she touched the hair on his neck, mothering, soothing him.

"Hey," came Candle's voice, "where's the lovebirds."

"We'll be right out, Mr. Wick," Elizabeth said.

Candle stood at the end of the hall. "You're missing the show."

"We'll be right out."

Duck stepped away from her and struck the palm of one hand with his fist. "Goddamn him," he whispered. "Who does he think he is?"

"We have to go out there," Elizabeth said.

"If he touches me again, I'll kill him."

Elizabeth dried his eyes. "The rockets—they're getting to you again."

"No."

"They are. You're shaking."

"It ain't the goddamn rockets, Elizabeth."

"Is it the other thing? Your trouble?"

"No. It's him. It's that fat son of a bitch who wants to make himself at home here and cheat my father. He's cheating my father."

"Maybe your father'll do better in a place of his own."

Duck turned from her. "You don't care about him. You never did. Don't you see he can't watch out for himself anymore?"

"I care about him, Duck."

"You never liked him from the first."

"No," Elizabeth said. "I'll tell you what I didn't like—I didn't like how much he took you away from me—and from the children. But I was wrong. It isn't him—it's never been him. It's you. Tonight is the first time you ever let me get close enough to you to mother you a little. To love you the way I want to."

"Leave it," Duck said.

"I'm going to have a child, Duck. You wanted to fill the house with children. What's happened to you?"

"Just please shut up."

"Hey," came Candle's voice again, "you're going to miss it."

Elizabeth went first. Down the hallway in the dark, toward the large shadow at the end.

"Can't hide yourselves away tonight," Candle said.

She heard Duck's voice behind her. "You got that one right."

Outside the light was blue: falling sparks trailing down the east. The children were very still out in the yard as though they were posing for a photograph. Alphonse Bexley sat back against the porch rail, pouring more whiskey.

"I took the liberty of getting glasses for you two," Candle said, "so we could have a toast."

"I don't drink," said Elizabeth.

"Oh, come on. Just a little."

"Elizabeth doesn't drink," Alphonse said.

Candle poured two drinks anyway, and Elizabeth watched Duck gulp his down.

"Toast," Candle said. "Wait. Toast."

Duck stopped.

"To the little mama." Candle poured more into the empty glass. Duck gulped that too.

The rockets were going in clusters now, high and loud and bright, and the sky was full of ashes, falling. They all watched quietly, and when it was over, Priscilla and Harvey brought the younger children back up onto the porch. Candle insisted on kissing each of them good night, and then Priscilla took them in to bed. Harvey stayed for a little while, sitting with his arms folded, between his grandfather's knees. The quiet, after the noise of the rockets, seemed thick, like the humid summer air. Elizabeth sat in her chair with her hands in her lap, and Duck stood at her shoulder. Candle roamed the porch, talking about the fireworks in a low, respectful voice. A slight breeze carried the odor of gunpowder to them.

Finally Alphonse Bexley said, "Hell, even the bugs are quiet after all that noise."

"Harvey," said Duck, "get on in the house now."

The boy rose, yawned, walked up to Elizabeth, and lay his head in her lap.

"Go on," Duck said.

"Got a handshake for Uncle Candle?"

Harvey put his small hand into the thick palm.

"Atta boy."

"Get on inside," said Duck.

The boy went in, and Candle walked to the top step, stood above Alphonse Bexley, and tipped his glass back. "That's a nice boy," he said when he had swallowed.

"Yeah, that's right," said Duck. "You got that just right." Then he said, "I want to know about this place you think you're going to rent to my father."

"You shut up, boy," Alphonse said.

"I am the head of this family now, Daddy, and you know it."

"No, I don't know any such thing."

"You're drunk."

"I don't know any such god-damn thing."

"Now hold on a minute," Candle said. "Let's not ruin a nice evening like this—a holiday—with an argument about something that—"

"You stay the hell out of it," Duck said. "You just stay the hell out of it."

"Alva, tell that boy to go to bed."

They were all quiet for a moment. Alphonse stood up, whispered, "Goddammit."

"Well," said Candle, "I guess I ought to be going."

"Duck," the old man said, walking toward him, "you don't give me any room, boy. I have got to have some room. A man has got to have a little dignity—"

"You got all the dignity you need right here, old man."

Alphonse turned. "I want that place, Candle."

"Sure."

"Where is it?" asked Duck.

"You never mind where it is, boy. You just never mind."

"It's out on Grace Road," Candle said. "You can't miss it. Right on the fork there. Grace Road and Larker Road. You've prob'ly seen it. It ain't much—but."

"We're going out to look at it tomorrow," Alphonse said.

"That's the agreement," said Candle.

"Yeah, well, we'll just see about that," Duck said. "We'll just god-dammit see."

"You come get me tomorrow, Candle," Alphonse muttered. "You hear?"

"At the agreed time. I'll be there if you want me to, Al." Candle went down off the porch, his small feet on the gravel below. But then he stopped, turned, walked back up, took Elizabeth's hand, bowing with elaborate grace. "Congratulations on the new addition to the family, Elizabeth," he said. Elizabeth, for an unpleasant instant, thought he meant himself. She turned from Candle's bowing and watched Alphonse enter the house.

"Congratulations again," Candle said to Duck, who did not respond. "Good night." He went carefully back down the steps, looking down, and when he reached the sidewalk, he straightened, striding jauntily into the dark. Elizabeth and Duck were as they had been, watching the lights of his car come on, hearing the engine, the smooth whine and whisper, the tires popping stones as the car went down the drive and away. Then, gradually, the sound of the summer insects came to them.

"I'm sorry about biting you," Elizabeth said.

There was no answer.

"You know you can't stop him if he decides to move out."

"Made up my mind," Duck said, "a long time ago, that if I have to feed and wash my father like a baby—if I have to change—if I have to put goddamn diapers on him and change him like a baby, I'll never see him at the mercy of people who ain't family." He did not wait for her to respond to this. He left her there, and she put her hands out on her knees, smoothing the cloth of her dress, and listened to more fireworks, far off, as if remembered.

Then Duck came back out of the house, without speaking or looking at her; he went down the steps, around toward the garage.

"Duck?" she said. "Duck?"

He came back, hands shoved down into his pockets, pacing back and forth in front of the porch.

"What is it?" she asked.

"Go on," said Duck. "Go on inside. Just leave me alone for a while."

"I am always having to leave you alone."

"Elizabeth—" He held his fists out in front of him, seemed about to scream at her; but then he pulled himself back, letting his hands down. "Elizabeth, just—please."

He walked toward the willow tree, slowly, as if he were half asleep.

"Mommy?" came from the door.

Elizabeth turned, saw a shadow there. It was Priscilla.

"What is it?" Priscilla said.

"Go on inside and watch TV," said Elizabeth. But Priscilla stood there until Elizabeth got up and, entering the house, guided her back to the sofa.

"I don't want to watch," Priscilla said.

Elizabeth sighed. "Then go on outside if you want—your father'll just send you back."

"I don't want to be in here and listen to that old man cough."

"Granddaddy's coughing?"

"Since he came in. He just stopped. You didn't hear it?"

"No."

"I heard it over the television."

A moment passed. There was a woman standing at a window looking out on a balcony in the silver light of the television screen. The screen made the only light in the room.

"I hate this house," Priscilla said. "I hate this family."

The words seemed to fall out of the filmy shape of the girl's face; and it was the haggard look of that face in the dark, as much as it was the cruelty of the language, that made Elizabeth want to cry. But she did not let Priscilla know that she felt this. She muttered something about getting to bed, turned, and walked to the kitchen, putting lamps on as she passed them. Then she could not remember if she had said that *she* should get to bed or that Priscilla should; so she called from the kitchen, "You get to bed right now, young lady." As she turned to look at what she thought would be an empty doorway, she saw Alphonse Bexley with the girl in hand.

"Now you tell your mother you are sorry."

"I'm sorry," Priscilla said.

"Now get your little ass in bed."

The girl turned and was gone, and Alphonse stepped into the kitchen, smiling, his eyes bright, his face coloring as if he suffered some undue praise. "I just started out of my room to get a beer, Elizabeth, and I heard her say that to you."

"Duck's out there wandering around—"

"Yeah, I know." He stood quite still. His face seemed to give in to some inward pressure—the eyes let down; the cheeks went ashen and pushed out bone. "I'm just—sorry."

"Thank you for—"

"She's a good girl," he said, waving his hand across his face. "She didn't mean nothing."

"Yes."

"Elizabeth, he's got to give me—a man has to have some kind of a life of his own."

"He loves you," Elizabeth said. "He loves you terribly."

"But I got to get out—I—" He stopped, seemed confused. A half smile worked its way into his mouth. She took his hand and led him back to his bedroom. By his breathing she knew that he was about to cough, but he held it back. She could feel him holding it back, and then, quite suddenly, she knew how much she had loved him all the time. She held tight to his hand, leading him into his bed. The room smelled of his whiskey and his age. On the small table by the bed were four or five paperbacks creased and fanned and dirty. The bed itself was in disorder, and she had to pull the spread from beneath him, with the cover sheet, which she let down across his chest and tucked under his chin. His large, watery eyes looked at her as if to forgive something, and then he brought his hands out from under the sheet and just barely touched her chin.

"You go to sleep now," she said.

"Elizabeth?"

"Go to sleep."

"I was going to get a beer." Now he did cough, a deep, rasping thing that took him down and down into it, so that when he breathed in, it was with a loud gasp. Elizabeth put her hand on his chest.

"Okay," he said. "I'm okay now."

"You want me to get you a beer?"

"No."

"I'll get you one if you want—it might soothe your throat."

"No," he said. Then he seemed confused again. "Elizabeth?"

"Yes?"

"There was something I had to—"

"You were going to get a beer."

"No."

"Try to sleep now."

"I want you to know, Elizabeth—I always thought Duck did well with you, that he was a lucky man."

She leaned down and kissed his forehead. As she was lifting back, he touched her breast. She stood very still, first from surprise, then from something else: It could do no harm.

In a moment he lifted his head, put his mouth to her ear, and whispered, "Thank you."

"Go to sleep now."

Outside, in the thick dark, she stretched her arms out wide and took a deep breath. She was suddenly quite tired and sleepy. Above the willow tree a hazy moon shone like a hole in the sky. She walked down the steps and a little way down the drive, looking for Duck. There was something she wanted to tell him. Twice she said his name, but she did not want to shout. As she turned back toward the house, she saw him coming from the garage.

"Honey?" she said.

He was carrying a gas can; she could hear the liquid splashing against the metal.

"Duck," she said.

"In the house, Elizabeth." He walked past her, toward the truck.

And before she could get to him, he had pulled away, swerving crazily down the drive and on, the truck rattling and banging over the bumps. She watched until the twin red lights dipped out of sight beyond the end of the road.

She waited for him, sitting on the top step of the porch, watching the occasional lights out on the road. She believed that this was the end, that her family was pulling apart as if something in her private wishes had already set things in motion; yet she could not bring herself to cry or call out or move. She had lost time: an hour might have passed. The moon was higher, brighter, and the air had begun to cool, little breezes stirring like the breath of some far-off storm.

"Duck," she said, as if he were standing there on the porch, "don't do anything, please."

At length Alphonse Bexley came out, his movement in the door startling her. He was careful not to let it slam, shuffled across the boards of the porch in his stocking feet—he wore his brown gabardine slacks and a white shirt. A dark tie was draped over his shoulders.

"Can't sleep," he said.

He sat down on the step below her and she looked at his thin back, the bones of his shoulders through the white shirt.

"So where'd he go?"

She put her hands to her face and began to cry. But she made no sound; the whole thing clutched at her abdomen and took her voice away. Alphonse put his hand on her shoulder, then went inside, and she heard him in his room, opening and closing drawers. The light from his window let out onto the lawn to her left, and she saw his shadow in it twice. When he returned, he had a pair of shoes with him. He sat down below her again, struggling to get them on.

"So you're leaving me too," she managed to say.

He looked back at her, smiled as if she had marked some pleasantry of the night—the way the moon fell out of the dark and lighted the grass, or the thin song of the insects. When he busied himself with the shoes again, she said, "Damn you, damn all of you."

He was not listening. His hands wouldn't work as he wanted them to, and he groaned with each failure of his fingers. In a little while, as she watched him, she knew he had forgotten what he had set out to do.

"Don't know why God put us here," he said, drawing breath in, a loud, cold, sniffing sound. "Work your ass off all your life and then die."

"I don't want to hear it," said Elizabeth. "I'm sick and tired of it. He's out there doing God knows what—he took a gas can with him. A gas can, dear God." She put her hands over her mouth.

Alphonse Bexley did not seem to hear. He stood up, looked down at his feet. The shoes were on. When he had reassured himself of this, he took the tie by its ends. "You know, I just —I was going somewhere—" He held the ends of the tie down tight against his chest. "Damn," he said. Then he turned, climbed back up the stairs and went into the house, again careful not to slam the door.

．　．　．

Perhaps an hour later, a pair of headlights pulled into the drive and came toward her. It was the truck: she could tell by the sound of it before she could make its shape out of the light. It pulled straight toward her, stopped; the lights dropped from it and the engine clanked dead.

Elizabeth waited.

Duck got out, walked with the can around to the garage. There was the sound of metal sliding on wood. Elizabeth got up, moved to the top step, and stood there, watching him come back around. He had removed his shirt.

"I'm leaving you," she said as he came level with her.

"Just leave me alone *now*," he said.

"What did you do," she asked.

He sat down heavily in the chair, his legs out straight. "Nothing but a god-damn wood shack."

"What did you do—please, Duck." She stood above him with her arms wrapped tight under her breasts.

"Burned it down."

"Oh," she said, struggling to the porch rail. "Jesus Christ God, I knew it."

Presently she murmured, "It doesn't matter that you have a wife and five children—"

"You got that right—not where this is concerned. I'm telling you it was a shack. One room, with a dirt floor."

"Now what," said Elizabeth, staring out at the road.

"Nothing what. That's what. Let him do what he thinks he can do. Let him prove it. Would've burned down anyway— and my father *in* it, if I didn't do something."

They didn't speak for a moment. Elizabeth thought she could hear sirens, but she could not be sure; then she believed she had been hearing them all night.

"Thing went up like a cinder," Duck said. "Come on, let's get inside."

She did not move.

"Oh, yeah. You're leaving me."

"Duck, your father is dying," Elizabeth said. "And nothing you do will stop it."

He went inside, let the door slap to. Then he spoke to her through the screen. "You think I don't know that? You think I don't know that, Elizabeth?" His voice was thin, shaking, a boy's voice. "Think I'm going to let him die alone, in a god-damn shack like that?"

"There are laws, Duck." She had turned, and now faced him through the screen.

"*Fuck* laws," he said, and walked away from her.

In the morning they ate without speaking, in the noise of the children. Alphonse, as usual, slept late. Duck went to work and the older children walked through the trees in back to a playground that had been built to accommodate a new housing development there. Elizabeth let Sandra June and the twins play outside—they stayed on the porch, afraid of the bees that lifted and settled among the clover blossoms. It was like any summer morning: bright, already hot, birds singing and sailing through the shade, squirrels darting in the trees. A beautiful morning, and Elizabeth sat crying quietly in the kitchen. She wanted to go home, wanted to walk down her street, swinging her arms, in the sea-salt air of the gulf, and stand at the end of the sidewalk, looking through perfect shade at the rain porch, where her mother and the old women sat on summer afternoons. She remembered standing on that porch on just such a summer day as this, hearing her mother say, "Cross-stitch, one-two, cross-stitch, one-two," and thinking that she could never be those women—not ever. And she remembered walking into her father's den one night—how old had she been? Thirteen? Fourteen?—while the aunts laughed at a quiz show on television, and finding her father facing the window of that small room, his hands up over his ears. "Fucking stupid," he said, turning. "Bitches."

"Daddy?" she had said.

He saw her, his face changed twice, quickly, from concern to a smile. "And what brings you here?"

She could not be sure, then, that she had heard him speak those other words: she never saw another sign of discontent in him. He had always been a man of orderly habits and quiet temper, and when Elizabeth had first taken Duck, he had stood with the old women against her. Oh, how she had wanted to get away from them all; and now, how much she wanted to be able to return. To go back clean of everything, somehow, and start over.

But then there was the sound of a car in the driveway, and she busied herself with the breakfast dishes, her hands shaking in the water because she knew who it would be—and damn Duck for going off to work and leaving her to face this alone. There was the lumbering noise on the porch, the banging on the screen door. Elizabeth waited a moment, then walked out to meet Candle, who stood pressing his round face against the screen.

"There you are," he said.

She pushed the door toward him and stepped out, stood arranging her hair with her fingers. "Alphonse is asleep," she said.

"I don't want to see Alphonse—I want to see your husband."

She bent down and picked up Sandra June.

"Where is your husband, Elizabeth."

"Gone to work." She was aware that her voice shook, so she smiled: "Is something the matter?"

"I'm afraid we have got a serious problem." His face was

like a big white balloon letting out air; the air smelled of sausage and eggs. It made her a little sick. "Was your husband here all night?"

"Of course," she said.

"All right," said Candle, rocking forward on his heels a little—he seemed about to pull out a pad and pencil, like a policeman who would take names, would ask for license and registration. "Where's the old man. I want to talk to the old man."

"He's asleep."

"Wake him up. Would you please wake him up."

She let Sandra June down, managed to say, "I couldn't do that." She felt a muscle jump in her neck, near the shoulder line. Putting her hand to it, casually, she tried to keep smiling. But she was too frightened to make it convincing.

"Look," Candle said, "I don't want to get mad here. I asked you to wake up the old man. Now I could just go to the police—"

But then Alphonse Bexley was there, standing in the door. He was naked. Elizabeth herded the children out into the yard, and when she turned, she saw that Candle had moved to the porch rail and put his hand on it. Alphonse came out, pushed the door out, and stood looking through the screen at Candle.

"Who is this man, Alva?"

"Al," said Candle. "It's me."

"It's Mr. Wick," Elizabeth said.

The old man stepped away from the door, letting it swing shut, and approached Candle, who backed against the rail, his wide buttocks covering it.

"Jesus Christ—I was here last night. Remember? I'm a friend."

"I believe you got something on your mind, the way you were talking to Alva, here."

"Put your clothes on," said Candle. "God-damn."

"I am aware how I'm dressed, sir."

"Elizabeth," Candle said. "For God's sake."

"What is your problem," said the old man.

"All right. Dammit. It's your loss. That son of yours burned down the place I was going to rent you. . . ."

Elizabeth stood quite still, watching the two men, and, without having to turn her head, she came to know that the twins and Sandra June had stopped their play and were watching too, standing just a little to the side and behind her.

"Alva, what the hell is he talking about."

Elizabeth kept silent.

"Look," Candle said, "don't do anything crazy. . . ."

And now Alphonse seemed to straighten, his hand going up to touch his cheek.

"I'm telling you, he burned it down. And I am going to go to the police about it."

"Alva," said the old man. "You know anything about this?"

"Nothing," Elizabeth said, crying. "Alphonse."

"Duck Bexley will go to jail for burning down my property," Candle said. "Now that's all I have to say about it."

"You want me to send this man away, Alva?"

"For God's sake," Candle said, "do you know that you're naked? You ain't got a stitch of clothing on. *Na-ked.*"

The old man looked at him.

"Wake up, man. You haven't got any clothes on."

"I told you," Alphonse said, straightening, his voice thin, but full of dignity, "I am aware how I am dressed. It's a hot day and we're a close family."

Candle was silent.

Elizabeth looked at Alphonse. He seemed weak and confused, so skinny and white and unprotected there in the sun on the porch. She tried not to look at the gray bush between his legs, and wondered that Candle could be afraid. *Alphonse,* she wanted to say, *Alphonse, it's all right, we're all right.*

"You ought to take your clothes off," Alphonse muttered. "You'd be cooler."

"Your son burned down the place!" Candle screamed.

"No, I burned it."

Elizabeth became aware that the children were taking their clothes off. She began to unbutton her blouse. "It *is* hot," she said, loud enough to be heard.

"Christ," Candle said, "you're all crazy. You've all gone crazy."

"Take your clothes off," Alphonse said in an exultant voice.

"I want you out of here. You all have one month to be out of here."

"Duck was here," Elizabeth said, "with us. Naked."

"That's right," Alphonse said, "and then I went naked over to Grace Road and burned that shack down. Sorry." He was dancing now, his arms high over his head. "Sorry."

Elizabeth let her blouse fall to her feet.

Candle stepped away from the rail, edged past the old man, and came down the stairs as if he might pitch forward and fall. He turned. "Al, for Christ's sake." Then he got into his car and drove away; he did not wait to see Elizabeth drop her bra.

The children played naked on the porch. Elizabeth helped the old man back to his room, and again he touched her breast. "Pretty," he said, lying down. She cupped her hand over him between his legs, but only for a moment. She felt like a child again—one of those outside who, naked, had lost their fear of the bees and were now running in the grass under the window. She left Alphonse and went to see that they stayed in the yard, but in a moment he had wandered out into the kitchen and got himself a beer. She hurried in to him, found him back on his bed with the beer on his chest, a dark, sweating bottle. Now he halfheartedly pulled the sheet over his loins.

"There won't be anything to worry about, Elizabeth," he said.

"You're—" she began.

"No," he said. "Right at the end there I—I knew everything."

She was silent.

"I'm sorry."

"No," she said.

"I think it'll be all right."

"Are you okay?" she asked. She was aware that she was still naked from the waist up, and she pulled part of the spread around her.

"I'm in and out," Alphonse said. He sipped the beer, not looking at her.

"Do you think Candle will go to the police?"

"Naw."

She waited for him to go on.

"This the damnedest thing?" His face tightened and he jerked back deeper in the bed, letting his head fall against the pillows. "Elizabeth, I'm afraid something is happening to me."

"Want me to get help?"

"No."

She was quiet.

"Hate ambulances."

"I'm scared for you," Elizabeth said.

"Don't be." He coughed. A fleck of blood appeared on his lips. The sun came through the window and burned there.

"Alphonse?"

"Like I go to sleep—you know? Like I'm walking around half asleep."

"Let me call somebody for you—"

"Like I dream—" He drank the beer, lifting his head. The beer spilled on his cheeks. When he brought the bottle away from his mouth, the fleck of blood was a pink smear. She put one hand under his neck, but he let his arm come hard against her shoulder, as if to push her away. "Elizabeth," he said, "don't be afraid now. Don't be scared." He grew wide-eyed, let the beer drop over in a quick, foaming puddle at his neck. "Elizabeth."

Presently she reached down and touched his cheek. Then she wiped the smear of blood away with her thumb, soaked the beer up with a fold of the spread that covered her. She felt old now—older than Alphonse had been.

"Oh," she said, "Alphonse."

Then, gently, she shut the lids of his eyes, arranged the sheet over him as if he slept. "I don't care about it anymore, Alphonse," she whispered. There was a sound at the window and she went there, saw Wallace running away from the shadow of the house, his little buttocks shaking. The other two ran and jumped in the blue shade of the trees yonder, as if their nakedness had given them the power and speed of animals. And her children would soon learn of this in the room behind her, this strangest thing under the sun. She went back to the bed and cried a little, wiping her eyes with the backs of her hands, thinking about what she must tell Alphonse's son.

6

Now she walks through the dim house, hearing the television upstairs. She hates to go up there, hates to put herself where the old priest can regret her: whenever she is with him, she feels all her anger and sorrow clamoring to the place behind her eyes: but she must know what Candle has told him.

She climbs the stairs, her hand on the smooth oak banister, and the sound of the television is louder. Perhaps he has seen her crossing from the social hall and will not answer when she knocks. The hallway is darker than the rest of the house; it is like night here. She stands outside the door, lifts her hand, hesitates, touches her mouth. A voice from the television, a woman's voice, talks about perfume.

Elizabeth taps the door.

There is no response. She waits, thinks she hears movement behind the door, imagines that he stands just on the other side, his ear pressed to the wood. She knocks again, lightly, and now there is no sound from the television.

"Yes?"

"It's me," Elizabeth says. "I have to talk to you."

Movement, bed-creaking, footsteps. The door swings open an inch, and part of his face looks out. "What is it?"

"I have to talk to you."

He sighs. "Just a moment."

She walks back to the top of the stairs and stands there looking down into the rainy light of the living room.

"What is it," he says, coming toward her. He is as he was this morning: unshaven, red-eyed, his hair uncombed. They walk down to the living room, and he sits on the sofa with his hands up to the sides of his head.

"I didn't mean to disturb you," she says.

"I know," he says. "You never do."

Before she can respond to this, he raises one hand. "I didn't mean anything but exactly that, Mrs. Bexley."

"You never do," she says.

He gives a half smile, a rueful turn of the lips. "Yes, that's right."

"You had a visitor this morning—"

"You saw him?"

"He came over to the hall."

"I watched him drive away."

"He came back—walked back and . . . found us."

"Yes," says the priest, "I lied to him. Can't believe I did that. But I did. I'll probably wind up—" he stops. "Well, never mind—so he found you."

"Yes."

"Mrs. Bexley, what does he want?"

"He wants money."

"Is he a detective?"

"No."

"Well, that's a relief."

"Did he tell you that?"

"I couldn't get anything out of him—he wanted to see you. Alone. I didn't—well, I just wasn't sure of anything and I wanted to wait until I could talk to your husband about it."

"No," Elizabeth says. "Let me tell him—I know how to tell him. It's better if it doesn't come from a—from outside the family."

"Who is he?"

Elizabeth tells him. As she does so, his face changes, becomes incredulous. He lets his hands fall between his knees.

"He kept hinting around about your husband, Mrs. Bexley. That I shouldn't trust him. He said Duck was in jail, in prison once."

Elizabeth is silent.

"Is that true?"

"When he was younger," Elizabeth says. "It wasn't anything."

"I'll tell you, I thought he'd come to arrest him—"

"No, he wants money."

"There's something else I should know, though—right?"
She hears reluctance in his voice; and, she thinks, a little fear.

"When he was younger," Elizabeth says, "he worked in a
gas station—he'd just come back from the—from Korea. He
was working in Galveston. See, when he got out of the army,
he couldn't find anything. So he got these jobs in gas stations—that's—this is all before I met him. And so he was
working there and he hated it, and so he got into some
trouble."

"What kind of trouble?" the priest asks.

"It was nothing . . . an . . . argument. Some man with a
Cadillac asked for a dollar's worth—no, wait. He asked for
a fill-up, and so Duck filled it up, and then he said he only
asked for a dollar's worth. He got the manager in on it—
and the manager let Duck have it in front of him, chewed him
out, sort of. And things—got out of hand. Duck blew up, took
a tire iron to the man's car."

"Yes?"

"He got two years."

"And that's all?"

"Yes, that's all," Elizabeth says, suddenly angry. "It was
a long time ago."

"Mr. Wick was hinting around about something more
recent."

"What did he tell you. You tell me what he told you."

"He just said—I shouldn't trust him. That he was—outside
the law. That was how he put it."

"There's nothing else," Elizabeth says.

"All right—and you want to be the one who tells your
husband."

"That's right—" She feels exposed, somehow: coldly examined. The first thing you lose when you get into trouble is
privacy.

"Mrs. Bexley, why do I feel that you're holding something back?"

"All right," Elizabeth says—it is almost a shout. "All right —I thought you didn't want to be bothered with our problems. . . ."

"I am doing the best I can," the priest says. "I don't know why you expect me to be overjoyed with the situation."

"You want it all?" Now she is shouting. "You want everything? Every last ugly detail? Why I got five children and no place to put them—you want me to start from the beginning?"

The priest stands up, but then he seems to have forgotten what he was going to do, so he sits down again, crossing his legs and bending himself over them. "Why don't you just tell me what I need to know. That's all I'm asking. I had to find out about Wick from Mr. Torgeson."

"I did not know that Can—that Mr. Wick was—that he followed—oh, damn you, why can't you understand—" Elizabeth paces now, back and forth in front of him.

"Please," he says. "All right—please. I can't have this."

"You can't have anything."

"Mrs. Bexley, I am trying—"

"You're trying—everybody's trying. So why am I made to feel like a beggar? No—a—a thief."

"Oh, now that is just—"

She stops, is standing directly over him. She looks into his red eyes and says, "My husband—let me start with that. My husband killed a lot of men in one fight, by himself, defending a damn hill nobody needed. He has nerves so bad, he still sits up nights thinking he can hear the guns. That fight happened twenty-seven years ago. He never had no education beyond the tenth grade and he spent two years in prison." She turns from him, sees her own pregnant shadow on the floor—the sun has come out; it pours through the window— she feels ugly and exposed, and suddenly her anger leaves her;

it is replaced by a weariness so profound that she thinks she can see the shadow sag away, as if falling from her: but the sun has gone out again, and she is just standing there looking at the place on the floor where her shadow had been. "Then," she says, "he met me. He had a family with me. Do you want me to go on?"

"Mrs. Bexley," the priest says, "you don't—please don't say any more. The whole situation is difficult for all of us."

"Difficult," says Elizabeth. "I am trying to hold my family together. I'm trying to keep a man from—"

"I understand, please. You don't have to say any more. I just—hoped there wouldn't be anything else—that I wouldn't have anything sprung on me again."

"When I met him," Elizabeth says—she is talking to the room now—"I was just fifteen. He was with a friend's sister. So quiet. Just so careful of me. I remember how his hair wouldn't behave, and how he talked about his father. It was like the movies or something. I felt like I was in a movie about falling in love. He was tender—real tender, and honest. Told me right away he'd been in prison. He had the softest laugh—"

"Mrs. Bexley—"

"Even later," Elizabeth says, "when he knew there wasn't a future for him—working in that dairy, driving that milk truck to all those big houses in Richmond. He'd get up every morning before light, and I'd hear him moving around and sighing—always a little mad at something, and keeping it all to himself. Even then, even when his father was dying, he'd stop and bend over the bed and give me a pat before he went off in the morning."

The priest had stood up, and now he touches her shoulder.

"Lately," Elizabeth says, "it's like he—like he's—not here anymore. Like Duck Bexley just went off somewhere and all that's left is this—this bitter man looking for something to hurt." She begins to cry; she can feel it beginning in her. The priest's hand is still on her shoulder, and she walks out from beneath it into the dining room.

"It's going to be all right," the priest says. "We're going to find something, somehow, before that baby is born. You'll see."

"I'm going to take a nap," Elizabeth says.

"Yes. Lots of rest. You need rest."

"Oh," she turns, and he nearly runs into her. "The money —I—Candle—Mr. Wick—I have to send him installments."

"How much?"

"He said it didn't matter how much."

"All right," the priest says. "We'll send him one dollar a month." He smiles. "Suppose we send him one dollar a month."

"But then he might come back—"

"Oh, yes. I meant it as a—well, yes."

"I won't ask another thing of you."

"What's the total amount, Mrs. Bexley."

"Four hundred dollars. He said four hundred dollars."

"We'll send him fifty. Is that all right?"

She frowns. She does not want Candle to come back.

"All right, more. We'll send more. More." Again there is the note of frustration, of impatience, in his voice.

"Send what you can," Elizabeth says, and feels her eyes widen with the last word. "I'll repay you for every last penny." Then she walks out, into the last fall of the rain. She sees the truck in the lot, Harvey and Priscilla climbing out of it. Duck is still behind the wheel.

"Mama," Priscilla says.

Elizabeth glances at her, but walks on to the hall and in.

7

Sandra June and the twins are still asleep; they lie in a rumple
of the blanket, and they do not move when she enters. It
is quiet. The rain has stopped now. Elizabeth lets her coat
drop to the floor, walks into the bathroom, and runs water
over her hands, touching it to her face, her forehead. There
is heat under the skin there, the beginning of a headache.
She dries her hands and face on a paper towel, returns to
the children, lets herself down on the bed as quietly as she
can. The bed creaks, but they do not move. When she is
down, she closes her eyes and her head swims, whirls, hurting, and she does not hear Priscilla come in. Priscilla touches
her arm.

"Oh."

"I'm sorry, I didn't mean to scare you."

"What do you want? I have a headache."

"Daddy wants you to come over to the house."

"Tell him I'm asleep," Elizabeth says.

"He won't believe that, Mama—he saw you come in here."

"I'm not moving, Priscilla. Tell him that. I have a headache."

"He's in a good mood, Mama."

"I have a headache." Elizabeth reaches out and takes her
daughter's hand. "There's nothing the matter. I just have this
headache and I'm going to take a nap. Tell him I want to see
him—over here."

They are whispering, but the children begin to stir. Elizabeth puts one finger over her lips.

Priscilla nods, backs away. Then she comes back, leans
down. "I don't know why, but I feel happy."

"You got used to things," Elizabeth says. "That's what happiness is—getting used to things."

Priscilla kisses her on the forehead. "You feel warm."

"I have a headache. Tell Daddy to come over here."

"Okay."

Elizabeth watches her daughter go out, then closes her eyes—the surfaces ache; she can feel blood pulsing through. She thinks Duck will come any moment, but then she drifts. She has a vivid dream: She is sitting in the truck on the way to Demera, everything—the accumulation of more than four-teen years—packed against the window behind her; Sandra June sleeps on a pillow at her feet, and Priscilla sits with Mackinley on her lap between Elizabeth and Duck; Harvey and Wallace are on the mattresses in back, in a cave of boxes and clothes. This is all just as things were on the trip out, except that now the road is yellow and stretches endlessly before them, winding among yellow hills and long, deep val-leys, like gashes in the land, on into the distance. She glances out the window at a field of dry grass, above which the odd sky holds, as though suspended by invisible wires, two enor-mous black crows. A strand of her own hair, dry as the grass, pelts her cheeks, as if something wants to wake her—and then she is aware that she dreams, that this is all in sleep; she fills up with horror as if horror were a liquid that could be poured into the body.

She wakes up to Sandra June's crying.

"I want down," the child says. "I want down."

"Let me take her," says Priscilla. She stands by the side of the bed and holds out her hands.

"Just get her to shut up." It is Duck. He is in the bed with Elizabeth. She looks across the room and sees Harvey sitting under the lamp with a piece of slate in his hand. Harvey turns the slate over and over, examining it, holding it under the light. The twins, she sees, are still asleep, though they have been moved to their mattress.

"I want down," Sandra June cries.

"Be quiet." Elizabeth brings her over her chest, and Priscilla reaches down to help.

"Down."

"Jesus," Duck says.

"What time is it?" Elizabeth asks.

"It's afternoon. Go on back to sleep."

"I'll keep her busy," Priscilla says, carrying Sandra June across the room to Harvey.

"Just be quiet," Duck says.

"Is it very late?" Elizabeth asks.

"It ain't late. Go on back to sleep."

"I have a headache—I don't feel good."

"You got a little fever."

Presently Duck says, "You stay in bed the rest of the day."

"Candle was here," she whispers toward his ear.

Duck comes up on one elbow, looking down at her. "Say that again?"

"He wanted some money—I told him we didn't have any."

Duck lies back, his hands behind his head. His feet are moving as if to keep some rhythm he hears. "Let him do what he thinks he can do."

"He's doing what he thinks he can do, Duck."

"Which is what."

"He wants installments. Until we pay him four hundred dollars."

Duck is silent, though his feet move faster. She knows this is anger building in him. She touches his hair.

"The priest is going to help pay him—"

"No, god-dammit!"

This makes the children stop what they are doing—and wakes Mackinley, who wipes his eyes and groans.

"Duck, you got to find something—you got to."

Duck jerks out of bed, holding his hands out as if he is afraid what they will do if he lets them go—the fingers outspread, tense, the bones tight under the skin.

"Duck," Elizabeth says.

He points at her. "If you send that son of a bitch one penny, I'll kill him. I'll drive out of here in that truck and go back to Treetop and kill him for sure."

Now Mackinley and Sandra June are crying, and Priscilla is muttering, "Daddy, don't. Don't, Daddy. Don't, Daddy."

"I want everybody to shut up."

"Duck," Elizabeth says.

"That goes for you too."

"Oh, no—it does *not* go for me. You don't tell me to shut up—*ever*."

Then they are all quiet. It is as if they wait until they can resume without anger or fear.

"He said we left without notice—and it cost him that much," Elizabeth says at last. Duck sits down on the bed and puts his fingers into his hair. "He says he'll forget the other thing if we pay him."

"He told us to get out. You said he told us to get out."

"Yes, but he went back on it—at Alphonse's funeral. You know that. He came over three or four times after that."

"It's blackmail," Duck says. "Four—Jesus Christ—four hundred dollars."

"It might as well be four million."

"You don't need to rub it in my face, Elizabeth."

"I am not rubbing it in your face."

He gets up again, seems anxious to get away, to do anything but remain where he is, under her gaze.

"Duck," she says, low, so only he can hear, "your father died and you just—what's happening, Duck—what is it? You've—you can't just give up. We can't stay here all winter—"

"I been getting pain," Duck says.

"Bad?"

He seems to consider. "No." Then he sits down; a slow falling, his back bent. "Bad enough."

"I had a bad dream." She did not know she was going to say this.

"You go on back to sleep—go ahead. I'll work it out."

"Duck," she says, "what're we going to do." She feels the baby climbing her ribs again. The headache burns now, and she arranges herself in the bed; it is less like settling down to sleep than gathering an invisible armor around herself.

Duck touches her hip, once, lightly.

8

It is morning. The rain has given way to a cold sun that sails among clouds dark as smoke. The wind is unpredictable and sudden and when it gusts, brittle red leaves swarm out of the trees as though startled. Elizabeth had walked the edge of the field at dawn, and now she makes her way across to the house and up onto the stoop. The old priest opens the door before she can reach for it, and she nods politely at him.

"You're very early for Saturday," he says.

"I have to talk to you," says Elizabeth.

He sighs, but she is not certain it is a sigh produced by what she has said. His face is friendly, concerned, and—she notices now—clean-shaven. He closes the door behind her and they walk into the dining room, where he has set himself a cup of tea.

"Can I make you—"

"No, thank you," she says. "You go ahead."

They sit at the table. There is a strange formality between them now, and so for a moment they sit in uneasy silence. Elizabeth nervously picks at the cuticle of her thumb with her index fingernail; the little sound is the only thing between them. Then he lifts his cup, sips the tea.

"I"—she begins—"I don't know if Duck has told you everything about this—sickness he has."

He puts the cup back on the saucer and looks at her.

"Has he?"

The priest thinks for a moment. "Well, I don't know what you mean by everything—why don't you tell me and then I'll be able to know."

"He's had it since he was nineteen years old," Elizabeth says.

"Yes."

"It never did anything to him before except give him sores on his skin—mostly in the summers."

"Is it fatal, Mrs. Bexley?"

For a moment she is at a loss: the bluntness of the question frightens her.

"Is it?"

"If it—if it turns a certain way. It can be."

"And he thinks it's turned."

"Did he tell you that?"

"No—no, he didn't."

After a moment he says, "Mrs. Bexley, could you stop picking your thumb that way? I'm sorry, but I have a terrific headache and it's bothering me."

"We don't know—" Elizabeth begins. Then she realizes

what he has said, looks at her thumb, puts it against her teeth, trying to bite the cuticle.

"Go on," he says.

She lets her hands down in her lap. "We don't know much about it—or I don't. I know it can turn, though. And that my girls have a good chance of getting it too. It's mostly girls that get it."

"What is it called?" asks the priest.

"It's some funny name. That doesn't matter. It's just that it's hurting him now, and that's why he hasn't been any help to you—I mean looking for a place—"

"I see."

"So that's what I wanted to tell you," Elizabeth says. "That it isn't him. That he's not—" She can't finish.

"Lazy?" the priest says.

"Yes. No—not lazy. That he hasn't—given up."

"Mrs. Bexley," the priest says, "I'll tell you, I've about given up—even if he hasn't."

"It's killing him," says Elizabeth, trying to keep from crying again. She does not want to cry in front of this man anymore, feels that she has already shown him too much of herself, though his eyes now are at least kind, if still red, racoonlike for their dark circles.

"The disease is killing him?" he says.

"No, no, no. This. He just—he fell apart after his father got sick. He can't make anything work for him anymore. . . ."

"You've got to help him pull himself together," the priest says.

She rises, says nothing.

"You've got to bring him back."

"He's always kept so much of himself away from us all," she says. Then she moves toward the kitchen. "I'll leave you alone now."

"Perhaps if you could get him to go to Charlottesville and look for something there. It's only a couple hours away."

"Do you know someone in Charlottesville?" she asks.

"I'm afraid not."

"His daddy was sheriff there a long time ago."

"See?" the priest says. "If you could just get him to move a little. I'm sure he's letting it all get to him."

"He's a proud man," says Elizabeth.

"Yes," says the priest, sighing. "I knew that."

9

"Lookie here," Duck says.

He holds it out, coming toward her from the open door of the hall, which lets in cold and twilight sun.

"Close the door."

"Mackinley and Wallace did a little exploring this evening." Duck goes back to the door and closes it, comes around the bed and sits down, letting the chalice fall on the bed between them.

"Oh, you got to put that back," Elizabeth says. "What's got into you, Duck?"

"I can't put it back—you want me to walk in on him and his television and just say how my boys snuck into his room and got it?"

"Yes," Elizabeth says. "Tell him that—and tell him you're sorry."

"No," says Duck, shaking his head, "I'm sick and tired of apologizing to everybody. Specially to *him*."

"Then what're you going to do with it?"

"Maybe keep it—till we leave."

"That's stealing."

"No. Borrowing. Look—you give it to him."

"I will." Elizabeth picks it up; it shines, gives off a hundred little sparks of light. She looks at herself, grotesquely elongated in it. And then Harvey comes in. She watches his face as he sees the chalice. He comes to her side of the bed, lifts it from her fingers as if it contains some incredibly fragile thing. His eyes, she thinks, are wide and beautiful.

"It is so very beautiful, isn't it," she says.

"You like that thing, boy?" Duck asks Harvey.

Harvey nods, looks as if he is about to cry. He takes it over to his cedar box, holding it in tight to his chest, as if to protect it from the air. Slowly, carefully, he lifts the lid of the box, tries to set the chalice down into it. Then, as if afraid of it in there, with those things he has collected and drawn, he stands, looks about him.

"What does he want?" Elizabeth asks Duck.

Harvey comes back to her, touches the blanket.

"Cloth," Duck says. "He wants to wrap it in cloth."

"Duck," says Elizabeth.

"Let him be."

Harvey moves back toward the box, stops, bends, picks up the pillow from his mattress, removes the slip, wraps the chalice gently, comes back. Now he smiles, kneels, slides the wrapped chalice under the bed.

"Duck," Elizabeth says.

"Quit. You want—just let it be now."

"Harvey, honey—" The boy smiles at her, nods: he understands, she thinks. Then what is he doing?

"Harvey, that's not ours."

Harvey nods again.

"Just wants to keep something fine to look at now and then, right, Harv?" Duck winks at his son.

"But you must give it back tomorrow," Elizabeth says.

"We'll give it back," says Duck, growing impatient. "Hell, we got a right to something pretty every god-damn thousand years or so."

"Duck, why do you want to make him mad at us?"

Harvey leans over and kisses her cheek. His lips are cold and moist. Then he walks around the bed and embraces Duck.

"That's a boy—now go on over and tell the—go get the others. The old man won't be back down tonight, anyway." The boy is moving toward the door, but Duck keeps talking. "Him and his TV. Ain't that right, boy?"

Harvey looks back long enough to do his special thing—a rare thing he uses to let his parents know that he is happy, that he doesn't mind his inability to speak—he bends down and pretends to press the rubber end of a hand horn, like Harpo, his eyes mischievous like that. Duck laughs, and the boy straightens proudly, goes out, shutting the door so quietly, they don't hear it.

"God-damn," Duck says.

"He understands that he can't—" Elizabeth begins.

But Duck interrupts her: "Aw, lay off it, will you. Let him alone for Christ's sake. The old man'll get his precious property back." Then he gets up, presses his knuckles to his eyes. "I'm going for a walk or something."

"You want me to come with you?" Elizabeth asks.

He lets his hands down to his sides, looks at her. "No."

"I didn't mean to hurt your feelings about Charlottesville, Duck."

"You didn't hurt my feelings."

"I just didn't think you should get your hopes up—"

"There'll be somebody in Charlottesville," Duck says, "and I'm going to go, right after Thanksgiving."

"Yes, good."

"I'd go now, but I want to get these—this—pain behind me a little. I got to rest up some."

"Yes," says Elizabeth, and watches her husband walk out into the dark. Her baby, her new baby, moves in her, and she is filled suddenly with some of the horror she had felt in her dream of the morning before. It is like a premonition: something final is approaching.

IV

1

Vincent discovered that the chalice was gone the week before Thanksgiving. The blue-velvet case had lain behind the television since the first days of the Bexley Invasion, as he now privately called it—this with some humor and not a little rancor, though the rancor was aimed mostly at his fate now, rather than at the Bexleys themselves. There had been no reason for him to look at the chalice or check it: the blue case lay there where he had put it, and he assumed that the chalice was in it. He had picked the case up to wipe a thin cover of dust away, and its lightness had startled him. Opening the case, he looked for a cold minute at the empty imprint in the satin.

Those infernal children.

It was morning: they were all out in the snow that had come with the turn of the month like an exact demarcation between fall and winter; it had come three times since, and it was coming now, with a steady wind that lifted it and made a dust. When he burst out into it, he could not tell if it hit him from the ground or the sky; he thought it was probably both.

"Hello," the children called. "Hello, hello, hello." There were only two of them: the twins.

Vincent ignored them, pushed through the stinging dust,

eyes half shut, and came to the door of the hall. He saw the twins enter the church, and he cried out to them, "Stay out of there. Out of there, you two." But they were already inside. Now he felt his anger like energy in his fingers. He knocked once on the hall door, with his fist, and entered. The hall looked empty. It was dark, the door behind him giving an alley of light with his shadow in it. He could just make out the shapes of the furniture, and thrown shoes and clothes, and then something moved to his left. As his eyes grew accustomed to the dark, he saw Duck Bexley rising from the bed, part of the blanket around his middle. Vincent saw white, hairless skin, marked or pocked, all goose bumps.

"Oh," he said, "I didn't mean to wake you up."

"Wake me up—yeah, that's good."

"It's just that I have discovered—"

"You hear that, Elizabeth—he's sorry he just barged in on us like a damn cop and woke us up."

"I did knock, Mr. Bexley."

"Yeah, and came in. One-two. Like that."

"I'm sorry—I just discovered—"

"He's sorry, Elizabeth," said Bexley. "Shut the goddamn door."

"Mr. Bexley, I am aware that you have rights and that—"

"Will you just get the hell out of here?"

"If you will allow me—"

"What, old man? Allow you to watch? We were *not* sleeping. You get it? We were not sleeping."

"Oh," Vincent said, the smallest letter out of his mouth. "Oh, I—she's pregnant, Mr. Bexley, and I—" He turned back toward the snow, wanted to hurl himself out. "My chalice—someone has stolen my chalice—"

"If you don't goddammit mind, old man—we're busy now."

"I'm so very sorry."

The snow swept at him like something that would ridicule him. The door shut behind him and he was alone.

Fever. A profound stillness and a sleep in which he saw the children in their various attitudes of play, in the dim vigil lights of the church, the windows giving back the wavering blue flames in the cups at the Communion rail, one of the children having lighted every candle. Their bodies lying on the altar in a sexual leisure, changing the poses as the light changed, showing themselves, cavorting like centaurs. The tabernacle doors open and the Host on their lips; the Stations of the Cross brought down and piled like firewood for some primitive tribe on the floor under the altar; the books opened and torn and thrown; the virgin's stone breasts grown enormous. These images plagued his sleep, yet he could not wake up, could not lift his eyelids and look at the room and know it as his room, his bed, and the walls and the severe curtains that opposed this lewd vision. He was too old to be the prey of such passions, and if he knew that one was not responsible for what transpired in sleep, he felt no less sullied when he did awaken, remembering what he had dreamed: he preferred the nightmares of heart attack.

But this was not the second heart attack: he was alive, and down with flu. He was still feverish. He wanted to sleep, or his body did; but he was afraid of the lurid scene and so he lay staring at the ceiling, telling himself the day, the hour, the word for his illness. When he was fully awake he felt cushioned, bandaged, shrouded. The ceiling was white. Mrs. Bexley entered, touched a cold rag to his forehead, smiled at him, and left. Priscilla did the same a moment later—or was it a day later? Was he that ill? Had he been that utterly exhausted? He could now remember that he had walked over to the church after stumbling out of the Bexleys' privacy, had found a shambles—the children gone wild: they had broken into the tabernacle and had sailed the Communion wafers back and forth to each other; they had drunk the holy water and draped their coats over the statuary. He had driven them out of there as Christ had driven the money changers from the temple, had felt a flying elation at the sound of his own temper. And he had gone to sleep early that night—last night?—his legs and the muscles of his back aching, the first symptoms.

Now he waited. The fever was gone; the room had carried its old expression of severity to the front of his mind: he would not think about the dreams of fever and he would not think about the Bexleys.

Except that he could not keep from thinking. And every thought led to some sort of quick lewdness.

"What time is it?" he said aloud.

Then he got out of the bed, experienced the dizziness he'd expected. He was in a nightshirt. The window was dark and he saw himself—a spirit on the flat, cold glass. On the nightstand was the blue-velvet case, still empty. *Damn them,* he thought. He dressed quickly.

Downstairs he found them all. Duck Bexley sat in the middle of the living room floor, legs crossed, as if he owned the house. He was drinking the I.W. Harper. Elizabeth Bexley sat on the sofa, with Vincent's breviary. The children sprawled everywhere, as if spun in all directions by centrifugal force.

"You're up," Mrs. Bexley said. She held the breviary out to him. "What's this mean."

Vincent looked at his own handwriting in the inset: *God is that than which nothing greater*

"I'm a little woozy," he said. "To tell you the truth I can't remember where it's from." This struck him as odd: he actually couldn't remember.

"What does it *mean.*"

He looked carefully at the words. This was a little frightening. Had the fever ruined part of his memory? *I am Monsignor Vincent Shepherd.* "It's a passage. It's from a book
about God. Part of an argument." He was distracted, weak,
nervous; he wanted to be alone to work it out, what damage
there might be. He thought of poor Father Grayson, who
smiled and nodded and who could not even say the Paternoster. He shook.

"You shouldn't be out of bed," said Mrs. Bexley.

"I'm sorry."

Duck Bexley still sat cross-legged on the floor, the bottle
of whiskey in his lap. Vincent now saw that Priscilla lay with
a blanket over her knees at one end of the sofa.

"I'm sick," she said, seeing his eyes on her. "I got what
you got."

"We'll go back to the hall," Bexley said, rising, "if that's
what you want."

"You've been staying *here?*"

"Sleeping on the floor. Last couple nights."

"You want us to leave you alone," Elizabeth Bexley said.

"No," said Vincent. "Forgive me. I'm a little confused.
I'm going back upstairs."

"You want anything?"

"No, no." He wanted his chalice. He wanted to be alone
and he wanted his mind clear. He vaguely remembered having been angry. She took his elbow and led him toward the
stairs. Part of him wanted to wrench free, but then it was
more than just the wish to make his own way unaided; he
longed, by some profound motion of his very spirit, literally
to shake everything away, to be new and clean and clear and
alone. Her hand on his elbow was like the hand one lent to
old age, and he felt his body begin to totter, his own feet
barely touching the floor, it seemed, his shoulders quaking.

At the foot of the stairs, as if to make up for what had

transpired in his mind—that something in him that had
wanted to break free had foamed with hatred for the touch
of her hand—he touched Elizabeth Bexley's elbow and said,
"I am grateful. Please understand."

She smiled. He thought it was a hopeful, childlike smile. It
made him sad.

2

Thanksgiving dinner had been arranged by Mrs. Bexley, and
there was no deterring her, though she, too, before the week
was out, had suffered from the flu. Some members of the
parish had provided turkey and ham, two cakes—one choco-
late and one lemon coconut—one apple pie, and an assortment
of side dishes: creamed corn, egg noodles, cranberries, yams.
It was a feast of the town's generosity, Vincent had said at
the mass that morning, though inwardly he considered it a
ransom of sorts, a payment of tribute, so that no one would
have to think about taking the Bexleys on. This was a mean
thought and he knew it; nevertheless he was convinced of
its truth. He had made, finally, more than one reference to
the Bexleys and their problem in his sermons: he may as well
have spoken about starving children in China or the plight
of the elderly in The Bronx. He had watched Mrs. Trevinos's
hard, staring face change at the mention of the name, her lips
tightening, her eyes boring into him from the first pew. It
was the only time he could be certain that she heard him. He
spoke of charity, the greatest of virtues, the liveliest of human
traits. But, as always, his halting voice, his birdlike voice,
merely sent waves of restlessness through the congregation.

And when mass was over, as they filed out before him, they all wished him good morning, and one or two said how good the sermon had been, speaking in the same tone of voice one might use to compliment an amateur singer who had tried to entertain everyone and had, of course, quite obviously failed. So Mrs. Bexley had taken the offerings of the parish and had cooked a meal much too large even for the eight people who would be eating it; and as the hour drew close for the meal, Vincent began steadily to lose his appetite. He sat at his window and looked out at the grounds, half threatened, half wooed by sleep, and knew that he would not be able to eat. He told himself this was a holdover from the flu, but he knew better. Outside it rained again, a warm rain that had beaten down all the snow. The sky was dirty: a thin, gray cover beneath which tatters of raglike cloud hung. He could not get himself clear, could not unlock the front of his brain. His chalice had been stolen, his heart had palpitated twice in the past two days, the fever had left him shaky and weak, and he felt nothing. It was as if, now, he only reacted, as if the nerve endings in his body had become antennae. There seemed to be nothing of Vincent Shepherd left.

He brought Death with him to the table. It was in him, it clung to every inner crevice. *You can all stay*, he thought, watching Bexley carve the turkey. *You can all have everything. I'm not hungry.*

"I'm not hungry," he said.

"For Christ's sake," said Bexley.

"Duck," Mrs. Bexley said.

They ate in silence. Vincent did not even say grace. Bexley did. He put his hands before him and said: "If You're out there, thanks for the food."

The five children sat at the dining room table, while Vincent and their parents sat in the kitchen. The two tables were not ten feet apart, and all five children were visible through the doorway, but Mrs. Bexley seemed a little forlorn, as if her children were a great distance away and she could not close the gap; she kept glancing at them. Her face was colorless, and her eyes were like glazed coins.

"You really ain't going to eat anything, are you?" Bexley said.

Vincent put some creamed corn on his fork and lifted it to his mouth. It was hot. It lay on his tongue like something that had come up from his stomach. He put the napkin to his lips, as if to wipe them, and perhaps that was what he had intended to do, but then he was spitting into it.

"Sorry," he said.

He watched them eat.

Presently Bexley spoke about Mrs. Trevinos. "See," he said, holding his fork out, waving it up and down as he spoke, "that old lady is a perfect example of a waste. She's got all that money and she holds on to it like it was life or something and she don't need half of it." His eyes were wide and bright, and he kept waving the fork. He sat hunched forward as if there were something in his lap that he wanted to keep from sight, and with his free hand he tapped the table with each word: he might have been counting them in his mind. "It just ain't right—a slug like her with that kind of money laying around, that she didn't have to do a damn thing to get except climb into bed with some half-dead rich son of a—except get married. It ain't right."

Vincent looked at Mrs. Bexley, who sat examining a morsel of ham on her fork: she didn't seem to be listening. The children ate like wolves, noisy and quick and single-minded.

"You're a little old to be worrying about what's fair in life," Vincent said.

Bexley seemed to smirk. "Yeah, well, maybe I can make things a little more fair."

"Mr. Bexley, it's Thanksgiving."

"Yeah, and you're celebrating real good."

"Duck," said Mrs. Bexley.

After a moment Bexley leaned toward Vincent and said, "I been wanting to ask you—talking about life being fair. Ever strike you what you're missing, being a priest and all?"

"Yes," said Vincent, before he could think. But then he said: "Of course. That's natural. One gives up certain things with any choice. . . ." This, he knew, would be lost on the other man: yet he felt compelled to explain.

"It ever bother you?"

"Does what bother me, Mr. Bexley."

"You know—being a priest." Bexley considered a moment: "Have you ever—" He paused.

"Yes?"

"All right. You ever had a woman? You know, *had* her?"

Vincent glanced at Mrs. Bexley; she, too, apparently wanted to know: she sat looking at him with the kind of interest one gives an exotic animal in a cage. He felt plumed, suddenly— arched, knobbed, beaked, red.

"Well?" said Bexley.

"The question is rude. The answer is none of your business." The overly dignified tone of his own voice made Vincent inwardly sneer at himself. *Fool*, he thought. Exaggerated dignity had answered the question. Bexley smiled. "Life ain't fair, all right," he said.

3

Oh, Lord, why have you sent these people here?

He had closed and locked the door of his room, and now stood by the bed. The dinner was over and he was safe for a while; but Mrs. Bexley would be back to clear away the remains. She had promised this over Vincent's protestations that she wait until morning. He lacked the energy to be heard, to make himself heard. *What time is it?* He seemed always to be asking himself what time it was. It was just past seven o'clock. Too early to go to bed and chase sleep, yet as he thought about this, he was undressing. On the bed, jutting out from a fold of the coverlet near the pillow, was something white; it looked like part of the sheet, except that when he brushed against it with his bare leg, it stung the skin. He bent down and examined the leg, looking for a cut or a mark. The skin was all goose bumps, chicken flesh, under the coils of dark hair, but there was no cut. Here he was, with the old trouble of a world broken into things, details tiny as this: his own leg and its aggregate of parts. He put his face to the white something, touched it, brought it out; as he did so he heard Mrs. Bexley downstairs. He held a piece of paper in his hand. The telephone rang, loud and sudden—like an accident.

It was Mrs. Trevinos and she was drunk.

"My heart," she kept saying. "My heart, my heart, my heart."

"Mrs. Trevinos," Vincent said, "for God's sake."

"My heart, my heart, my heart."

There was breathing in the wire—large, healthy, drunk breathing. She sang to him: "My heart, my heart."

"Stop it. Stop it. Damn you, stop it."

"Forgive me, Father, for I have sinned."

"Mrs. Trevinos—"

"Forgive me, Father, for I have sinned."

"No," Vincent cried, "I will not forgive you for this."

The voice began to hiss at him through the line. "Yes, you have to, yes you have to, yes you have to."

"Mrs. Trevinos, why are you doing this to me?"

The line clicked. Vincent stood holding the phone.

The note read: IT'S UP IN THE BALKNY OF THE CHERCH For a moment he was puzzled. He pictured one by one the Bexley children. Who among them could write? When he realized that this note was about his chalice, he was enraged. All the blood seemed to flow back into him as he dressed again. The dinner, Bexley's nerve-wrecking behavior, the phone call—everything washed through him down to a single point of rage about the chalice, the one thing that belonged to him. "Mrs. Bexley!" he called.

He met her on the stairs, she coming up and he almost running down. He thrust the paper at her. "Look at this."

She took it, held it up close to her face.

"Which one wrote this?" he asked.

She gave it back to him, her face showing no expression at all; when she spoke, only her lips moved. "Can't tell you."

"You know whose it is."

"No," she said.

"You mean to tell me you can't tell which of your own children wrote this?" He did not wait for an answer. He went past her, down the stairs, hearing her come behind him. In the kitchen he pulled his coat on, and she talked about how it was silly to go on over to the church because there probably wasn't anything in the balcony. Vincent turned his back on her to go out: he was conscious of leaving her while she was in midsentence: she had irritated him beyond his capacity to control his temper, or that was what he told himself. He crossed the lot with his temper, letting himself feel the frowning of his brow, the stiff, angry breathing; he butted through the wind, kicked the soggy remains of snow, and quite suddenly saw himself as from a distance: a ridiculous, crooked figure, the butt of children's jokes, an old man glad of a rage that made him foolish.

4

In the first days of December the weather turned warm. The sun shone all day in a sky that was the darker blue of winter, but the air was soft. Warm days in winter are like kindnesses done to us by strangers, Mrs. Bexley told Vincent. In the mornings there was a cold dew, which glistened like snowfall out over the fields, and a mist rose from the beaten grass, smelling of earth and loblolly pine. By midmorning it was past sixty degrees, windless, fresh. It filled Vincent with obscure and bittersweet sadness, like the sadness of temporary parting. He opened the windows of the rectory, sat on the stoop in the cooler shade, and watched the children play in the puddles of the lot, their voices shrill as summer. He watched their parents walk along the edge of Torgeson's property, Mrs. Bexley stopping from time to time to fetch something out of the wild tangle by the fence—a dark leaf or a broken sprig of laurel. Now and again a car came by on Sixteen, windows down, and once Torgeson went past, waving from his

Lincoln. Vincent saw that someone was in the car with him, a woman, though he only caught a glimpse of her.

The light drew down behind the mountains and left a balmy dusk with little stirrings of wind, like promises of warm days to follow. The children played on, and periodically one of them would amble over to speak to him. Priscilla talked about her problems in school—almost everyone in Demera knew where the Bexleys were staying, and she was a little ashamed of this, though she would not come right out and say it. Vincent told her to be herself, and not to worry about things too much. He said, "You don't want to get into the habit of worrying." And then he added: "Honey." He had not been quite certain that he would say this. Then he went on: "That's what I do, you see. I spend almost all my time worrying."

"Thank you," she said, and curtsied.

"I don't suppose you know who is hiding my chalice from me," he said.

She smiled. "Naw."

It was all very good-natured. He watched her run back out through the long shadows of the afternoon and felt an extraordinary sense of a benign presence at the very center of things. Somewhere far down inside him, like the faintest beginning of memory—it was incredibly tentative and fragile —he felt a species of joy begin to rise. It frightened him a little, yet he sought it, reached for it, watching the Bexleys come back into the lot, arm in arm, her one hand resting over the place where her new baby lay curled, probably asleep.

At night it grew cold, the wind rushed down out of the mountains, and Vincent lay in bed gazing at the stars outside his window. He didn't care whether he slept or not. The weather reports had predicted seventy degrees in the morning. When he did sleep, he searched his dreams for the chalice, like someone wandering after the Holy Grail. The Bexley children, oddly enough, were with him in the search; he greeted them all and spoke about how warm it would be.

But the weather reports were wrong.

The fourth day of December dawned cold and windy, though the sun still shone in a cloudless sky. The wind made the runnels of water in the lot into brittle, corrugated blades of ice, and the eaves of the house groaned and shook with each cold gust.

Vincent spent most of the day in his room, but he did come down for dinner. It was a quiet evening. The children seemed as subdued as they had earlier seemed excited and glad. It was, finally, rather discouraging. He supposed that everyone was thinking about the cold months ahead. At one point, near the end of the meal, Mrs. Bexley broke into tears. "I'm sorry," she said. "I don't know what's the matter with me."

Her husband patted her wrist.

"Can you imagine?" she said. "I don't even know what brought it on." She held a napkin to her lips, brushed her eyes, sniffed, said "Ah," her fingers trembling. "I'm so sorry."

The children sat very still, watching this, and Bexley kept patting her wrist.

"It's just being pregnant," she said.

"Sure," Bexley said, taking her hand now.

That night Vincent lay nodding over his breviary—*I will give unto him that is athirst of the fountain of the water of life freely*—and Harvey came to him. Vincent was startled, put the book down, and lay watching the child fumble with the folds of the blanket at the foot of the bed. Then he was aware that it was a dream. He said: "Go downstairs, Harvey."

The child did not move.

"Harvey," he said.

And then Harvey spoke to him. It seemed that he opened his mouth and a word came out.

"What," Vincent said.

"Something awful will happen."

Vincent felt himself filling up with fear and he tried to get out of the bed, knew that if he could stir, the dream would break up. "Harvey," he said. "Harvey." He struggled upward, and then he was just lying there, looking at the room, which was empty. *But the door was open.*

"Harvey," he said.

He was absolutely certain that he had closed the door before he had lain down. And now he could hear the other children downstairs. It was after two o'clock in the morning, but he heard them. They were laughing and singing. From where he lay in the bed, leaning on his elbows now, he could see the top of the stairs, and he didn't know if the faint light on the wall was from his own lamp or from the lights down in the living room, which were supposed to be out. He had turned them all out. Yet he could hear the singing and then, quite suddenly, it seemed to be crying. He was awake and they were crying and he went out of the room, to the stairs, shaking all over.

The living room was dark.

But he had come down here, and now he was fully awake. He trembled for a while, getting his bearings, his hands on his chest. He went into the kitchen and looked out at the field and sky beyond the hall; it was clear, and he knew it was cold, and he almost stepped out. He wanted the sharp clarity of the frozen air. But then he was afraid of another fever—and he saw, with a shock that threatened to buckle his knees, a shadow cross in front of him, going on, across the grass just below the stoop, and out toward the field on that side. The figure disappeared in the deeper shadow of the church. Vincent stood there with his face against the window, faintly aware of his own breathing, and now the shadow came back. He watched with mounting terror, and then without thinking, he opened the door violently and shouted, "Who are you?"

But he could see in an instant who it was.

"You scared me," she said.

"What're you doing out here? It's cold." Then he realized that he was the one who was shivering: he was in a night-shirt, and his legs were bare.

"Just walking," she said.

"Please," he said. "Come in here."

When he had put on the light and made some tea for him-self—she refused any—he sat at the table in his nightshirt and told her of his dream; he was too nervous to risk a silence between them and it was a little while before he realized that he was undressed, that he still didn't know how they had come to be sitting here in the middle of the night. He could see that she was too frightened by his dream for him to leave her there for a robe, so he pulled his chair close to the table and sipped his tea while she bit the cuticles of her fingers.

"What does it mean?" she said finally.

"I wish I knew."

She gave a little shudder, as if she had thought of some-thing damp and loathsome. Vincent wished fervently for daylight. He had always believed that if God did not exist, then only evil did—that accident was chaos and chaos was evil and if the universe was random, it was also evil. But sit-ting there in that little lighted room with her, both of them fearing the dream as if it ordered events, was a revelation of some order, he began to hope randomness was true. He could feel blood pulsing to his knees, and it was as if anything might happen next—something foul and dark on the other side of each dragging minute. He gulped the tea. She seemed to be waiting for him to tell her what his dream had meant. He breathed, and he breathed again. "It was—it was just a dream," he said.

She put her hands up to her face.

"Are you all right?"

"I'm scared. I'm so scared."

He said again it was just a dream.

"I don't like dreams," she said.

"I don't like nightmares," said Vincent.

She gave a weak little smile. "I don't think I've ever had a good dream."

"Sure you have."

"Maybe. I never remember them if I do."

"What were you doing out there?" he asked.

"I walk at night sometimes, when I can't sleep." She sighed.

He drank the tea.

"What in the world are we going to do," she muttered.

"It'll all work out."

She put her hands out on the table, spreading the fingers. "I see your shadow in the window a lot."

"You've done this often? This walking?"

"Yes."

"All this time," he said. He had almost gone on to say, *You've been watching me. You know.*

After a moment she said, "Duck is talking about Charlottesville. It'll be soon now."

"All of you?" he asked stupidly.

"No," she said, frowning.

"When will he leave?"

"Maybe tomorrow or the next day."

Then she got up and walked to the door and went out. She

nodded at him, smiled quickly and awkwardly before she closed the door. He sat there for a moment, sipping the last of his tea, and then he went upstairs and turned his light out and stood at his window for a while, looking for her. But she had either gone back to the social hall or she walked out of sight of the window.

5

"So," Torgeson said, shuffling a deck of cards, "this isn't a social call either."

Vincent watched him arrange the cards in his hand.

"I've kept my end of the bargain, haven't I?"

"There's a new problem," Vincent said.

"Shoot."

"Duck Bexley is gone."

"Gone."

"That's right."

"*Dead?*" Torgeson's mouth spread out over his teeth, so while his lips smiled, his eyes narrowed and the expression of his whole face was a clownlike grimace.

"No—gone. He picked up and went to Charlottesville this morning."

"Charlottesville." Torgeson made the face again.

"Mrs. Bexley and those children are alone with me at the church now."

"What do you want me to do?" Torgeson shuffled the cards. Behind him the fish kissed and smacked the green ambience of the aquarium. "You know," he went on when Vincent didn't answer, "there's an old couple in Point Royal who might take them. They live in a big place and their children are gone—they might take them off your hands. Point Royal is quite a ways, but it's near enough and it's closer to Charlottesville than we are."

"Why didn't you mention these people sooner?" Vincent asked. But he spoke mechanically. A little knot formed at the back of his throat, a mobile something that felt as if it might come up. He did not know whether this was fear or anticipation: to think that the entire solution might be at hand: an old couple with plenty of room, whose children were gone and who might therefore want the sound of children again. He imagined two thin old people in a setting that was mournful as well as spacious. Now he was suddenly dizzy—or rather, *light:* as though he were floating or the chair beneath him had shifted downward an infinitesimal space. "Can you arrange it?" he heard himself say.

Torgeson considered. "No."

Vincent breathed, "Why not?"

"You'd have to arrange it. I can give you their phone number and you can call them. I don't get along with them anymore, you see, because they're my wife's relatives—an aunt and uncle. Nice people, but you know how it is."

"No," Vincent said. "I've had my fill of wandering the countryside looking for a home for the Bexleys."

"I was unaware that you had done so."

Vincent said nothing.

"Well, so why is Bexley's trip to Charlottesville a new problem?"

"I had to give him quite a bit of money—for gasoline and a place to spend the night, and food—"

"You need more money."

"Yes."

"This is getting expensive."

"Yes."

"How much?"

"As much as you can spare."

Torgeson put the cards down, spread them out as though
he were about to perform some sleight-of-hand trick. "Now
you see it," he said, "now you don't."

"I suppose," Vincent said, "I couldn't ask you to help get
the children to school tomorrow morning."

"You suppose right—I have another appointment. Sorry."

Vincent stood up. "I just don't see any end to it if he
doesn't find something soon," he said. "I'm afraid she might
have that baby in the social hall, for God's sake."

"It's a warm place—a lot of people have entered this world
in worse places than that."

"How can you be so blithe about it?"

"Look," Torgeson said, "just call me if she starts to have
the baby—I've had experience with it. I drove an ambulance
for almost ten years. Believe me, that's the least of our
problems."

"*Our* problems."

Torgeson smiled, waved his checkbook.

6

By late morning of the following day Mrs. Bexley had begun
to worry. It was not like Duck to stay away without getting
in touch. "He ought to have phoned by now," she said. It was
as though she spoke to the room. As usual, they were in the
kitchen. Outside it rained, and the windows ran silver. Mrs.
Bexley had come to the house alone, though she had kept
the older children out of school that day, perhaps inwardly
hoping that Duck Bexley would pull in with a new job and
a place to get to. Vincent had watched this hope, if that was
what it was, flicker and die: she had not spoken of it—indeed

she had said little—yet he believed it was so. Now he searched
his mind for something to say to relieve her, console her—
whatever.

"I thought . . . he'd call. He would've called me by now.
He's never stayed overnight anywhere without calling."

"It's just been a day, Mrs. Bexley."

It struck him that he had thought she would be afraid of
something else: that Duck Bexley might be on his way to
California. There was, he told himself, no justification for
such a thought, beyond the knowledge that men like Bexley
were . . . were what? he asked himself. Untrustworthy? Un-
educated? Unaligned somehow? Presently he began to feel
that he had not been fair to Duck Bexley, and this opened in
him a desire to make amends, to correct himself.

"Don't worry," he said lamely. Then he said: "He'll call
today if he doesn't come home."

She looked at him with an odd sort of questioning, though
not remote, expression; it seemed to recognize him. She had
been standing by the sink. He was seated at the table. Now
she walked over and, leaning down, took his hand. "Thank
you," she said. "I am so scared."

He felt the pressure of her fingers, knew that he should
speak.

"Are you scared too?"

"No. Duck will be all right."

Then she seemed to hesitate. "No," she said, "I mean—"
But she did not finish. She let go of his hand, walked back
to the sink. Vincent heard himself breathe.

"You going into town?" she asked.

"Yes."

"I made you a list of things."

"Thank you."

He left the rectory, walked to the Ford in the slanting rain,
leaving footprints in the softening ground that filled and

overflowed almost as they were made. The windows of the Ford were foggy as soon as he settled in behind the wheel.

Demera was festooned with Christmas lights, brilliant tinsel cones meant to suggest decorated trees—every streetlamp was capped with one—bulbs, stars, ribbons. In the lobby of the bank was a white tree that looked like cotton candy. Vincent felt that if he touched it, it would stick to his fingers. In the window of the drugstore, farther down the street, a mechanical Santa Claus laughed crazily through knobby red cheeks and a silken beard. Because he saw this from the car and therefore could not hear the laugh, he had a moment of uneasy distrust of his senses, as if he were having a hallucination. And so when, as he pulled to a stop at the last intersection, he saw, gliding in a long slow turn out of the street to the left, Bexley's truck and Mrs. Trevinos—her face empty of color and her eyes staring through the rain like a doll's eyes—leaning out of the window on the passenger side, her stubby fingers lying over the bottom edge, he blinked, grabbed his door handle, thinking to get out of the car to assure himself that what he had seen was real, or to hail them. Yes, call them. But he couldn't get the door open, and so he sat watching the truck gather speed until it disappeared in the rain and mist ahead. They were heading north, toward the Interstate. He pulled the Ford around, stopped, untangled his coat from the door handle, got out. The rain pelted his face and neck. On the sidewalk he saw a woman with an umbrella, a clear plastic thing that fit down over her head like a bell.

"Hello," she said, smiling.

He sat back down in the car, closed the door, thought of following Bexley. In his mind he saw a chase, a wild movie chase, with no end. He pressed the pedal, sped toward the Interstate. But then he caught hold of himself, turned around, and headed back through town, racing. He was so confused and his memory so repeatedly gave him the image of Mrs. Trevinos looking out of the window of the truck (she had looked—she had been *dead*—she was dead!) that he drove past Torgeson's and was at the church before he remembered he had wanted to tell Torgeson what he had seen. But it was too late now to just turn around and go back, because Mrs. Bexley was waddling toward him from the house. The rain beat down on her and matted the hair over her eyes. He watched her walk around the car, filled with dread of what she would have to tell him.

"Where is he?" she said, getting in. "Why doesn't he call?"

"What are you doing out here?" Vincent said. "What has happened?"

"I'm so scared. We got to go to Charlottesville now."

"No—wait."

"Please," she said. "Please."

"It'll be all—it's—don't, don't cry."

"I wish I'd never *seen* this place," she said, and her eyes opened wide with the word *seen*; they rolled, crying.

Vincent touched her hair. "Don't." He lifted it from her face. "We don't know anything yet. Don't upset yourself like this."

For a moment she just stared out at the rain, shivering, her eyes like two wet stones, her mouth slightly open, the water running down from her hair, beading up on her cheeks. "I'm sorry," she said. "I just got so scared and I had to do something. I can't stand to have to just sit around and wait for bad news."

He said nothing.

"It just got too much for me—I can't stand being alone here. And something's happened, I know something's happened." She wiped her eyes with her fingers—quick, brushing movements, as though she removed dust. For a dreadful minute the rain was like a presence, a knowing thing that listened. Vincent thought she huddled toward him an inch, the slightest distance; then he remembered the groceries: she would know something was wrong because he had come back without them. As though on cue she said, "Where's the groceries?"

"I . . ." he stopped.

Now she sat watching him.

"I cashed Torgeson's check and came home. I'm sorry."

Yes, she believed him.

"I won't take long," he said.

"I'm better now."

"All of you stay in the rectory."

"Yes," she said. "We are."

Presently she opened the door and walked bent over in the rain to the house.

"Elizabeth," he said, and was astonished at the sound of her name on his lips.

Oh, he must be careful now. He must not misconstrue what he had seen, as he must not misunderstand what he felt. But he did not know what he felt, beyond the most profound worry. He hoped, with all his heart, that an explanation would come—from Bexley or better, from a live Mrs. Trevinos—that he would not have to watch Elizabeth Bexley suffer anymore.

The Torgeson house was all light; the rain had let up some, but the sky was so low and thick and dark, it was like an early night sky. He knocked three or four times, with long intervals of waiting, before Torgeson opened the door. Torgeson was wearing a bathrobe and holding a drink, though it was only a little past noon. He had been smiling as he opened the door and now he frowned, pulled the bathrobe tight around his neck. "Monsignor Shepherd," he said.

Vincent moved to step inside, but then he stopped. He could not be certain, yet it seemed that Torgeson had been about to block his entrance: there had been the slightest motion of the arms, a motion that Torgeson retracted as soon as Vincent hesitated.

"Ah—I was getting ready to take a nap."

"I've got to talk to you. It's important."

"Can't wait, huh."

"Something's happened. . . ." Vincent was almost pleading now. When he stepped past the other, into the house, he again noticed that motion of the arms—no, it was the whole body now; Torgeson seemed to flex toward him, and when Vincent hesitated, there was again that same awkward retraction. Torgeson shut the door, turned, held the drink up to his mouth.

"I'm sorry to disturb you," Vincent said.

"What's the problem?"

"I don't know quite how to put it." Vincent walked into the room. There was a fire in the fireplace, and country music came softly from a radio on the mantel; it was a transistor radio in a pink case. He thought he smelled perfume.

"I'm sorry," he said. "I'll leave."

"Tell me what you came to tell me."

Vincent now looked at the bathrobe. The sleeves were bell-shaped, fringed with white fur; they came to the other's elbows, fanning out.

"Oh, this robe."

"I saw Bexley today," Vincent began. And then a young woman came down the stairs, wearing a raincoat and red high heels. The heels sounded on the floor as she approached.

"It's not—" she said.

"No," said Torgeson. "It's not."

The woman laughed. "It's the minister. Oh, Lord, the

minister." She extended her hand quickly, still laughing. "Well, let's see. I'm Cousin Marie." Then she said, "That's right, I'm Cousin Marie Trainer from Point Royal."

"Marie," Torgeson said. "Shut up."

"Oh, I ain't Cousin Marie?"

"There's nothing to this," Torgeson said.

"You don't have to explain anything to me," said Vincent.

"That is something—the minister is at the door." Marie pointed at Torgeson. "And you in that getup."

"All right, all right, you've had your laugh," Torgeson muttered.

"See," she said, looking at Vincent, "we heard the door and we thought it was Judy—friend of mine who's staying with me this week?—and so I sent him down here to answer the door like this." She took the end of one of the sleeves as if Torgeson were a mannequin and she wanted to sell the robe to Vincent. "And believe you me, it cost me a lot of coaxing to get him down here in this." She seemed to grow more serious. "To get him down here to surprise Judy. . . ." She stopped. Her voice was thick and southern and loud; it was still on the air as she looked at both men. "Hey, what is this anyway? Why're you looking at me like that? You," she said, poking Torgeson in the chest so that his drink shook over the lip of the glass, "you get that damn look off your face, Victor Torgeson. I didn't exactly force my way in here on you, did I? Maybe you ought to remember it takes two to tango, sweetheart." She put one hand on her hip, gazing at Vincent, smiling again, only now it was obvious that she meant to challenge with this smile. "Right?"

Vincent could not speak for a moment.

"Right?"

He nodded dumbly.

"You got the same thing under your belt, right?"

"Jesus Christ," said Torgeson. "Leave him alone."

"I didn't mean anything by it except that he is a man."
She said *may-un*. "Like any other man."

Then they were quiet. She stood with her hand on her
hip, looking at Torgeson, who gulped his drink. A car horn
sounded outside. It made Marie straighten herself, draw herself up. "That's Judy," she said. "Let me have my robe back."

Torgeson gave her a look of abject supplication.

"Come on," she said as the car horn sounded again. "Fork
it over."

"I have to go upstairs," said Torgeson.

"All right, go on. But hurry."

He set the glass down on the coffee table and went up the
stairs, his head down, one hand flying up to his mouth as if
to take something bitter off his tongue. Vincent watched him
go, felt the woman's eyes on his neck, where the collar
was. He nervously buttoned the top button of his overcoat.

"You Catholic," she said. It was not a question. It was
something to assert, as though she had just now remembered
it. "Huh. You're a priest, right?"

"Yes," Vincent said.

"You get a lot of confessions, right?"

"Right. Yes."

"I'm Catholic."

"You are."

"Yeah. Catholic girls have three choices in life. They can
be nuns, mothers, or whores. Period. You want to guess which
I am?"

"No."

"You hot under the collar, talking to me?"

"No."

"Maybe not—you're old enough to be my grandfather."

"I suppose so," Vincent said.

"You ever read Rimbaud?" she asked.

"I don't believe so."

"French poet. Baudelaire? Villon?"

"No."

"Too bad."

"You?"

"Over and over."

"That's nice."

"Nice," she said. Then she cocked her head to the side. "What do you think of me?"

"I think you're too intelligent to worry about what I may think of you."

"I ain't asking for evasions."

"I don't know what I think of you."

She made a snorting sound. "You think you know me." Vincent was silent.

"But then you get that too, don't you. You're a priest."

"Yes," said Vincent. He could not look at her, so he studied his hands.

"You seem like a nice old man to be wearing that collar."

He did not know what she meant and he did not want to know. He did not want to know or be or do anything just now.

Torgeson came back in one of his own robes, Marie's draped over his arm. He put it over her shoulder and took her by the elbow, guiding her to the door with his free hand.

"We were having a nice little talk," she said.

When he opened the door, another woman was standing there.

"What the hell is going—" she began.

"Good night, ladies," said Torgeson, and slammed the door, leaning against it. Vincent waited for him to turn around. He did so with what seemed like effort, his eyes not settling on anything. "Man," he said, "I could use another drink." He started toward the kitchen, paused, turned, gazing at the floor. "You want a drink?"

"No."

"Look," said Torgeson, coming back, "I don't know what you're thinking. . . ."

"I'm not thinking anything," Vincent said.

"I—will you sit down and have a drink with me?"

"All right."

"You know," Torgeson said, his voice cracking, "my divorce is final now—this morning." He cast his eyes at the floor. "Now I'm officially 'Uncle Daddy'—you've never seen my kids, have you?"

Vincent was faintly irritated by the idea of looking at pictures of Torgeson's children. The other man was already reaching for his wallet, which was on the mantel. From the transistor radio came a mild, feminine voice, talking about rain, bad weather, storm systems crossing the plains.

Torgeson kept him for over an hour, and got drunk in the process. He talked about his children and about his wife, whose divorce of him, since she was Catholic, was an aberration he neither understood nor could accept. He kept asking Vincent how a thing like that could happen. She had been so religious, and granted he had not been the best of husbands— he was twelve years older than she, and seemed to feel that this was the major problem. He just could not understand how a woman so religious could so suddenly throw everything away. He dismissed Vincent's news about Bexley and Mrs. Trevinos with a wave of his hand and a comment, mumbled through or over the lip of his drink glass, that the only thing to do was to wait and see what the whole thing meant. He went on to tell Vincent that his wife had never really wanted him in bed, and then he talked about the children again: they were not really *his* children, though he felt about them or for them the same love any father felt for his children, natural or not. Did Vincent know that he loved children? Everyone loved children, and Victor Torgeson loved them in a special way, since it looked like he would never have any of his own. He and Ellen (his wife) had tried, oh, how they had tried, and that was hard to do, try to have children when one party to the whole thing had no liking for the sex act. Vincent must excuse him for talking about the sex act and his own problems in such a direct way, but then Vincent was in the business, so to speak. Would he like another drink? Did he know that the single most important reason he had taken steps to find the Bexleys a place to stay for the winter was those children—and the woman, too, of course. Did he mention to Vincent that he had experience in delivering babies? He was an ambulance driver in his early twenties; that was how he got interested in hospital work and hospital equipment. Had he ever shown Vincent the little piece of equipment he had invented to make all the money he now had? It was so simple, and Vincent couldn't leave yet. Victor Torgeson wanted to explain himself, had to say some things that Vincent would want to hear. Vincent was not to worry about Elizabeth Bexley: she could handle anything, wasn't that obvious? Yes, she might have been upset, but for all anyone knew, Duck Bexley had just done the old woman a favor and was back at St. Jude's right now. Wasn't that probably so? Hell, the old woman always looked half dead, didn't she? Vincent must be careful not to imagine things. He, Torgeson, had felt ill at ease with Duck Bexley, but then the man had that effect on people, and Torgeson was sure that Duck Bexley was as fine a man and as considerate of his family as any man was.

It went on. It lulled Vincent in a way he could not fully understand. He was aware that part of him wanted to cling to the steadily more drunken voice because this was easier than facing Elizabeth Bexley with what he was afraid he had seen. But there was more to it than that. And then he began

to understand that, because he too had been drinking—
though not nearly as much as Torgeson had—there was,
even in that small amount of alcohol, an easeful feeling, a
sense of the abeyance of things, a relaxation of all his nerves
that carried with it a wish to prolong and ratify itself.

He left after the hour, went to Demera, and bought two
bags of groceries, vaguely troubled, but still the slightest
bit quiet inside, calmed, almost reassured. Coming back
toward St. Jude's, he realized how much time had passed
since he had left Elizabeth. *My God*, he thought, *how I have
failed her. Cowardly, cowardly*, he thought. He sped, pressing
the pedal too far: now he could risk anything. The whiskey.
But he had no time to think about this: as he pulled into the
lot, he saw Bexley's truck, in its usual place. All the lights
were on in the rectory.

7

Bexley had apparently come in only moments before. He was
still in his coat, and he stood under the kitchen light em-
bracing Elizabeth, who put her hands to his chest and backed
away from him as Vincent entered. Priscilla and Harvey sat
at the kitchen table with Sandra June. The twins were in
the dining room, on the floor, pretending to be Indians waiting in ambush for some imaginary cowboy. Vincent took his
coat off and hung it up on the rack, and Bexley followed suit
with his. No one spoke. Elizabeth began to dispense with the
groceries, moving about the room with an air of dispatch that
made Vincent feel entirely mistaken about everything: this
left him vaguely disappointed. Until it struck him that he
wanted to be mistaken.

"Well," Bexley said at long last, "now everybody's here." He had the baseball cap on, still, and the shadow of the folded bill cut down across his face. Vincent could not see his eyes.

"Where were you?" Vincent asked.

"Why, Charlottesville, sir."

"You didn't go anywhere else?"

Bexley shook his head slowly, looking at the floor; he seemed to study it. "No, sure didn't."

Presently he said, "Suppose I should've," and he looked at Vincent almost apologetically, though there was, Vincent was sure, an element of something like defiance ready to surface on the instant. He said, "I didn't get a thing, there. Nothing. Nobody's hiring."

"You went to Charlottesville and stayed overnight and came straight back here."

"That's right." Now there was doubt in the face. The lips tightened a little. This was fleeting, though: it crossed under the precise shadow of the cap like an air current and was gone. Bexley smiled. "Why?"

Vincent let his eyes wander from Bexley to the children, then to Elizabeth: they were all watching him. "I'll be in my room," he said. "I'm not hungry, so don't make dinner for me. Please remember to lock the door."

"Not going to eat," Bexley said. "Got to keep your health up."

Vincent walked out of the kitchen, stepping over the twins, who still pretended to wait in ambush.

"We'll lock the door," Bexley said.

Vincent turned. They might have been any family in any kitchen. The light came down on Elizabeth's hair, and she let her hands come together over the baby in her womb. *Blessed Mother*, Vincent thought. *Hail, Holy Queen. Ma-*

donna. Then he saw that her ankles were swollen far beyond their normal size; they overflowed out of her shoes, brown shoes, he saw, with black laces; white socks bulging; her eyes, looking at him, bulged—black, brilliant, moist.

"It's all right," he said, though he had no idea why.

"We'll work it out," said Bexley, and touched the bill of the cap.

There had been a woman. Long ago now. When he was a curate at St. Dominic's in Chicago. Janet Miller of White Lakes, Illinois: she had traveled to the city to study at the university and, because there was trouble for her there and at home, had come back to church after years away ("not since I was seven, Father—you see Mother is an alcoholic and my father has despaired of her or anything, and it's just hell."). Janet had a pointed nose and small hands and a tiny black mark on her cheek, and when she cried into her little turquoise handkerchief, she broke Vincent's heart. There was no explanation of this, but he had felt all his love go out to her, had felt it as she cried and had felt it later when she showed up in church, a sharp-nosed face under a black felt hat that he had been looking for all that time and that appeared, without fail, every Sunday of that year. Those mornings the bells rang out from the stupendous gray stone edifice of St. Dominic's, rang all the way to the lake, in any wind, any storm; and, preparing for mass, he would think about how those bells called her to him. He gave little time to the significance of these thoughts because they filled him entirely and because they never called attention to himself as a priest and her as a woman: it was a perfect love, he believed, that only wanted her well-being and peace. He spent hours every day thinking about her problems, which were myriad: she told him she was afraid of everything; she feared that she was suicidal, schizoid, cancerous, alcoholic; she hated her parents, had no friends, no money, and she believed that her chain-smoking was subconscious self-destruction; she was failing every course at the university and a professor there had attempted to seduce her, had promised to fail her if she did not relent. Vincent was certain that he was her only contact with the world, and what could he do about her problems? He was tied to his parish, his duties. He never saw her anywhere but in church. He never talked with her for more than a few minutes: she was always in a hurry; she was nervous about wasting his time. She always carried the little turquoise handkerchief and always wore the black felt hat. These two things grew to symbolize her in Vincent's mind. Her hair was auburn, and cut short; it lay over her ears like part of the hat—a dark, red edge. He never saw a hat like that without searching for the tight, auburn curls. Below the curls her neck was blue, with tiny maplike veins, as were her cheeks. He called her "Miss Miller." Perhaps once or twice, when she was particularly upset, he used her first name. There was never a time when he could have told anyone what her hips were like, or her legs; yet he seemed, during that year, to notice the hips and legs of other women more, no matter how arduously he tried not to. Janet, lifting the turquoise handkerchief to her eyes, was a shape that folded inward to a point, a center. And, as in the beginning he had seen no danger in what he felt or in what he thought, this inward-folding idea became fixed in his mind in a way that seemed very dangerous indeed. There were times, toward the end, when every woman he looked at—from the nuns of the parish school to his own mother—seemed to fold inward that way, to that center, that secret place his dreams told him was damp, warm, only itself.

And one Saturday night, during a long, sleep-inducing

stint in the confessional—how could anyone believe that sin
was enticing, or that sins, of themselves, were interesting: it
was all, always, so horribly the same, so mean, so colorless: it
was the deepest boredom—he thought he recognized her
voice, wondered if he had fallen momentarily asleep and
dreamed it, sat up, put his ear close to the screen, concentrat-
ing on the words that came murmuring through as if formed
out of the close, stale air of the booth.

"I didn't think I'd go through with it, Father."

"What," he said. "Go through with what."

"With—that. You know. I was so miserable and he was—
different."

"I'm sorry," Vincent said, "but I missed the first part of
your confession."

A sigh came through the screen.

"Go on," he said sadly, "I believe I know what you're
talking about."

"That's all."

He waited.

"I—*liked* it. But I feel—wrong."

"Yes."

"But I feel wrong about everything."

There were two small whimpering sounds that Vincent
did not know for sure had come from the other side of the
screen. He held his hand up to his mouth, imagined the turquoise handkerchief, the black felt hat, the auburn edges. *A
Catholic girl. How old are you?* He had never asked how old
she was. *Twenty. Twenty-one. How could you do this to me?*

"Now I don't care anymore how I feel. I just want to be
forgiven."

"And," Vincent said, certain of the facts as if he had heard
them and had not guessed, "the young man?"

"Young man?" she said doubtfully.

Had he been wrong?

She said, "It was—I told you, Professor Glick. At the school."

The one who tried to coerce you? The words clustered on the point of a shout that he barely kept down.

"He's not a young man, Father. He's in his fifties."

"Oh, Lord," Vincent muttered.

But she hadn't heard him. She went on. "He wants to see me again. He said so. He said he could fix things with his wife."

"His wife."

"He said she—understood his . . . needs."

"Do you want to see him again?"

"Yes."

Presently she said: "Is that a sin?"

"Do you think it is?"

"I don't *know*."

Now he had to wait for the sobbing to stop. He sat hunched in that dark—gathered, it seemed, around his own pain: a prodigious, expanding knot of something just under his heart.

"Is it a sin if I want to see him?"

Vincent drew in air, opened his mouth to speak.

But she went on: "I've tried the Church, Father—it doesn't do anything for loneliness."

"Then," Vincent said, trying to control his voice, "the answer to your question makes no difference."

"Answer it," she said. It was a demand. Almost, he thought, given the nature of their previous relationship, a challenge.

"It's a sin if you want to see him to repeat the sin you've come here to confess."

"No exceptions," she said.

"I'm afraid not."

"No provisions—no circumstances. Father, for the first time

in my life I felt something . . . like I might even want to see what happens tomorrow and the next day. Like there was some reason for me."

"You said you felt *wrong*." He could not control the sententiousness in his voice. He added, gently as he could: "Didn't you?"

"I feel wrong because I can't decide about it—can't say the hell with your church and my parents and all their torturous, mind-crippling guilts and all their damn *death*."

There was a moment, then—less than a moment, though it was palpable—when he could have said something, anything gentle or kind or understanding, to keep her from jerking out of the booth. But he said nothing and with a last sob she parted the curtain, let light into the booth, was a thin shadow going out. He watched the curtain come swinging back over the light, and knew he would never see her again.

He was wrong. He saw her everywhere, in every female face, saw her in the knowledge that he had done something truly evil, though he could not quite define it for himself in any specific terms—this would have required thinking about her, and he was now engaged in a daily battle with himself not to do so. There was, at this time, a housekeeper in the rectory, a Mrs. Elliot, who was fifty-something, heavy, motherly and devoted, and who carried within her the memory of some ancient grief that she was always bearing up under, since she believed herself to be heroic and grieving as any woman of the Bible. She was a good woman, conscientiously humble in spite of her high sense of what she had suffered, and so it seemed unjust to Vincent's monsignor—a golfer named Blackman; Father Blackman of the Three Handicap, as the curates called him—it seemed unjust to Blackman that Vincent should so passionately insist on Mrs. Elliot's removal. Vincent, to protect himself, insisted, and conscientiously sought inadequacies in her work to justify his own desire to have her dismissed. It was nothing personal; it was merely that she was a woman and the proximity of any woman was torture. Mrs. Elliot bore this trouble as she bore all trouble, and Vincent knelt alone in his room at night, aware of his own meanness, begging the dark for an end to the misery that made him behave so. Blackman would not be moved, of course, and Mrs. Elliot had stayed on. Vincent became the pacing figure in the upstairs room, having broken off friendships, associations, habits that brought him into contact with parishioners in any but the most ceremonial, and therefore impersonal, way. He had begun to receive letters from his mother that hinted about the possibility of her moving to Chicago, and the idea both horrified and discouraged him. Wasn't it sad, her letters said, how life pulled people apart. And how lonesome it was in Virginia, in the old house, and her only surviving family member so far away in Chicago.

Finally he came under the bishop's eye. The bishop wanted weekly reports on him; the bishop liked his priests to get out and be pastoral servants of the parishes: "We keep the vineyards," he said. "That is for us to do—we humbly till the fields." Vincent thought of leaving the priesthood. The idea came to him quite suddenly while he said mass one morning, and it caused his hands to shake as though he had a sudden palsy. It took all of his strength to get through the Communion and the blessing: he had never in his life more meant the passage: *Go, the mass is ended. Thanks be to God.* "Thank God," he said. And walked out of the church as though it were on fire, nodding at those who wanted to speak to him or greet him, but speaking to no one, answering no one. In his room he wept, his hands knotted together over his bed, his face down, the hard floor punishing his knees.

"Father," he heard behind him.

It was Mrs. Elliot.

"Get out of here," he said, but then, as she turned to go, he made himself rise. "Wait."

She waited, her hands at her sides. Her eyes were moist and empty and sad, like the eyes of a suffering animal: some blind, small, suffering creature. He walked across the space of floor that separated them, and gave himself over to his tears, touching her shoulder. She stood quite still, but only for a moment, and then she put her arms around him as though she were his mother, patting the back of his head.

"There," she said. "There now. There."

He was, twenty-nine years old.

He wrote his mother and begged her to come to Chicago. He hurled himself back into his priesthood; he did everything with all his might, and gradually the memory of Janet Miller began to fade from him, though he liked to believe he had seen her one other time.

This had been some years later: he had been transferred to New York, first to a small parish in Syracuse (four of the most peaceful years of his life) and then down to the city itself. He had taken a train south to visit his mother, who had never been very communicative and from whom he had not heard in a long time—and whom he would discover this time to be quite alert, quite active, with new friends and a new garden as if she had, at that late date, decided to become gregarious and sunny. It was summer, 1952. A lot of men were running for President. As the train passed through Newark, it was slowed by the passage of another train on the other side of one of the platforms, from the back end of which a minor candidate spoke. Vincent glanced out at the crowd on the platform, and at the body of the other train, and thought he saw, in the window of one of the forward cars, Janet Miller, pregnant, bouncing a baby in her arms, leaning forward so that the baby might see Vincent's train go by. It seemed to Vincent that she looked right at him, and that she recognized him; but there wasn't time to smile or wave—his train had begun to pick up speed—nor was there time to decide what Janet Miller was doing on a presidential candidate's Campaign Special. Of course, later, he doubted that it had actually been she—yet this didn't matter: the vision of that woman, whoever she was, seemed to have put the memory of Janet Miller to sleep, because whenever he remembered her now, he remembered that face he had seen on the train, that face of a woman who smiled and who was pregnant with at least a second child, and who was, in some way, involved in presidential politics. He seemed to know, even then, even as he sat back in his seat and watched the ugly skyline of Newark give way to marsh grass and pine, that this was the end of his torment over Janet Miller.

Until now.

He dreamed about her all night. She came to him fitfully, in odd tangled combinations of clothing as if she were modeling them for him. She sobbed at him and her eyes burned, and there was something terribly wrong but he could not know it, and he understood that he could never know it. She was pregnant. She became mixed with Elizabeth Bexley and Jane Trevinos and the woman he had seen at Torgeson's. It was the face of Jane Trevinos, staring out of the window of Bexley's truck, that woke him.

Morning. The light at the window surprised him, and he lay staring at it as if he expected some figure to take form from it and speak to him. The old, weightless feeling came back, and he tried to fix his mind on what he must do. But his mind flew off in all directions, and he hurriedly dressed, without shaving (that would make two days) and went down to the kitchen. Elizabeth Bexley was crossing the lot, a blue shape in the shade of the house. The sun seemed to spill out of the sky onto the church and the social hall.

"You're up," Elizabeth said as he opened the door for her. She hung her coat on the rack. "You must've slept last night —I didn't see your light."

"You were out walking again?"

"Yes."

Then there was nothing to say. She was putting cereal bowls on the table—red plastic bowls that she had brought over from the social hall in the first days.

"How do you feel?" Vincent asked.

She seemed puzzled by the question, frowning, a strand of her hair lying over her forehead. She pushed it roughly out of the way. "I feel all right. You?"

"I seem to have lost track of the time."

"It's seven forty-five."

"Wednesday."

"No, Thursday."

"Of course."

And there is something wrong, Vincent thought.

She busied herself, her back to him now. He looked at the suggestion of her spine through the thin cotton sweater she wore over her dress.

"You shouldn't work so hard," he said.

She did not respond.

"You look tired."

"We're all tired," she said. "Everybody's tired."

"Did your husband say anything else about his trip to Charlottesville?" he asked suddenly.

She looked at him. "No."

Presently she asked: "Why?"

He saw again the grotesque swelling of her ankles. He could not look away.

"You want something to eat?" she asked.

"I'll fix myself something later." He took his coat from the rack, carefully putting hers aside to do so. It was as if the coat contained some part of her that he must be careful of. *Oh, what sort of man is Bexley anyway?*

"You growing a beard?" she asked.

"No. I'll shave."

"It's nothing to me."

This hurt him in a vague way. He was silent.

"I was just curious."

"Of course."

He went out, passed Priscilla in the doorway, nodding as she nodded. There wasn't a cloud in the sky. The ground gave under his feet and the puddles in the lot were like large pieces of brilliant glass. He went over to the truck, looked into the front seat, thinking he might find some sign of Mrs. Trevinos. But he saw only gum wrappers, a broken pencil, and a map that had been folded and refolded so many times, the creases were torn. As he stood there gazing into the truck, something moved in the other window.

Bexley.

"You look a little ragged, sir."

"So do you," said Vincent. He could not believe how quickly the anger rose in him, tinged with something like fear.

Bexley smiled. "What's the matter? What's so interesting about my truck?" His eyes were bright and friendly and uncertain.

"I saw you yesterday," Vincent said.

Bexley's face did not change.

"I saw you in Demera with Mrs. Trevinos."

"No, not me." The eyes were now clearly afraid. "You couldn't have seen me because I was in Charlottesville. Must have been somebody else."

"It was you," Vincent said.

Bexley just barely moved his head, as if he had thought to deny it, and then had changed his mind. But now he was indeed denying it, his hands on the edge of the window. "That is just not so, now. You seen the wrong man. It wasn't me."

"Yes it was."

"All right—what if it was?"

"Where is Mrs. Trevinos?" Vincent asked.

Bexley waved his arms, walked away from the truck. "How should *I* know where she is? I gave her a lift. I don't know where she is."

Vincent went around to face him. "When you first came here, you denied that I had seen you at her door. You told me not to tell your wife that you'd been there."

"What of it?" Bexley said. "That's got nothing to do with anything."

"Why did you lie about it? Why are you lying now?"

"Leave it, old man."

"No, I will *not* leave it."

Bexley stepped toward him. The cloudy eyes had narrowed, and the mouth pulled back over the teeth. "You better— you're going to get hurt if you don't."

"Oh," Vincent said into that face. "What have you done?" He had not intended to say it. For an instant he thought he could feel the blows that were about to rain down on him. But Bexley walked away, walked back to the social hall and in, without looking back. Vincent stood very still, and in a moment the door to the hall opened; Bexley emerged, with his children. The children surrounded Bexley like willing hostages.

God, he thought, *I have been living with a murderer.* The force of the words in his mind took the air out of his lungs. He drove into town, to the feed store. It was closed, locked, dark. He stood with his hands cupped at the sides of his face as Bexley had the first time Vincent had seen him, face pressed against the glass; but there was nothing to see. He realized now that he had inwardly believed he would find Mrs. Trevinos there, understood that the extremity of his fear was an attempt to charm the object of that fear out of existence: all the way into town he had imagined himself breathing the long sigh of relief into the old woman's face. As he went down the rickety stairs in the cold, sunny wind, he could feel himself filling up with the conviction that it was all so: Mrs. Trevinos *had* been dead; Bexley had murdered her. He drove to the police station—the highway patrol office on Sixteen—and sat listening to the idling of the Ford, looking at the closed door with the wooden badge painted gold on it, the windows with their brown shades. Two squad cars were parked at the entrance; they were freshly washed, polished, looked ready to go. A clipboard with paper in it gleamed on the dash of one.

Officer, I want to report a missing person.

Murder.

Officer, I have a murderer in my social hall. He's there with his wife and five children.

No, Vincent told himself. *No, get ahold of yourself. No. Other possible explanations. She looked dead, but she stared that way from the fourth pew all year. He wouldn't have come back. He would never have come back. Sure, he would. No, he wouldn't have driven her through town in plain sight of everyone. Yes, he would. Bexley would.*

Oh, God, Vincent thought, *what sort of man is Bexley? He is not a murderer and I am not going to make a further fool of myself. Murder.* It hurt his chest. He almost longed for the heart attack. A patrolman came out, saw him, waved. Vincent waved back. The patrolman hesitated, then approached. He was a tall blond boy with wide, flaring nostrils and a mouth thin as a pencil line.

"Something wrong, Father?" he asked.

Vincent had rolled the window down and now he got out of the car. "I don't know—" he said. He could feel his panic roiling up his middle. It was about to come shouting out of him.

"Something I can help you with?"

"I'm looking for someone." Vincent put a shaking hand to his mouth, to hold back, control himself.

"Yes, Father?" The patrolman frowned. His voice had become all business. Vincent was now truly terrified, but he held on somehow.

"A Mrs. Trevinos—Jane Trevinos."

"I know her—yeah. Lives over the feed store. Used to call her *witch* when I was a kid. She ain't there?"

"No," Vincent said. He had thought the young man might say her remains had been found. An inordinate sense of relief washed downward in him—he seemed to feel it flow that way as if he had swallowed a gallon of some warm liquid in one gulp.

"She supposed to be there?"

"I'm just . . . looking for her."

"Is something wrong?"

"I just think it strange that she's not there." As he spoke, Vincent was certain that he was all off-base, absurd, completely hysterical. Yet he had begun, so he went on: "It looks suspicious to me. I'm afraid something has happened to her."

"Well," the young man said, pulling his helmet off and scratching tight, blond curls, "she has that house, you know, and that boy in New York. You been up to the house?"

"No."

The young man put the helmet back on. "Well," he said. His voice had now become incredulous, but just slightly so. He smiled, and this made Vincent feel very foolish.

"I'll try her tomorrow," he said.

"Try the house," said the patrolman, strolling away in the direction of one of the cars. "She goes up there a lot when it gets cold."

"Wait," Vincent said.

The young patrolman stopped, turned, the faintest irritation showing around his eyes. "Yes?"

"Would *you* check the house?"

"You *are* worried."

"Probably nothing," Vincent said, and tried to smile.

8

He would talk to Bexley again. He would talk to Torgeson. He must be certain. It was crazy to jump to any conclusion. "Bexley is capable of murder," he said to himself as he drove toward St. Jude's. *Bexley is not. Yes, he is. Everyone is.* Oh, why, why had they ever come into his life, his peaceful, ordered life? Why could he not have it all back as it was before they came? Torgeson was not home—or he was not answering his door. He thought about the woman Marie— "You think you know me," she had said. The things he did not know about everyone. How could he have come this far through life and not found anything out about it? A voice in his mind said, quite clearly, as though it were another person in the car with him, *You are afraid of what you will find out.*

He stayed in his room the rest of the day. Five or six times he tried to call Mrs. Trevinos, but there was never any answer. He watched, from the window, holding the curtain an inch to the side, Bexley drive away in the truck, was about to rush over to Elizabeth when he realized that it was afternoon, and time for the children to get out of school. Elizabeth came over to the house with the twins and Sandra June, but he did not go down to her and when she came to his door, asking if he would eat dinner, he told her, in as polite and unswerving a voice as he could muster, to go away. Bexley came back with the children and everything seemed quite normal, but Vincent had no will to face any of them. He was exhausted. He believed he had reached the end of his tolerance and his strength. He thought he might be having a nervous breakdown. And since he could neither sit still nor pace, he did both, would discover himself pacing and then sit down, or discover himself sitting down and then pace. It went like that for hours. He tried to call Torgeson, and Torgeson wasn't there. He tried to call Mrs. Trevinos and Mrs. Trevinos wasn't there. He called the State Police, but the voice that answered was so calm and reasonable and bored, he lost courage and hung up. He called them again, perhaps an hour later, and got no answer. The Bexleys went back to the hall, and he wandered the house. It seemed that the world had managed to empty out secretly, and had left him alone in an awful quiet, a disordered, sick silence. He believed that he had made his fear up in his mind, that everything outside glided toward midnight as reasonably as ever; but there was something else, something so alien to him that its slightest mental touch made him ache to know for sure there had been no crime and sent shocks of heat up the back of his head. Midnight came and passed without his knowing. The lateness of the hour when he went back up to his room surprised him as if he had awakened from a sort of dream of hiding to find the house abandoned, quiet and cold. He sat at his window in the dark and looked out on the social hall and the church. They made a deeper dark—were half-formed shapes on the other side of the glass. Clouds covered the moon—what had been only a sliver, like a piece of cut fingernail. The stars had gone out as if snuffed. Nothing moved save the occasional branch in the wind, which gusted like the separate shocks of an invisible tide: waves rolling in on a reef—and indeed it was as though he were a lighthouse keeper on a barren promontory over the sea. Except that his light was only a little rhomboid on the dark below. And now he realized that he was waiting for Elizabeth to come from the hall and do her walking. His stomach filled with air, and he waited, with spreading horror—aware that he must get up quickly, must not think it—for the rest of the thought. It didn't come immediately. It hovered in the dark behind him like a spirit, sure of him, a separate thing that would settle over him like an enormous bird with cold, wide wings.

You want it to have been murder.

Vincent got out of the chair and away from the window, and now he could not remain in the house another moment. It was almost four o'clock in the morning and he was half dead, but if he did not get out where he could breathe and move, he would go mad. He bundled himself quickly, like a man desperately late for some crucial appointment, and went out and started the Ford. He drove north through town—the Christmas lights dark, the shop displays and decorations mute and abandoned as the artifacts of a ruin—the window open on his side so he could breathe the air. He had no idea where he was going or how far he would go: he was not thinking of destination as much as he was thinking of escape. The cold air stung his nostrils and made his breathing visible, but it was clean and cold and clear, and he sucked in great gouts of it. His headlights went out into the dark, a wide, white cone; and he traveled down that cone toward daylight.

On the outskirts of Demera, coming back from the long, aimless flight, he stopped at a small roadside diner for some tea. He was only partially awake, sheepish and wracked by a headache. Dawn had come: red, cold, factual as a number on a calendar. His panic was now like something he had witnessed in another person, though its effects still clung to him like an odor. In the diner he breathed frying eggs and bacon, and coffee. These fragrances taunted him as if his long night

had left him unworthy of them. He sat at the counter, though
there were empty booths along the windows. The windows
were dirty and the counter was dirty and the waitress, who
wore muddy-colored lipstick, had a glazed, sullied look about
her. He kept his coat on, ordered his tea, drank it too quickly,
anxious for its warmth. There was a man in a white car-coat
next to him, eating eggs. The man had a transistor radio,
which lay on its back between Vincent's little metal urn of
cream and the plate of eggs. A rough voice talked about Nash-
ville, and then a chorus sang about toothpaste. Gum disease
was deplored by a female voice, heavy and sexual. The fight
against cavities was the fight against evil. Vincent felt old and
solitary and useless. Now a voice, backed by the sound of
Teletype machines, was announcing the news. He sipped the
tea while the voice went on about the Point Royal City
Council. There had been a mass resignation, a scandal that
would cause ramifications in Washington. Vincent thought
he might speak to the man at his side—a bell-shaped, balding,
swarthy man, who kept glancing at him as if trying to remember his face. But now the voice was talking about a body
that had been discovered in a wooded area north of the little
town of Demera early this morning.

". . . identified as seventy-six-year-old Jane Trevinos of
Demera. . . ."

Vincent put his cup down as if it contained some sort of
explosive. The little corrugated leather screen over the speaker
seemed to cover a gaping mouth. *Cause of death not de-
termined. Termed suspicious by police. County sheriff's office
seeking information. No immediate signs of sexual assault.*

"You want something else?" the waitress said. Both she
and the man in the white car-coat were looking at him. He
could not speak. His hands shook at his mouth.

"He can't pay for his tea," the man said. "He's a drunk.
Look at him."

"No," Vincent said. "I'm a priest—I haven't shaved. . . ."

The waitress held her hand out: stubby, short-nailed, nicotine-stained fingers. Vincent reached into his pocket, but now a tall, thin boy in a navy pea coat leaned toward him from his other side, two stools away. "Here, I'll pay for your tea, pop."

The county sheriff's office was in the basement of the courthouse. The courthouse was a white clapboard building across from the old train depot; it had been erected in 1862, just in time for Mosby's Raiders to fire the porch and much of the upper floor. There was a cannon and a solid pyramid of heavy shot on a little square of sandstone in front of the building; a green metal plate in the ground, like a grave-marker, gave the story of the raid. Beyond the cannon was a flagpole, and a small reserved parking lot, nearly empty at this hour of the morning. Vincent parked out on the street and walked across the lawn to the side door, above which a sign with dark blue lettering read:

SHERIFF

PLEASE COME IN

He opened the door, which was heavy and which resisted him, and went down a flight of stairs to a green room that was divided by a partition. A stocky man with thick black eyebrows and short, blue-black hair got up from a green desk and walked over to him.

"I'm a priest," Vincent said, unbuttoning his coat so the man could see the collar. "I haven't shaved."

"Yes?" the man smiled and frowned at the same time.

"I'm sorry. I haven't slept."

"Can I help you?" the man said. There was a blue name tag on his chest. The white letters read GREEN.

"Mr. Green," said Vincent. He was thinking about the

green walls, the green desks, Mr. Green. "Mr. Green," he said. He thought of Elizabeth Bexley and the children, and his mind froze on an image of her swollen ankles.

"Can I help you, sir," Mr. Green said definitely.

"Yes," Vincent said.

Mr. Green waited.

"I just heard," Vincent said.

"Yes."

"The woman. You found—the body. Jane—Jane T—"

Mr. Green went back to his desk, brought back a yellow pad of paper. He held it up, as if he were writing a ticket. "Name," he said.

"No," said Vincent.

"No?"

"Let me just tell you."

"I have to have your name. Aren't you the visiting priest over at Saint Jude's?"

Vincent spelled the last name out for him, and he wrote it down. It was terribly quiet. There was an exhaust fan in the wall to the left; it was still, the blades coated with a fur of black dust. This was what had to be done: there was no question.

Yet he could not do it.

"Never mind," he said.

"Do you know something?" Mr. Green asked. "If you do, you have to tell us."

"I'm not sure—no." Vincent could not look at him now. "I can't be sure."

"Isn't there a family staying with you?" the other man asked.

"Why, yes."

"By the name of Bexley?"

"Yes."

"I have a report here," said Mr. Green, turning the pages of the pad. Vincent looked at a gold ring, which was imbedded in Mr. Green's little finger. "A Mrs. Louise Warren—yes—she claims she saw your Mr. Bexley with the old woman two days ago in the rain. You come to talk about Bexley?"

"I—I don't know. I saw him with her too. Wednesday. But he—"

"That's what you want to report?"

"Yes—but I talked to him about it. He came back and I spoke to him and he said—he said he gave her a lift."

"Well, we're going to talk to him too."

"It's all a mistake," said Vincent. "Isn't it all a mistake?"

Mr. Green looked at him from under his black brows. "You go on home now, Father—we'll see."

"There must be a mistake. He's back at the hall—at the church right now."

"No," Mr. Green said. "No, he's not there—we're looking for him, Father."

Vincent said nothing.

"We got people out looking for him right now," Mr. Green said. "He seems to have disappeared."

"He was there this morning when I left."

"What time did you leave?"

"Early," Vincent said. "Pretty early—I couldn't sleep, and I went for a—I drove around a little—"

"This is all very upsetting, Father, I know. Why don't you go on back home. Nothing's certain yet. We'll be in touch when you're more—clear."

"I—" Vincent began. But there was nothing more to say.

"Let's just see what happens," Mr. Green said.

V

1

❧❧❧

The signs had said Charlottesville, but then Duck Bexley found himself on the road to Richmond, across the mountains into the sun. The road was dry and the sun burned everywhere, though there were still patches of ice in the pools of water below the roadbed. Treetop: Bexley knew where to go, but he did not do so right away. He drove around Richmond, wound up back at the dairy—the white trucks lined up at the docks, and that smell on the air. He sat in the idling truck and watched, and then he got out and walked over to the first platform, where Wainright stood. Wainright was an old yellow man—colored man, he called himself. Duck Bexley had worked with him for ten years and had never called him anything but Wainright to his face.

"Well, Bexley," Wainright said, "how you doin'." He stood there with his hands on his hips, great yellow paws folded up. Two boys, strangers, were with him.

"How you doin', Wainright."

"Jes' fine."

They loaded the truck, metal racks of bottled milk rattling. Their breath was white.

"Got new boys," Duck Bexley said.

"Yeah." Wainright worked on, grunting. "You ain't coming back to work, is you?"

Bexley felt himself shaking.

"Cold," Wainright said.

"Lotta changes. Such a short time."

"Jes' these two," said Wainright. "What brings you here anyway? Boss is mad at you for runnin' out."

Bexley shrugged, but the other man had turned away, had looked at one of the boys. The boy jerked his head back, getting the hair out of his eyes. "Who's driving this one?" Bexley mumbled, standing below them. "I had to get. Had better things to do." The crates rattled and he walked away.

"Nice seein' yeh," Wainright called from behind him.

Bexley turned. Wainright was gray now, standing up there in the shade. His tight wool hair, white above the ears.

"I got nowhere to go," Bexley said, barely moving his lips.

"What's that, man?"

"Bye-bye."

The pickup shook and groaned to life. Bexley looked across at the dock, where Wainright worked, calling commands to the boys, as though nothing had interrupted him. Wainright's days would go on and on, with those boys or other boys, on and on, like that. A man set down into his job like a fence post. Bexley's throat burned, thinking this, and he drove on, out of Richmond, on to where Alphonse was buried. The Gates of Eden Cemetery off Larker Road. It was getting colder, though the sun poured down out of gaping holes in the clouds. The grave was tucked back in a cluster of white markers on the down side of a knoll. There were small fir trees scattered over the grass, in no apparent order, and beyond the knoll was a great white stone mausoleum. The grass was green, like summer grass, and the wind rolled across it in waves. ALPHONSE BEXLEY, SR. 1897–1978. The plain white marker had been all Alphonse's pension would pay for. Bexley thought about how his father had never owned a house. How he bore a son, Alphonse junior, but hated the name Junior and called him Duck. Little Duck, because things rolled off him like water off a duck's back. Bexley stood there on that cold little hill, the sun lost behind a long gray cloud, and felt empty, dead under the heart. *I'm running away and I don't know where to run.*

"Nothing ever rolled off me, Daddy," he said. "Not ever. Nothing."

2

Mrs. Trevinos had shown him the money. He had been working for Torgeson, driving Torgeson's car—the rich man wanted the feel of having his own driver. Or that was what he said. Bexley would take anything, even this, if Torgeson would provide the house. There were really no other choices but to do what Torgeson asked and take the car into Demera on Fridays, to drive the old woman wherever she took it in her mind to go: Charlottesville, or south to Danville—sometimes across the state line into Carolina. The country was beautiful down there, and the old woman would name trees and flowers, sitting in the backseat with her hands folded across her stomach. "That's silver maple. There's beech. Pin oak. Pignut hickory. Red Rooster, celandine. Lots of Jimson." Bexley drove on: *Torgeson's chauffeur*, and his eyes hurt for his anger. The skin on the backs of his hands showed the blotches of his condition. He was past forty years old and there was no help anywhere, and life had gotten away from him. There was nothing he knew how to do except drive, and people like Torgeson knew it. Torgeson was abrupt and suspicious, seemed more and more anxious to keep command in his voice, to let Bexley know who was boss, who supplied the money and the house. Bexley said little, having lived through a lifetime of bosses—except for that time in Korea, when he wandered the hills with a rifle in his hand, and everything counted. That, he thought, had always been his trouble: making things count somehow; in Korea he had shot forty-four Chinese in a hole from which they could not escape, nor even see him, and he had been given a medal for it. Alphonse had put his name in the Treetop newspaper, had sent him copies. "Christ," Bexley had said, "I'm a hero." And had come home and found that it didn't count, that nothing counted and the war was not even a war. He had been able to find work in a gas station—one gas station after another—had wandered south, away from Alphonse and his questions about what he wanted to do with his life. He did not know, and not knowing, not being able to find something definite to fix on, made his anger grow. He could not explain it. And then he had wound up tearing an automobile apart with a tire iron, carefully as if he had been instructed to do it, astonished at his own fury.

Bexley, at twenty-five, was a convict.

He grew used to the sound of Mrs. Trevinos's voice on the long drives, and he heard some of what she said: her queer son and her dead husband and what ached her. The flowers, the trees.

One Friday, when he had brought her back, she asked him in, sat forward in the seat and said, "Come with me." She stopped at the base of her stairs and motioned to him. "Did you hear me?"

Bexley got out of the car. "I got to get back."

"In a little while. Come here." She motioned to him again. "Do as I say."

He went up the stairs behind her, into the rooms, which smelled of something dead: an odor of rotting fish and dampness, like a touch, from the crowded walls. It was the cats—cat dung; open cans of tuna on the floor.

"You like cats," she said, as if she answered him.

"I got to get back."

"You want coffee?"

"No." He waited a moment. "Thanks."

"You believe in God?" She stood facing him, her heavy face gleaming in the heat. She folded and unfolded her hands. "Do you?"

"I guess so. I don't go to church."

"How old are you?"

"Look. I got to get back—"

Mrs. Trevinos came to him, took his hands, cried suddenly and noisily down into his fingers. She knelt, asked if he would rub her neck. "Here," she said, rising. She walked him to the sofa, and he sat, conscious of himself dropping down, as if he broke through something.

"I am getting out of here," he said.

"No," she answered. "Not yet. I want to talk to you—you never have anything to say." She turned her back and bent over, then stopped, faced him again. "Get up."

Bexley stood. If he left her here, she would complain to Torgeson. His breathing rolled up out of him. "Got to get."

"Look," she said, bending again, pulling the cushion of the sofa up. Bexley looked at money—new, green, wrapped, like decks of cards. "You don't think you can massage my neck and shoulders," she said.

"What in the hell," Bexley said.

"You don't think you can touch me."

"You offering it to me?"

She told him to never mind, put the cushion back down

carefully, as though she were afraid she might wake someone, whispering at him. "Sit down."

He did so, thinking about the money, what was under him. The old woman got down on the floor, her back to his knees— he felt the heavy shoulders, round and solid, saw her hands pulling the hair up off her neck.

"Go on and rub," she said.

He touched the skin.

"Just like it used to be. You don't mind."

"Used to be."

"It's an old neck," she said. "Rub an old neck." She held her hair out of the way, talking about having a man in the house again, holding her neck open for him like someone waiting to be slaughtered. And then Bexley thought about squeezing the neck, watched his fingers move, thinking. It was as if his fingers, each of them, entertained the idea, touching down to the shoulders and back up. He looked at his knuckles and waited for them to stiffen. *Just an old woman who has no need*, he thought, pretending to himself, *this next minute, this one, this.*

"Goddamn."

"Good," she said. "Harder."

He stopped.

"Go on," she said.

He moved his legs, pulled them out on either side of her so she fell back against the sofa between them. "What if I do it too hard," he said.

"That's right," she said. "Yes."

His own neck was hot: she had understood him. "Jesus Christ."

"Don't go," she said.

"For Christ's poor sake."

She got over on all fours, crawled away to the chair on the

other side of the room, turned and sat, legs out. Bexley looked at the stockings rolled around her ankles, like chokes—the ankles themselves, the jutting feet, as though she were already dead.

"Can I have some of that money."

She drew her mouth into a line. "Get out."

"Look. What do you want me to do."

"Get out."

He could see up her dress, was sick, felt himself about to gag something up. "The money," he said, looking at her head above the eyes. He saw spots there, her matted hair.

"You just get out."

"You're crazy—you're a crazy woman."

"If you don't leave, I shall call the police."

He went out, down the stairs into the street. It was now even hotter than it had been, cloudy and hazy and getting early dark, as if winter had sneaked through the heat somehow. It struck him that he would remember this as a winter dusk, in spite of the heat. He held his hands up in the first bath of a lamp on the corner, looked at the knuckles, the tips of the fingers. Then he got into the car and drove away fast, speeding into the falling dark, until he was approaching the farm. The air was cooler under the trees, whose branches knotted over the road. He thought about this as he stood at Torgeson's door, waiting for the other man to come for the keys. He did not remember getting out of the car and he did not remember knocking on the door. He knocked once, waited.

"You've been gone a long time," Torgeson said.

Bexley held the keys out to him. He could hear a woman singing somewhere in the room, and he could see the aquarium, fish darting through white bubbles.

"Well?" Torgeson said.

"I don't think she'll . . . want my . . . want me to drive

her around again." He felt himself closing up inside. Always the reaction of his cells to the bosses. As if he grew stupid, lost his sight, his memory, his voice.

"What did you do?" Torgeson asked.

"It ain't what I did. It's what I didn't do."

"All right," said Torgeson, moving the door an inch, as if he were about to slam it shut. "What didn't you do?"

"Wanted me to sit and talk—talk to her."

The other man handed him a check, took the keys. "I'll let you know," he said.

"Let me know what?"

"When—and if—she wants you again. I'm going to assume this isn't any more than you say it is. So she'll go next Friday. Let's stick with that."

"Why you doing this anyway?" Bexley asked.

"You don't have to know why—you just have to do what you're paid to do."

The door slammed. Bexley stood there looking at the wood grain of it. Then, suddenly, Torgeson pulled it open again, seemed surprised to find him still there.

"What do you want?"

"Nothing."

"Look, I didn't mean to be abrupt with you."

"Yeah."

"I've got her on the horn right now. Wait a minute." Torgeson walked away from the door, and Bexley stepped inside, looked at the fish as they grazed the glass. There was a TV on in the next room; music; a woman laughed just inside the entrance. Torgeson's voice was there too, talking low. The fish moved into the dimmer parts of the tank, then glided back into light as if coming through a dark curtain.

"All right," Torgeson said, entering the room. "I had to work on her a little bit, but it's all fixed. You'll take her to Point Royal next week."

"What did she tell you?"

"She said next week."

"No—"

"Look. She said she doesn't like you very much. You're moody."

"Next week," Bexley said.

"What did you think she might tell me?" Torgeson smiled, but his eyes were hard.

"Nothing."

"Just remember," Torgeson said, "you're representing *me* there."

Bexley wanted his own smile as brittle. "Yeah," he said, "I got to remember that."

All week, he saw the Chinese dying. They died without noise, dropped over each other like sacks, though there was no blood. Bexley remembered blood, but couldn't see it and did not want to: did not want to see any of it.

"What's the matter with you," Elizabeth said. "Tell me, please."

"I don't know why I don't feel just wonderful, Elizabeth."

"You have a job and we have a place to stay."

"Yeah."

"You have a family that loves you."

"I never said I didn't."

"Where are you ever, Duck? We don't even see each other anymore."

"Don't make it worse than it is."

He lay in bed at night, listening to the insects—millions of them, so many you couldn't count. And as he began to drift toward sleep, Mrs. Trevinos spoke to him. "Nasturtiums." He woke to the pantomime of guns, dying Chinese, so many. Elizabeth turned uncomfortably in her sleep, her belly already swollen like the bellies of thousands of hungry children.

Birds sang in the trees, and he could believe he heard insects eating the leaves. Twice during the week he went into town in the truck, and stood in the street outside the feed store, watching the cars, watching the people go by him, women in white shorts, boys with skateboards, shoppers, men with jobs, things they knew how to do. Bexley carefully imagined ways to ask Mrs. Trevinos for the money—long, polite monologues of harmlessness: a gentleman, father of children, family man. Anything she wanted done around the house; she would be safe with him. But his heart quickened and he was aware of every inch of the lining of his stomach. He drove home groggy with his own racing mind, and when the children greeted him, it was as if he had already done something they would revile him for.

Friday came: cool, bright, breezy. A true fall day, though it was still September. Bexley drove Torgeson's car into town at the appointed time, and his hands shook on the wheel.

"What is it?" Elizabeth had said as he made ready to leave.

"Nothing. Forget it."

"Is it your trouble?"

"No." Bexley walked away from her.

"Duck—maybe don't go today."

"I got to. It's my job."

"Anybody can get sick."

He drove away without answering. He played the radio as loud as it would go, watching his hands shake, and tried not to think, but saw the old woman's neck, the hair pulled up. There was a grease spot on the dashboard and, looking at it, he thought for the first time, clearly, as if he had spoken it, the word *murder*.

3

He drove past the feed store, all the way to the Interstate and west toward Kentucky. He drove without paying attention to the signs, and when he turned around to come back, taking the long, slow arc of a cloverleaf, he could not remember having shut the radio off. He was surprised and frightened to see that he had crossed into Kentucky. Now he would lose this job—had probably already lost it: the old woman would have called Torgeson. Bexley felt something like relief.

But Torgeson took the keys and said nothing, and so there was another week of waiting—waiting to be fired, or for the next Friday. Perhaps the old woman had died in her rooms, and if he had gone in to her, he would have been the one to find her. He drove Torgeson to the bank on Wednesday, and they passed the feed store. Neither man spoke, and when they returned to the farm, Torgeson said, "Friday, for the old lady."

"I'd like to go back to the gulf," Elizabeth said that evening.

Bexley lay in bed, hands folded under his head.

"Do you hear me?"

"Yeah, I hear you."

"I'd like to take the train down there all by myself, and just wander around."

"Go ahead."

"You wouldn't care if I did, would you."

He was silent.

"Do you love me?"

"No, hell, I'm just hanging around."

"Here," she said, and began to unbutton his shirt. He lay

quite still, and when she had unbuttoned him, unzipped his pants, she stood by the bed and let her clothes fall at her feet.

"You're pregnant," Bexley said.

"So?"

He moved over in the bed, and she lay with her head on his arm.

"I'm sorry," he said.

She kissed his neck. "Come on, do it to me."

"Elizabeth, I am scared to death."

"Of what? Tell me."

But he could not think it clearly.

"Come on, get these off." She pulled at the open top of his pants. He lifted himself, let her. But as they were together, she ranging herself above him and letting herself down, at that moment he felt a grief so profound that all the blood seemed to run out of him.

"Wait," she said. "I'm sorry."

"No. Can't—Christ."

In a moment, she lay back down. "It's all right."

"Elizabeth," he said, "I just don't know what's going to happen."

Friday he drove through town, back to the Interstate, this time east, toward Point Royal. And in Point Royal he was ill, had to pull the car over by the side of the road and get out. It was warm again, like summer again, and he sat on the hood of the car, rocking with pain in his joints. A young man drove up in a Jeep, a boy with long red hair and dirty teeth, who chain-smoked and played the radio loud. The boy took him to the Point Royal Hospital, insisted on doing so.

"We got to help each other out, you know," he said. He said "You know" over and over in his talk, and he talked mostly about himself, all the way to the hospital. He was "into"

music, liked to work on cars, was a good skier. He was getting
ready to start college but didn't really want to go: his father
was insisting. At the hospital he said, "I'll wait for you,
really."

"Really," Bexley answered. The pain was almost gone.
"You're a nice kid."

"Better go in and talk to somebody."

Inside there were rows of blue plastic chairs with metal
legs. Four or five people sat scattered among them, tired,
waiting, hurt. He saw bandages, one pair of crutches, a man
smoking a pipe, standing by the far window, and a little girl
playing on the floor at his feet. No one looked at him. Across
the room was a counter at which a woman sat. She wore a
light-blue uniform and her hair was pulled into a tight bun
at the crown of her head. She was the central thing in the
room, but seemed absent somehow, as if the room were something she only remembered.

"I got to see a doctor," Bexley said.

She handed him a form, without looking at him. "Fill
this out."

"What?"

"Are you in pain?" she asked.

"No."

"Fill it out and I'll have a doctor look at you if you want
to see one—but you'll have to wait."

"Got to see one right now, miss. Somebody's waiting for
me outside."

"Sorry," she said. "But there are others here before you and
they are in pain."

"I was in pain—I couldn't drive my car."

She smiled—an official, narrow smile only of the lips. "You
don't look like an emergency to me."

"I got a bad sickness," Bexley said.

A little gray man came out from behind a screen to the left

of the counter. A man with laid-back ears, a bulbous nose, a little perfect ball of a belly coming down over his belt. He took the form from the counter and looked at it.

"He hasn't touched it," the woman said.

"Mister?" the doctor said, eyeing Bexley.

"Yeah."

"Your *name*."

Bexley told him.

"Are you from around here?"

"No."

"Do you have a doctor?"

Bexley was silent.

"Well?"

"Next question is, Do I have any money."

The little man put the form down, folded his arms. "As a matter of cold fact, Mr. Bexley, the next question is, Are you insured."

"I'm not."

"Well then, you'll have to make arrangements—"

"I'm sick."

"What is the name of your illness? Do you know what's wrong?"

"Yeah."

"Well?" Impatience in the voice.

Bexley told him.

"Lupus—is it discoid?"

"What's that?"

The doctor picked up the form again. "How long have you known this?"

Bexley had known since just before he got out of the work farm, but he did not want the doctor to know he had ever been there. "A long time," he said, and then he heard himself say, "I think I'm going crazy."

"Pardon?"

The woman picked up the telephone and began to dial a number.

"Do you want to check in to the hospital?" the doctor said.

"I—got somebody waiting—"

"If you're having pain, I'd advise you to check in to the hospital."

"I can't check in," Bexley said.

"Well, that's what I'd advise."

"It's going to kill me anyway, right?"

"Not necessarily. There are some things we can do for you, Mr. Bexley."

"I'm all fucked up, here—" Bexley spoke into his fingers, felt as if he might start to cry.

"Pardon?"

"Ah, just let me alone."

Outside, the boy waited, listening to the radio. A high, screeching guitar. Bexley climbed in, and the boy turned the radio off.

"So whud they tell you?"

"Waste of goddamn time."

"Can I take you anywhere else?"

"Why?"

"Be nice." The boy touched his knee. "We're all in this together, man."

"What're you—fucking queer or something?"

"Just doing a fellow human being a goddamn favor," said the boy. He drove fast out of the lot, back in the direction of the highway, Bexley's car.

"Hate doctors," Bexley said, loud into the force of the air on his face.

"You don't have to say anything," the boy said. He turned the radio on again.

"All right, then. Fuck off."

"Yeah, right. Just what I was thinking."

They did not exchange another word. The boy pulled the Jeep to a harsh stop just behind the car, and drove away without looking back as soon as Bexley stepped out.

4

In the first week of October Torgeson fired him. "You want to go joy-riding on my gasoline in my car, and then you want me to pay you for it," he said. "You're fired." Bexley had come in the early afternoon, at the usual time, and instead of handing him the keys, Torgeson gave him a severance check. "I want you out of the house, now," he said. "Do you understand? I want you to start looking for a place right now."

"Sure," Bexley said. "Where am I going to find a place."

"You brought this on yourself. Besides, I have someone else who needs the house. Because of your wife and kids I'm giving you this severance pay, which I don't think you yourself deserve."

Bexley felt relief, more like himself—angry now, not so much afraid. That evening, while Priscilla walked with the children through the trees behind the house, he and Elizabeth made love in a sorrowful quiet, and then he went out and walked with the children out to the far fence, the edge of Torgeson's land. He knew he had hurried away from Elizabeth, and was a little ashamed for it. But the twilight was beautiful and moist, the air smelling of honeysuckle and wild mountain laurel, and he watched his children, losing himself in their shrill play amid the uncut grass. He remembered something his father had said about Alva: how she liked a walk in the summer dusk better than anything. A chill breeze knifed down through the crossing branches to the east, and reminded him that this was the edge of winter.

"Daddy," Priscilla said, "we're going to have to move again, aren't we."

"Looks like it," he said. He did not believe he had ever lied to his children.

"I don't want to move again." There was distress in her voice.

"Don't bother about it now, girl. Look at the pretty moon."

In a red sky, the moon trailed low along the edge of a grassy knoll; Harvey ran ahead, one arm out, watching the moon over his shoulder, as if it were a kite he held on an unraveling spool of thread. The grass was white under the shadowless light, and Bexley touched Priscilla's shoulder, glad of familiar trouble, something he was used to. "Look at the color of that grass," he said.

"Every night just before dark it's like that, Daddy." Priscilla sighed.

He put his arm around her, watched the twins—so careful of Sandra June, walking on either side of her, holding her hands—and he felt almost good about himself, these others.

"Torgeson was here," Elizabeth said. "I talked with him about a place we could stay awhile."

The children all went into their rooms—the girls in one, the boys in another. Bexley sat down at the kitchen table and folded his hands on its surface.

"Did you hear me?" Elizabeth said.

"Yeah, I heard you."

"He wanted to talk to you."

"I bet."

"Please, Duck."

He got up and went out on the porch, and she followed him.

They sat in chairs on the stoop, looking out at Torgeson's land, the climbing moon that had contributed to what warmth he had felt earlier. He felt nothing now.

"We have to do something," Elizabeth said.

"I don't want to talk about it, Elizabeth." He looked at her hands, which lay in her rounded lap. He touched her wrist, but she did not respond.

"Duck," she said finally.

"Don't think about it right now." He took his hand from her wrist, lay his head back on the chair, watched the shadow of a bird drop from a tree out by the road. Beyond the tree the sky was sharply clear, like a winter sky. The insects were making a terrible humming racket.

"What's happened to you, Duck?" she said. "Did you even think of us?"

"I thought of you," he said. "There were—you don't know—"

"I want to go down to that little church on the other side— Torgeson said he would talk to the priest."

"Priest. That's the place Torgeson—"

"It would be a roof over our heads, Duck."

"We'll find something," he said. "We'll find something."

She sat back, faced the night sky, folded her hands. "You got to look for work tomorrow."

"Yeah."

"Maybe you don't believe it, but he's kicking us out of here," she said. "He had some woman with him. He was show-ing her the house."

"That son of a bitch."

They were quiet for a moment. Bexley thought, *I ought to kill him too.* Then he was breathing deeply, resisting the urge, like an electric current along his skin, to run anywhere, to get out from beneath himself somehow. The air stirred, was colder, for days the sky had been full of birds trailing south.

He looked at the bare, cold face of the moon. *Now it's got you,
whatever it is, it has you real good. What has you? Nothing.
Nothing,* he told himself.

Elizabeth got up and went inside. The wind was coming
down through the trees like something with a word to tell
him, and he went out into the wet grass, walking toward the
road. *Murder, murder.* "Jesus Christ," he said. *Is that what I
got born for?* There wasn't any sense to it, but here it was, as
though he had always known it would be.

He did not go back to the house. He walked down the road
for perhaps a half mile, watching the moon, and when he saw
the lights of Demera glowing along the edge of the night sky,
he went back into the trees and hid himself. He felt like a little
boy, crouching in the shadows of a game, a stand of summer
trees. Others were looking for him, other boys, so he made his
way through the thick growth, toward the house again. And
when he got there he went in to the children, kissed each of
them, told himself he was crazy, and lay down on the sofa in
the living room. He did not want to wake Elizabeth. *That's
right. You work your ass off just trying to keep it all at bay.
You stare straight ahead, all the time. And then it gets you. It
just comes up when it wants to and gets you good.*

He went to town the next morning, stood on the sidewalk
outside the feed store. So he had already come this far. He
couldn't believe that he had already come this far into it, but
here he was. It had grown cold, windy, leaves flying everywhere. Branches of trees were visible, the cold sky visible
through what had been the thick green, or burned red and
bright yellow of the maples and oaks along Sixteen. It was
all dropping away early, the air early cold, and there was no
reason to kill her at all. He could tie her up and take the
money or he could wait until she was gone or asleep and
sneak in and take it. Then he could get out of Virginia forever,

and go with Elizabeth back to the gulf. He was climbing the stairs before he was aware that he had begun to climb in the direction of the old woman.

When he saw the priest, he nearly let out a yell.

This is me, he told himself over and over, *this is me.* He gazed through the window at the old woman's rooms, at the sofa where he knew the money was. And then he seemed to stand apart from himself, watching himself do this; watching, too, the old priest drive away. He saw a cat come from under the window, and his heart banged against the bones of his chest.

All right. So it's got you. So now. Now.

He backed away from the door, went down the stairs slowly. Then he just stood there in the wind, at the bottom of the stairs, gazing up and down the street, as though he waited for someone.

I ain't no murderer.

5

In Charlottesville he had spent all one day and part of the night seriously searching for work. He imagined himself years into a job, an occupation, his children grown, or almost grown. The applications he was asked to fill out humiliated him. In the truck, on the way there, he had felt good, busy, finally having taken hold of things; but he hadn't counted on the numbers of forms he must fill out, the blocks he must check that defined him, put him in his place. In the late night he sat alone on a park bench, and when it began to rain, he walked across a baseball diamond to a pavilion. At one of four picnic tables a young couple sat, making one gray shadow in the faint light of a far-off streetlamp. The wind blew their hair and they snuggled. Bexley felt invisible. He remembered —as if someone goaded him about it—the sad array of his belongings in the social hall.

"Do you know what time it is?" the young man asked him. The young man had stood, and was lighting a cigarette. The flare of the match showed his face. A boy no more than eighteen or twenty, with the scars of acne.

"Don't carry a watch," Bexley said.

The girl whispered something.

"Thanks anyway," the boy said. He seemed nervous. The girl took his hand and led him away through the rain. Only when they crossed the baseball diamond and broke into a run did Bexley, watching them, begin to understand that they had been frightened of him. He felt dark, crouched, dangerous. Did something like murder creep into a man and leave a smell on him? Bexley got to his feet and paced between the tables, telling himself that anyone would be afraid of a lone figure coming out of the dark at that hour of the night and that he was Duck Bexley from Treetop, Virginia, nothing to be afraid of. *A man gets desperate and all sorts of things go through him. It doesn't have to mean a damn thing. I ain't afraid of nothing.* He went out into the rain, a cold knot of something expanding under his ribs. It just toyed with you, that was what it did; but you didn't have to let it mean anything. He had already killed forty-four people in a ditch. *Hero,* he thought. *Shit, here's your hero.*

He slept in the truck, in the lee of a blind alley. He dreamed that he was a boy again, and this boy was in a dark room, dreaming, until Alphonse, an elongated shadow, came from light to wake him. The light was blinding, but he knew it was Alphonse. There was the dim shape of a bed next to the boy, and he felt cold wood on the undersides of his legs. He looked along the shimmer of his own thighs as the shadow that was

Alphonse covered them. It was hot, it was summer, and there was the sound of a fan near him—perhaps at the window. He looked there, saw its pale square light; then he saw faces, a crowd of unrecognizable faces.

"Daddy," he said, "I was out walking with Elizabeth. Warmest day of the winter. Sixty degrees, Daddy, and I thought it had left me for good."

"Who are you?" Alphonse said, bending down.

"I thought it left me that time I stood outside her place, Daddy. It just brushed past me."

"What's your name, boy?"

"Oh, Jesus Christ," Bexley was crying. "You know me. You know me."

"Tell me your name, son. You had a dream."

"Murderer," Duck Bexley said. "Killer. There's nothing else for it."

"Easy going, kid—"

And then he awoke.

A man stood gazing at him through a gray drizzle—a yellow-hooded figure, the face back in under the shadow. Then the fingers of a fist touched the window.

Bexley rolled it down.

"Can I see your license and registration, please, sir." A cheerful, smiling face, neither young nor old. Bexley looked at the eyes, which were green, slightly crossed. "License and registration, please." The voice left little space between the words.

"I ain't done nothing wrong."

"If you'll let me see your license and registration, please."

Bexley made as if to get out of the truck.

"Please stay where you are, sir."

The policeman wrote him a citation for parking illegally and for loitering. It took a long time. Bexley sat in the truck, the rain coming in the window, and waited.

That afternoon he went to the county sheriff's office—the last stop, the last hope; that someone might recognize the name. *Does anybody know the name Alphonse Bexley? I am his son. Alphonse Bexley used to be sheriff a long time ago.* It turned out to have been a very long time ago, and Duck Bexley drove back to Demera thinking about the money under the cushion, drove straight to the feed store and went up the stairs and knocked, watching his hand ball up and hit the door. He remembered that at Thanksgiving he had been able to say someone ought to hit her over the head, as people will say who mean no harm; and he wondered—it was truly wonder—that he really was that one others were afraid of. Rain poured down his collar. In a moment he realized that he was crying.

He hit the door. "Damn you, answer. Answer."

Mrs. Trevinos walked up the stairs behind him. He heard her, turned, said, "You." She was wrapped in something canvaslike; it looked like a tent. There was a hood on it, which came to a point. She labored up to him, was almost to him before she saw him—and when she did see him, she gave a little cry, whirled and sat down so fast, he thought she'd fallen. He stood above her, looking at the water that rolled down the hood and off the shoulders. She was very still.

"You don't deserve all that money," he said. He was suddenly very calm.

She did not move, so he sat next to her, leaned around to look at her face. She just stared at the steps below, her mouth open, so that he could see her teeth.

"What do you want," she said.

"I want the money."

She laughed. "I gave it away."

"You're lying."

"Gave it to a lady in a blue Maverick. Iowa license plates. Lot of kids. I'm going to kill myself."

"You're lying to me."

"Two days ago."

"Two days ago what?"

"Gave the money away." She laughed again. He hit her once on the side of the head, hard. But she was a solid woman: she kept laughing, a high, thin, half-crying sound. He hit her again, and she stopped.

"Go ahead," she mumbled.

He saw blood on her lips, and then he was screaming at her. *How could she give it away to a stranger.* She nodded, as if to say she couldn't understand it either.

"My son is married," she said.

Bexley was silent.

"Can you imagine that? Married. They let them get married now."

He was planning how he would throw her off the stairs.

"Sent me wedding pictures—him and his—this . . ."

"Goddamn," Bexley said.

"Can you believe it?"

"What am I going to do."

"Kill me," she said.

"Shut up."

She got up and walked down the stairs, and he followed. But then she stopped, started back, holding her mouth. She walked up to the door and in, and he went behind her, out of the rain; he had no idea now what he would do or what would happen next: what *she* would say or do. She stood gazing at the room, the hallway from which, now, a cat came, walking slow. A large white tom with one pink eye and one green one.

"He's back," she said. "How'd he get in? I let the others go."

Bexley looked at the sofa.

"Will you take me to Point Royal?"

"No."

"I have more money there."

"You going to kill yourself in Point Royal?"

"It's a sin to kill yourself," she said. The cat wound itself around her legs, tail up. "That-a-boo," she said. Then she looked at Bexley. "Say my name."

"Trevinos."

"No, say my first name,"

"I don't know your first name, dammit."

"Jane," she said.

"All right: Jane."

"Jane," she said. "Say it again."

"For Christ's sake: Jane."

"God won't forgive me."

He was silent.

"Don't you believe God won't forgive me?" She smiled at him then. "What will you do to me?"

"Nothing, damn you."

"Take me to Point Royal."

"For what?"

"Money."

"How much money."

"A lot. More than you've ever seen. Barrels of it."

"You're lying."

"Find out."

"What do I have to do for it?"

"Take me to Point Royal."

"All right, let's go."

She walked in a little circle around the room, looking at the walls, the furniture. "Home. Good God."

"Let's go if we're going."

It took her a long time to get the cat arranged in the crook of her arm, but then she made a slight bow, smiled, as if they had just been introduced to each other, and went past him with a quickness that left him alone. Now he, too, glanced at

the room, backing out. Its meagerness made him vaguely sick
at heart, as if this place would lie here empty and wait for him
all the rest of his life. He was on the landing in time to see
her hit the last two steps, her surprised face looking at him
and the cat flying out of her arms. She lay over on her side,
one hand visible under her hip, the other, the free one, covering her face. For a moment she was quite still, but before
Bexley got to her, she had risen, stood white-cheeked, eyes
bulging, her mouth wide and bloody, gasping words he could
not understand. She gripped his elbow and he looked up the
street for help, but it was empty, a blur of cold rain.

"What," he said at her ear. "What."

"Broken."

"What. You broke what."

"All right," she said. "All right." She looked out at the
street, still holding his elbow. "Take me to—take me to Point
Royal."

"Are you hurt?"

She pulled him with her out into the street.

"What is it—where are you hurt?"

"The cat." Now she led him back to the truck. "The cat. I
want the cat."

He helped her in, put both hands under her, lifting.

"Get him. Get the cat. Where's the cat."

He looked at the raining street, the shining wet stairs, the
streaming windows; everything seemed gray and falling.
When he closed the door of the truck, she rolled down the
window and leaned out, watching him.

He walked up the street a little, peered down an alley, saw
cans, trash, a long, muddy stream coming from a drain
spout. At the end of the alley was a fence with a car hood
propped against it, but he would not go down there and look.
He went back to the truck and got in on the driver's side.

"No cat," he said. Water ran off him onto the seat, the floor;

his clothes made a spongy sound as he went into his pocket
for the keys to the ignition.

Her back was to him, as if she still searched out the window, the top of her head curving above her hunched shoulders
and the rumpled cloth of the hood. Her left hand held the
window frame and the rain beaded on it as if it were waxed.

"Did you hear me. I said, 'No cat'—he's gone."

The rain was pouring in. He touched her shoulder, then
brought his hand back to his face.

"Hey?"

Now he reached out, around, to her mouth, felt wetness—
the rain—and his hand went up to her eyes, which were not
closed, and did not blink.

For a while he only drove back and forth, carting her up
and down the streets of Demera. There was in him the faint
idea that he searched for the cat; but then he was going out
Sixteen, toward the Interstate. He had not touched her again,
nor had he uttered a sound. Along Sixteen, just before the
Interstate, was a gravel road, back in among trees, and he took
it, without consciously deciding to, still vaguely entertaining
the idea of the cat, as if, finding the animal, he might be able
to fix something. The gravel road wound through the trees,
and became a dirt path, grew thinner, slicing between tall
spines of dead grass. Finally he stopped the truck and got out,
stood leaning against the closed door with his hands over his
face. The sound of the rain made the silence behind him
bigger, and now, quite suddenly, he was in a hurry. He went
around the truck, averting his eyes from the open window, her
face; when he put his hand on the door handle she was a
blur above him. But he had to remove her hand from the
window frame, and when at last he got the door open, she
seemed to leap out of it, on him, driving him with astonishing
force into the wet grass. She lay head down on his shoulder,

the muscles of her arms already stiffening. As he struggled to get out from beneath her, he heard himself cry out, felt energy and strength rush into him with terror that he would not be able to free himself. But then he was free, and he sat with his head down on his knees, gasping. The body lay face up; he thought he could hear the mouth filling with water. He spoke to her. "I never would've hurt you." Slowly, with strength he did not know he had, he hauled the body back into the brush, lay it down, still trying not to see the face, and covered it with leaves, fallen branches, mud. It was dark before he finished, and when he was finished, he wandered on into the brush, stumbling and falling, letting his head down on his arms. It would never stop raining. He would never get out, never get away: he had wanted to kill her, had dreamed of killing her—in his confusion he was convinced of this—and now he would be accused of killing her.

He walked, and for a while he ran crazily in any direction, and when he came out into the path, perhaps sixty yards from where he'd parked the truck, he nearly fell face-forward in the mud. In the truck he let the heater run and warmed himself, his mind beginning to take hold of what had happened and what he must do. He could not run. He was absolutely certain that he must get back to Elizabeth and tell her; but as he started to back down out of the path to the gravel road—that awful quiet off in the leaves and grass—he began to know that he could never tell anyone, could not find the words to ever say it all in the right way.

At the church he parked the truck along the road and went along a ditch to the weeds behind the hall. He looked at the wide puddles of the lot, marking, with relief that swept over him like a chill, that the Ford was gone. When he had made it to the base of the house, he peered through the windows of the dining room, saw the twins on the floor. He could be reasonably certain that everyone was in the house. Yet as he opened the door of the social hall, he leaned in and whispered, "Hey?" Waited, tried again: "Hey?" Then he rushed in, closed the door, put the light on, and got out of his clothes, still trembling, though it was warm there. In a moment, after he had dressed, he began to think about getting rid of the wet clothes; he stood with his back to the door, holding the leg of his trousers, trying to decide. Then it struck him that Elizabeth would see that he had changed, so he left the clothes where they lay on the floor—he would tell her that the truck cut out on him and he'd had to work on it—put his coat back on, and the baseball cap, and walked over to the house, let himself in. It was as if he had come home from a long time away, from war, all of them running to him, pulling at his arms, shouting his name.

"Let up now," he said. "Let up."

He knelt and let Sandra June bury her face in his neck; her hair was in his mouth. "Daddy."

"Little girl," he said, and had to force himself not to cry.

"What is it," Elizabeth said. "What's happened?" She stood above him, had been studying him since he came in.

"Nothing, Elizabeth." He stood, his hands on the girl's shoulders. "There was nothing in Charlottesville. Nobody remembered Alphonse." His voice bumped over the words, broke. It was suddenly very quiet in the room.

"Tired," he said, crying. "The truck broke down. I got wet."

Elizabeth held him. Wallace touched his chest, smiling.

"Thank you, son."

"Daddy," said Priscilla. "We'll be all right."

"You remember that." He sniffed, took the napkin that Elizabeth handed him, wiped his eyes, blew his nose. He was ready to believe that this was all there was now, this room, his family—he would find his way back to them if he could just get some time between himself and the events of this day.

He picked up Wallace, held him high. "Which one is this— this one's Wallace." He did the same with Mackinley, and he kissed Priscilla and Sandra June—again—and Elizabeth.

"I haven't seen you like this for so long," Elizabeth said. "You *did* get something, didn't you?"

"No." He backed away from her.

"Come on." She smiled. It angered him.

"What the hell is this anyway? I said I didn't get anything. Nothing. Nothing happened." Now he had turned and moved to the sink.

"All right, Duck."

No one spoke for a moment.

"Why do you always have to make me feel like I'm being *watched*, goddammit?"

They did not look at each other. Priscilla coughed, tried to hold it under her fingers.

"Cough, if you have to. For Christ's sake cough. *Cough*."

"Duck," Elizabeth said. "That's enough."

"She's holding a damn cough back. Why? Why is that? She wouldn't hold a cough back if I wasn't here, and I want to know why."

Now they were all staring at him.

"Listen to you," Elizabeth said. "You want an answer, just listen to yourself." She moved toward the dining room. The twins went ahead of her. Harvey and Sandra June and Priscilla sat looking at him from the table.

"Elizabeth," he said.

"I'm listening."

"I missed everybody—" It seemed a lame thing to say, but it brought Elizabeth back.

6

Now he was driving out of the cemetery, through slanting sun, toward streets he remembered but did not know the name of, looking for landmarks—an oak tree thick as a silo, a field of winter rye where there had been corn, a pond. Houses he thought he could remember, and then the big green one with the mansard roof and the flagstone facade, among willows. The Cadillac was not there and the door was closed, but this was the house. The wind had picked up, and he stood on the porch and looked out at the willows drooping cold, and the dead grass. There was a fine, dark dust on the wood of the porch rail and he touched it, ran his hand over it, clapped the hand into the palm of the other, waiting. After a while he walked down the steps, around the house along a cracked pavement, thin and matted with leaves. There was a patio in back, which he did not remember, two metal chairs, and a portable grill. He sat in one of the chairs for a few moments, tapping the arm with his fingers, looking out at a redwood fence smothered by dead vines. Beyond the fence were a few top-heavy pines, thin as telephone poles and taller, and now the clouds had put the sun out, and the motions of the wind stung his face. Finally it was too cold to remain outside, so he walked back around the house and got into the truck, out of the wind. In the truck there were vestiges of his children and his wife, of his time as father, as son: they were far from him, as if he only remembered them, though he could reach out now and touch a hairpin on the dashboard—Elizabeth's, or Priscilla's. He felt the solitude of himself inside his body, and his body inside this truck: his mind seemed to listen, and as the wind slashed under the eaves of the porch and shook the truck, he watched his hand put the key into the ignition and turn it, the engine rumbling to life, groaning, dying as he pressed the gas pedal. He turned the ignition again, and now the engine raced. Perhaps an hour had passed since he had come here. He would come back.

As he pulled out onto the road, the idea came to him that he was, after all, innocent, that he could go back to Demera and explain everything and be believed. (No one could find out his thoughts, or accuse him for them.) But he was tired, and he thought about how tired he was: and he had tried everything. He had tried to make a life out of what he knew.

He stopped at the university, counted the money he had left. Eleven dollars and twenty-two cents. He was hungry, he must eat, he must decide what to do. The sun had broken through the clouds again, and he walked through a crowd of students down a tree-lined path toward an old stone building. The students all looked alike, male and female; they seemed, each of them, to know everyone but Bexley. He followed them into the building and down stairs, a long, polished hallway with more students sitting along the walls, talking. No one looked at him. Bexley watched one boy, with hair thick as Harvey's, playing a harmonica, eyes closed, mouth and cheeks sucking and blowing; no one looked at the boy either, and no one seemed to hear his playing. Bexley walked on. A man with a briefcase bumped into him, said "Excuse me," and did not look at him. He followed two young women into a large room, beyond glass doors, past rows of tables where people sat eating and talking. At the far end of the room was a line, too long to wait in, that led around to where the food was. He went to a table and sat down, looked at a heavy blond girl who sat at the other end. The girl's skin was red as cooked meat, and when she caught him looking at her, she frowned, the skin grew violet under her eyes, and Bexley trained his own eyes on the table. A tall thin boy with a scrap of a mustache and baby skin sat next to him, with a tray full of food—green beans, two hamburgers, French fries, and coffee, steaming. Bexley had not known how hungry he actually was.

"Food any good here," he said.

No answer. The fat girl made a squealing sound with her lips that he thought was laughter; but she had sneezed, and now held a handkerchief to her nose.

"Food any good here," Bexley said, leaning toward the boy. And now another, just as tall, but thinner, with no mustache but with a patch over one eye, sat down next to the first.

"He wants to know if the food's any good," the first one said to the one with the patch.

"Tell him."

"Poison. We're all committing suicide."

" 'One option among many in a world of choices,' " the second boy said, "according to good old Doctor Frank."

"*Herr Doktor* Frank," said the first.

"What do you mean?" Bexley said.

"There's another Frankism," the second boy said. " 'How does man make meaning?' "

"No," the first said. " 'How does meaning mean?' "

"Shit."

The first one turned to Bexley. "You go to school here?"

"No."

The fat girl got up to leave.

"Bye, doll," the first boy said, and the other, laughing, said, "How does a fat broad mean?"

"Fuck off," the girl said, and walked away.

"So," the first boy said, looking at Bexley, "you don't go to school here. You work here?"

Bexley told him he did.

"What do you do?"

"He teaches philosophy," the second boy said.

"No," Bexley said. He wanted to feel anger come but he felt nothing.

"Did you know," the first one said, toying with his mustache, chewing, "that you are condemned to be free?"

Bexley stood.

"Hey, sit down. I was only fucking you around, man."

"We just came out of an exam," the second one said. "A philosophy test. A pisser. A ballbuster, a motherfucker, and, in short, a very hard test."

"Yeah, man. We didn't mean anything by it."

Bexley let himself back down into the chair and watched them smile at each other. Then he was watching them eat.

At length the one with the patch said, "So how come you're not eating?"

"Waiting for the line—"

"Really," said the first. "So what do you do here?" He wiped his mouth, the mustache, which was thin enough to create the illusion that it would come off in the napkin.

"I mind my own business," Bexley said.

"Look, man. We're sorry."

"Will they let anybody eat here?"

"Don't know why not."

There was a pause.

"Course," the second one said. "Used to be only blacks could eat here. There were signs all over the place: BLACKS ONLY. No, BLACK ONLY. Then they had three bathrooms, you know? BLACK MEN, BLACK WOMEN, and then one that just said UNCOLORED. We used to have to ride in the back of the bus; we couldn't go to school. It was tough."

"That's bullshit," Bexley said.

"Man, you ought to go to school here—you picked that up right away."

"Ah," said the first, "let him alone, Patch."

Bexley said, "That—what you were saying before. Choices and options. What is that?"

"Those are Frankisms," said Patch. "Doctor William R. Frank. Nazi."

"Nazi."

"That's what we call him," the first boy said.

"Why?"

"He's mean, has a German accent. Likes Hegel and Schopenhauer."

"Yeah," Patch said. "For instance according to *Herr Doktor* Schopenhauer, Happiness, as we know it—that is, happiness with a capital *H*, which in my case would be pussy with a capital *P*, is negative. Happiness, says dear old Schopenhopen, is the absence of pain, and since life is a royal pain in the ass, Happiness is negative."

"Who is that—Schopen—"

"Why, he's a Nazi too. He's a Nazi she's a Nazi you're a Nazi I'm a Nazi too."

"Be serious," the first boy said.

"I am only serious when I talk about the capital *P*."

"Listen," said the first boy, leaning toward Bexley, "you don't know those names, do you—Hegel and that shit. You don't know that."

"Maybe I do," Bexley said.

"No—wait—I'm not trying to fuck you over. I really want to know."

"All right. I never heard of them."

"Bliss," said Patch.

"What?"

"Bliss. You, sir, are in what we here at Hahvahd call a state of bliss."

"You just come in here to eat, is that it?" the first one said.

"This is the first time."

"But you work here."

"Let's say I do."

"Oh, then you don't. You're just passing through."

"You're a cowboy heading west," Patch said. "On to the great divide."

"For shit sakes, Patch, shut up."

"You kids got a lot of money," said Bexley.

"You a robber?" Patch said.

"You got everything you want."

"Yeah, right—everything."

Bexley looked away. The line had not changed, or it was longer—he couldn't tell.

"You need money," the first one said.

"I got some money."

"We don't have a lot of money, man. Don't listen to Patch. I'm in student loans up to my ass."

Bexley watched the line. Girls not much older than Priscilla and boys not much older than Harvey. The two boys were now talking to each other, as if he were not there, and he put his hands out in front of him on the table. His eyes were burning, as if fresh from sleep, and when he closed them, he seemed to drift.

"Where do you live," the first boy said.

Bexley leaned toward him and smiled, surprised at himself. "I've killed forty-four people."

"Wow," said Patch. "Psycho."

"Are you serious?" asked the first.

"What do *you* think?" Bexley said.

"I think you're an alky," Patch said.

"Somebody ought to knock you around a little bit, boy."

Patch laughed. "Come on," he said to the first one, lifting his tray. "Let's get out of here."

The two of them moved away. Bexley sat by himself for a while, watching the line increase. There was a moment or two of a sort of drifting; perhaps he fell asleep. "I'm dying," he

said, or thought he heard himself say. "I didn't kill anyone."
He jerked up out of the chair and almost knocked someone
down. He looked at her hair, freckles, watched the mouth say
he ought to watch where he was going: dirty teeth.

"You," he said.

"What," the boy said.

"You're the one with the Jeep."

The boy walked around him, looking back. The same long
hair, the same face. "Wait," Bexley said, and followed him to
where he sat down, still glancing back so that his thin red
hands almost upset the tray as he put it on the table. Bexley
stood at his shoulder for a moment and watched him bite into
a hamburger.

"Food's poison here," he said, watching him chew.

"Look," said the boy, "I don't know who you are or what
you want."

"These two other guys, they told me the food was terrible."

No answer. Bexley watched him eat, looked at the bulge in
his cheek. The boy picked up a French fry and rolled it in a
dab of ketchup on the plate.

"You're the one. You picked me up along the highway outside Charlottesville. When I was sick. You took me to the
hospital in your Jeep."

The boy was chewing the French fry, looking off toward
the line of people still waiting to get food.

"Nice to see you again." Bexley extended his hand.

"I don't own a Jeep, buddy. I never owned a Jeep. I was
never in Charlottesville."

He was the one.

"It's you," Bexley said, touching his arm. "Why don't you
know me."

The other only shook his head, picked the tray of food up,
and moved to another table. Bexley sat down and watched
him. The boy was four tables away now, eating, staring down

at his plate and back up at the line, but never looking at Bexley, who continued to watch him anyway. "It's him," Bexley said, the words burning out of the back of his throat. "It's him."

It was after dark when he returned to the house. This time the Cadillac was there. Lights were on in the downstairs windows, and in one slender window above the porch. The wind had died down, and it had grown a little warmer, the air smelling of more rain, though stars were visible between tattered strips of cloud, which partially concealed the moon. The moon looked like a white thumbprint, the sky behind it flat and dark and clear. Bexley walked up onto the porch, under a dim yellow light, and found the door locked. He peered through the window—a gauzelike curtain on the other side— and looked at the hallway and part of the living room. He saw four bottles of beer on the coffee table—a loaded ashtray and a newspaper. He had been to this house as a boy, when Candle's father lived here. This was how he remembered it—the dark wood of the hallway, the ginger-jar lamp along the far wall in the living room. He knocked once, loud, waited, knocked again.

"Candle."

He put his face against the glass, and saw shoes on the stairs, high up. The shoes were very still, as if they waited, or were searching the air for intruders, like radar.

"Candle!" he shouted.

The shoes turned a little, as if they might back away. But then they stepped down, and he saw the legs, the belly, coming down: white pants and a black belt and a blue shirt, the tie lying out on the chest. Candle came slowly to the last step, a beer in his hand, a lighted cigarette in his mouth. He opened the door after he had peered through the curtain; now he looked through a crack, the smallest space, holding the door.

"Bexley."

"I come to talk to you."

"What the hell do you want?"

But Bexley did not know: he did not know why he had come here and he did not know what he wanted.

"You come to make up what you owe me?" Candle asked.

"That's right." *What I owe him*, Bexley thought. *That's right.* "Let me in, will you?"

"Did you talk to your wife?"

"What?"

"I was over to see her a while back—that's what you're here for." Candle closed the door. "Get out of here before I call the police."

"Candle, I come to rent another place from you."

"That's crazy," the other man said through the door. "I don't believe that."

"Look, I'm in trouble—let me in, will you. I come to you for help."

Candle opened the door. "You really want to rent a place?"

"The old place."

"I don't know why I should do anything to help you." He stood there looking at Bexley, just the tip of his tongue at the corner of his mouth. He held the cigarette between his fingers now, and the ash was long, the smoke running up his arm and around his neck.

"I'll pay you back everything, Candle, I swear it. Only let me in for a minute."

Candle walked away from the door, and Bexley followed him into the living room, watched him douse the cigarette in the overstuffed ashtray.

"What kind of beer you want?"

"Anything."

"I got four kinds of beer. I got Bud, Black Label, Miller, and Pabst."

"Pabst."

"I'm doing this because of your father, and for no other reason." Candle walked into the kitchen, and there was the sound of bottles and cans bumping in the porcelain hollow of the refrigerator. Bexley stood by the television and waited, looked at a gilt-framed photograph of a woman, thin as a girl, and a boy already—at nine or ten—balloonlike, round-faced and heavily thighed, both of them smiling into sunlight. He stared at the face of the woman and experienced an odd moment of sadness for whoever she was now: someone old, a widow with one son. It was a specific sorrow for the woman of the photograph and for no one else. And now he knew clearly why he had come here in the first place, why he had waited, why he had returned.

Candle came back, tossed him a can of beer, sat down on the sofa. Bexley sat down in the wicker chair across from him, watched him light another cigarette, held his beer in both hands, watching him.

"You didn't smoke before," he said.

"Not like this," said Candle. "Drink your beer."

Bexley opened the can, and it foamed like a fountain of soap.

"Damn," Candle said. But he did not move.

"Got a rag?"

"Forget it."

They drank the beer, watching each other.

"That your mother?" Bexley asked, staring at the photograph.

"Yeah, that's her."

"Skinny."

"That's right. Used to say I was—well, never mind."

"She living?"

"Yep. Altamont now. Can you imagine that? My father left her some money, and she sold her house and moved to

Altamont. Liked the name. Can you imagine it? I'll tell you, my father was a son of a bitch. First class. He might've been okay to you-all, but to me and my mother he was a dyed-in-the-wool son of a bitch. Once when I was about seven or eight years old—well, it was the year my mother left him, and we went to New York State: I'd come down to visit him that summer, and he took me on the train to Washington. Was going to show me the sights, as they say. So we're on this damn train, and I have to go to the bathroom. Now since I flew down from New York and I've never in my life been on a goddamn train, I don't know where or how I'm supposed to relieve myself. So I make the mistake of asking him—" Candle paused. "You want more beer?"

"No," Bexley said.

"This boring you?"

"What happened—tell it."

"So I ask him where is the bathroom, and he says people have to go out the window of the train, only they can't get any of it *on* the train, and because of the wind and everything, the force of the air, and the train is going so fast and all that —well, you have to find somebody who's willing to hold your feet while you dangle out the window and piss upside down. I wasn't old enough to know much, but I think I knew he was fucking with me, because I remember I said that was all right, I didn't have to go anyway, just asking. But I could look at him and get that feeling, you know, something so big, so much bigger than you and it's going to do what the hell it wants to with you and you have to let it or get your ass in a jam—although your ass is—" He spit, sipped the beer, took something, with some trouble, off his tongue. "Fucking hair. I'm losing hair, and let me tell you, I can lose a whole head of hair talking about this shit. Where was I?"

"Your ass is in a jam," Bexley said, trying to mean it.

"Yeah. So there you are, and you can't do a fucking thing

but take it. I keep saying no, I don't have to go, and he starts talking about water. Ever have somebody talk to you about water when you really have to go? It's like the word hooks up to your bladder. Niagara Falls, he says, lakes, pools, puddles, drops, running streams, glasses, and cups full of water, water, water. Then he starts tickling at me, grabbing me low under my gut—I had a gut as long as I can remember, and there isn't a goddamn thing I can do about it. Not even smoking. Did you know that smoking keeps your weight down? Anyway, that's what they say. Never works for me. Nothing works for me. You think I like being fat? Never getting the girl? I been laid twice in my whole goddamn life—both times the girl was fatter than I am, and both times I got the crabs from it. You ever had the crabs? Let me tell you, sex ain't worth the crabs. Itch and bite you till you're crazy, and then they give you this damn blue ointment. Burns like fire. A week of that damn blue ointment and if you got balls left after all that, you can thank God and never use them again. Or else get the crabs again like I did." He took the last of his beer. "You ready for another one?"

"I'm okay," Bexley said.

"Let me get another one. Where was I? Oh, the damn crabs. Called that girl up and said, 'Goddamn you, you gave me the crabs,' and she threw a fit, threatened to throw my ass in court, says, 'You got 'em from some damn toilet seat, you dumb ass.' And hell, I was nineteen—" He was shouting now, from the kitchen. He came back with two beers anyway, set one of them on the floor at Bexley's feet. "There, you'll want that. So I was saying, I was nineteen and didn't know any better and I believed her—said I was sorry, I didn't know anything, she was right, I sure did mess things up, and could she forgive me, and she says she can, but I better not mention it again. I say I won't and ask if I can see her that Saturday night. 'Not if you got the crabs,' she says. 'I don't want no crabs.' So I waited a few weeks and after that I called her again and told her I was over the crabs and I'd like to see her, and she says all right, if I was sure there was no chance of her getting the crabs, and I said there wasn't. And now, get this, I go see her and we have a fine old time and in three days I got the goddamn crabs *again*. Man, I called her up and said, 'You lying bitch, you whore.' And she says—get this— she says I'm a son of a bitch because now *she* has the crabs and I gave 'em to her and I said, 'Well then, the little sons of bitches are coming from outer space.' And she hung up on me. And I had to go through the whole mess again—blue ointment and all that. It's no fun, let me tell you."

There was a pause.

"You ever have the crabs?"

"No," Bexley said.

"Well, anyway, I was going to tell you what my old man did to me—"

"He held you out the window."

"Right. Son of a bitch put my ass out the window of that train and I was so goddamn scared, I pissed all over myself. And when it was over, he pulled me in and said, 'That's because you look like your goddamn mother.' And I never looked like my mother. And then the bastard turns around and leaves her all this money when he dies. And leaves me this house and Al—and your place—the place you had. I'll tell you, I can't figure it. Because we were never, any of us, very close—I mean like your family was. I used to—well. When I was coming over there, to see you all, I sort of liked to think . . . well, I envied you your kids and your wife and your father. I never had anything like what you had."

They drank. The silence was awkward.

"So," Candle said, "you come back. Where's the family?"

"Back in Demera."

"Your old man—he sure got sick at the end. . . ."

"You knew he was sick."

"I knew he had a little trouble from time to time."

They were silent again.

"She have the baby yet?"

"No."

"You really—you in trouble?"

"Yeah. I want to rent the old place back."

"Why? What kind of trouble?"

"Do you want to rent it to me?"

"Well," Candle said, "there is the matter of what you owe me."

"Yeah, I owe you." Bexley was now trying very hard to hate the other man, but it was not there; his anger and his desperation and his murderous will were gone.

"I'm glad we could talk like this," Candle said.

Bexley stood.

"The old place is empty. Rented it to some damn kids who played goddamn rock 'n' roll all night and got arrested for drugs—it was a mess. It's empty."

"Candle," Bexley said, "I don't like you—"

Candle stood up too. "The wife and kids—what?"

"I don't like you one bit."

"You don't like me—you. You cost me a lot of money, man. I want it back. Which is part of why you ain't in jail."

"You knew my father wasn't fit."

"I'd have fixed that place up for him—I liked him. We were friends."

"No," Bexley said. "That's bullshit." They were now face to face. Candle's left eye twitched, and he touched it with one heavy finger. "You tried to take advantage of my father."

"*That's* bullshit."

"You wanted to make a fool of him."

"Your father," Candle shouted, "was the only man I ever knew—including *my* father—who ever listened to me or gave me more than five fucking minutes! I liked him. I liked him a lot. I wanted him to have what he wanted."

Bexley looked down into the hole in the top of his beer can. Candle's shadow was on his hands.

"You want to look at the place or not."

"I don't know."

"I've made some changes. You want to or not. I'll rent it to you right now, sight unseen, if that's the way you want it, and even though you're being such an asshole about everything and have been all along. Asshole. And if you want to do anything about it, you go ahead and try."

"Show it to me," Bexley said.

The two men went out, down the steps of the porch, around to the Cadillac. When Candle opened the door, he said, "You don't really want to rent a place, do you?"

"I don't know anything," Bexley said.

They got in. Candle put the radio on, loud country music.

"Turn it down," said Bexley.

Candle did so. They went down the road in the direction of the old house. "Well," Candle said, "so why did you come— what kind of trouble are you in? Police after you?"

"No."

"What're you here for?"

"Wanted to pay you back for everything," Bexley said. Candle was a big white shape next to him.

"Everything."

"I *am* in trouble," Bexley said.

"Yeah."

"And you did it to us."

"Me," said Candle. "That's funny."

They rode on. There were no streetlamps now, and the sky was dark, low, thick. The dark closed over everything but the white fan of the headlights.

"So," Candle said, "you think you're going to kill me."

Bexley was silent.

"Is that it?"

"All right then—maybe I thought that."

"Jesus Christ."

They went on for perhaps another mile, and then Candle pulled the car over to the side of the road. "I don't know what I'm doing carting you toward a house you ain't going to rent, or why I thought we might get to some understanding—let me tell you something, Bexley. I could've had you put away. I didn't because of your father. I'm as nice a man as I know when I'm let be, but you cross me and I'll fuck you up good. Always been like that and I ain't stopping now."

"I'm in trouble, Candle—I don't know what's happened to me here." Bexley put his hands over his face.

Candle stopped the car. "You poor stupid son of a bitch. Get out."

Bexley opened the door, stepped out. Candle leaned over and took the silver door-handle.

"You poor goddamn fool," he said. He slammed the door and sped away, and Bexley watched the lights go. The road was empty, a long winding gray ribbon in the dark. Bexley stood in the quiet, listening to the faint sound of engines far off, gazing at the delicate hue of Richmond on the horizon. He went out to the middle of the road and began to walk, hearing his shoes on the pavement and his breathing. He walked for a long time. When the first set of headlights came, he went to the side of the road and stuck his thumb out. The car pulled over a few feet ahead. He ran to it, thinking *That's right. That's exactly right.* It didn't matter. Nothing mattered anymore. When it got you, it got you so good. It just took you all the way, and you never had a chance. Not one. *That's right. Exactly.*

VI

1

That Wednesday Vincent took Harvey and Priscilla to school. No one spoke, but as the school became visible in its blue field, Harvey moaned suddenly and began to cry. Vincent pulled the Ford into the entrance drive, listening to this, and when he stopped, Priscilla said, "I don't want to go."

"Your mother wants you to, doesn't she?" Vincent said.

She opened the door and got out. Harvey went with her, though he was still crying.

"Harvey," Priscilla said, "you got to stop it."

Vincent could only watch.

"Stop it, now." The two of them walked away, as if they had come alone. They left the car door open. Vincent reached over and pulled it shut, sat with his hands on the wheel, watching them go. They walked into a stream of other children, were swept away from him, out of his hands now, and he wanted to get out of the car and make sure of them, guide them through somehow. He caught a glimpse of them at the top of the stairs leading into the building: they still held on to each other. He had never been more miserable; yet he felt, too, a sort of dismal peace. There was no explanation, no bearable reason for this, so he clung to the facts: Bexley had been traced to Treetop; Mr. Wick had told the police what he knew —they had confiscated the truck. Bexley was officially a suspect: murder. Elizabeth hadn't spoken above a low, monotonous whisper since Saturday morning, when the police had made their first visit; they had been back twice. "My husband would not murder," she said. She would answer no questions, and if the police had been careful about not telling her who had seen her husband with the dead woman, they were brutal enough in their questioning: Had the suspect ever been in trouble before (they knew, or they had records, so she might as well tell them). Had he spoken about the old woman. Had he ever struck Elizabeth or the children, or anyone, to her knowledge. She might as well answer, because they would find out anyway. Nothing she said could be used against her husband; they just wanted to know.

"My husband is not a murderer," Elizabeth said, over and over, in answer to the questions and in the spaces between the questions. Vincent had wondered if she really believed it.

Now he drove back to the church in a blazing sun, and tried not to wonder or think at all. Everywhere there were signs of Christmas. The shops in town were decorated as before, but now they were busy, mostly with women, who bundled themselves up like Eskimos against the cold, and looked happy and full of anticipation. The world seemed to be perfectly at peace with itself. At the church he found Torgeson, who had apparently walked across the field. Torgeson waited for him to come up onto the stoop and open the door. He looked tired and weak. The kitchen was empty, though it had been cleaned, the breakfast dishes gone. There was no sign of Elizabeth.

"Where is she," Torgeson said.

Vincent wearily hung up his coat. "Must be in the hall. What do you want."

"I thought I'd—" Torgeson began. Vincent had not seen him since he had found him with the woman Marie.

"Well?" Vincent said.

"I have some news."

"All right."

"Duck Bexley is dead."

Vincent walked into the living room and Torgeson followed. He wanted to get away from the words, but Torgeson followed him.

"Did you hear me? Duck Bexley's dead."

Vincent sat down.

"The police wanted to talk to you, but you were gone. They want you to tell her. You're a priest."

"My God," Vincent said.

For a moment they were quiet.

"What happened," Vincent asked. It was not a specific question, but Torgeson answered it as if it were.

"He hitchhiked north. To Washington. Anyway he must've hitchhiked. He got into trouble in a bar. There was a fight. He cut a man with a bottle, and . . . they shot him."

"Who shot him?"

"The police. Somebody had called the police. He didn't have the old woman's money. He had a few dollars. Some change."

"My God. My God."

"You know," Torgeson said, "we're never going to know what really happened."

"Shut up," said Vincent.

They were quiet again. Torgeson touched the front of his coat. "You have to tell her," he said.

"I know, I know. Shut up."

"You can—they can come stay with me if they want. I'll let them stay as long as they want."

"*Now* you will let them," Vincent said.

Torgeson was silent.

"My God," Vincent said.

Again Torgeson touched the front of his coat. There was a

sheen on the skin of his knuckles, and his long fingers moved on the cloth as if to smooth some roughness in its surface. Vincent stood up, walked out of the room into the kitchen, where he had come to Elizabeth Bexley every morning of the past two months. He looked at the coatrack, at the clean table, the window in the door, bright as the sun, blinding. He went toward that brightness, looked out. The sky was clear, blue, indifferent. The social hall looked diminished, hunched to the ground, rickety and insufficient. He heard Torgeson behind him, a long sigh.

"There was a time when I would've jumped at what you just said, Torgeson."

"It's the only sane thing to do now."

"Sane," Vincent said. "Sane."

"She has no place else to go," said Torgeson.

"I know. But don't ask me to do anything about it now. I have to go over there and tell that woman something I'd rather die than have to tell her. . . . No, I can't tell her. I haven't the words."

"I think the police should've told her."

"Yes," Vincent said. "Well, they didn't."

At that instant, so suddenly it startled him, Elizabeth Bexley opened the door and entered. She looked tired, sleepless, her eyes glazed, quick, searching the room it seemed, as though there were an object whose shape might allow them to clear and focus once she found it. She did not look at either of the two men, nor did she speak. She took her coat off; then, hesitating, put it back on.

"Mrs. Bexley?" Torgeson said, as though he were trying to match a name to the face: a man in a bus terminal, met by a stranger whose name he has been given.

"They're asleep," she muttered. The coat lay over her shoulders like a shawl.

"I'll see you later," Torgeson said to Vincent.

"I left them sleeping," Elizabeth said. Her eyes had settled on the table.

Vincent watched Torgeson close the door. And now he was alone with her. He walked into the dining room because he felt sick to his stomach. She followed. The room was smaller, somehow, crowded with the two of them. Her shadow on the table there, the faintest suggestion of a shadow in light that had gone gray, seemed to be taking air from the room. He breathed once, deeply, braced himself, and faced her.

"I want him home," she said.

"Elizabeth."

"I don't know what to do anymore."

"Elizabeth, listen—"

She waited. He thought she must know, somehow, what he was about to tell her. The dark eyes were fixed on him now, waiting. Even knowing what it was, she would want it said.

"Elizabeth, it's all over." The words tumbled out of his mouth. The wrong words. Words too soon.

Still she waited.

"Elizabeth, I—" He stopped, tried to order it all in his mind. And then she let down, shaking, holding on to the table. The almost male hands, swollen and colorless.

"Tell me," she said. "Damn you."

He couldn't say the words out, though they rushed through him like icy water.

"It's bad—tell me."

"Duck is—Duck is gone. Dead." He'd corrected himself with the last word; he'd only tried to correct himself.

"How," she said. The whisper. Her lips barely moved.

"They—shot him. . . ."

She stood back, let her hands fall to her sides. And in the

next agonizing minute he told her the rest of it, rushing now, hurrying, as if what went out of him were only something to fill the vacuum her silence made.

Then she said, "All right." She waited.

"I'm so sorry," said Vincent.

"You tell me now," she said. "You tell me."

"That's—that's all. I don't know any more."

"I don't know any more," she said.

"Elizabeth." He touched her arm. His hand went around her arm all the way.

Elizabeth let out a long, low, sighing murmur. Then she brought her face up close to his, the black eyes giving off little brilliant particles of light.

"We have to go get him," she said. "We have to—we. . . . Where is he. We have to find him." Then she turned and was going out, pulling her arm out of his grasp, walking through the kitchen to the door and out. Somehow her coat had wound up on the floor. Vincent, following, gave it to her. She held it close to her chest, bunching it up under her chin. "Oh," she said, "God." They were on the stoop now. He put his hands on her shoulders. The great weight of her abdomen swept against him as she tried to free herself. "Oh, God," she said. "My coat. My *coat*." She held it in her fists on Vincent's chest. "I can't—my coat."

"Please," he said. "Elizabeth. Please."

Her head went down over her hands, and he looked through his own tears at the dead field beyond the church, holding her, saying "There, there, now. There now." He put his hand at the back of her neck, her hair like dry grass under his fingers.

"All right," she said. "Yes."

Carefully, slowly, she removed herself from his embrace and put the coat on. She did not look at him.

"I'm cold," she said.

She shook the coat, adjusting it over her shoulders, her fingers closed on the ends of the sleeves.

"I'll take care of everything," Vincent said. "I'll take care of you."

"Yes, leave me alone now," she said quickly.

He watched her move toward the hall. She did not look back, and her slow progress made him think of following again. But he didn't know what he would say to her now. She went in, closed the door quietly, and he stood alone out in the lot, coatless, shivering, as if he would stand a cold guard over this ground where he had tried to comfort her.

2

She drew into herself for what comfort she could find. To Vincent she was both distant and patient. She told the children by herself, in the privacy of the social hall, relieving Vincent of what he thought he would have to do; and she began, in a sort of supreme solitude, to make the arrangements, the preparations—all the sad, customary details surrounding death. She would ride with Vincent into Point Royal, where the body had been taken, to identify and claim it. She insisted that she be allowed to do this herself, or something in her carriage and voice insisted: there could be no sense in arguing with her or in trying to get her to let anyone do the cruel, practical things for her. Yet she was not in any way adamant: it was just that she moved in her solitary space out of any reach; it was as if she had curled up inside her own body somehow, like the infant closeted in her womb. The younger children, who did not comprehend what had happened but had sensed that this vague trouble connected to the absence of their father had deepened, cried almost constantly and would not be pacified by anything; Elizabeth held them, rocked them, prepared them for the stay at Torgeson's, without a sign of strain or irritation. Vincent did what he could to help, but there was, finally, not much he could do.

The children were left with Torgeson then, and Elizabeth agreed to move out of the social hall and into his house. She gave no sign of what she felt about this: she merely agreed, as if Torgeson had suggested something inevitable, like the coming of winter. And, as had happened with Vincent, something of the profound quiet that surrounded her made Torgeson's talk excessive and meaningless, as though it only filled the empty space. She kissed each of the children, while Torgeson went on about how much room he had and how much sense it made and how he would provide for her and the children until things were better, and then she turned to Vincent and said, "Let's go now."

In the car on the way to Point Royal, he thought he heard her whimper once or twice, but he could not be sure. Now and then she brushed the wings of her nose with a handkerchief, gazing out at the road as though it said some punishing thing to her over and over. Vincent longed to tell her to go ahead and cry; but she had so carefully gone about the business of this day, that he feared what the result of his interference might be. So he let her alone, riding at her side in a sort of speechless wonder, through shadows of low clouds that had gathered on the blue mountains and rolled down, heavy with snow.

The Point Royal Hospital was an old, red brick building, aggressively Victorian in style—gables, leaded panes, and fretwork balconies everywhere, it seemed, cupolas and spires along the rooftop. To the left of the main building was a great gouge in the earth, and two or three yellow bulldozers lay dormant, like sleeping animals, in the quickening snow. Point Royal was already dusted by a powdery inch, though the streets were merely wet, the flakes disintegrating where they fell. Vincent parked the Ford as close as he could to the building, and they walked up a wooden ramp to the ground-level door. Elizabeth put her hand on his arm as they walked, and he glanced at her, saw snow in her hair, like blown salt. She did not seem aware that he had looked at her, any more than she seemed aware that she had put her hand on his arm, or that, indeed, he was even there.

Inside there was a corridor, long and cold and damp. At the end of the corridor was a yellow door. Two bright plastic signs hung from the ceiling: one said MORGUE OF THE COUNTY OF FAIRFAX, and the other said CORONER'S OFFICE.

They walked slowly, almost warily, toward the yellow door. There were other doors on either side of them, and now one of them, just ahead, opened. A tall black man in a white coat came past them. He wore rubber-soled shoes that squeaked, and in one hand he carried a bundle of manila envelopes.

"Excuse me," Vincent said.

The man stopped, turned, smiled. "Yes?"

"We're—we've come about Mr. Bexley."

"Alphonse Bexley, Junior," Elizabeth said.

"Identification of remains?" said the man, not smiling now.

Vincent nodded.

"Through that door at the end of the hall."

"Thank you."

They walked on, the sound of their shoes echoing all around them. Vincent pushed the door open, saw a clock, a desk, a couch. There were glass doors to the right, the glass corrugated and cloudy. The room was empty, and so they sat on the couch together and waited, Elizabeth with her hands folded tightly in her swollen lap. She sniffed once, then was silent. Outside, in the corridor, voices echoed toward them, but words were indistinguishable. Presently a man entered through the yellow door and walked directly to them. He was dark, with thick brown hair that rose off his forehead in a widow's peak. Above his brown eyes brown tufts met, forming a ridge. He extended his hand to Vincent, rough flat fingers carefully manicured and faintly moist.

"I'm Mr. Walker," he said, reaching for Elizabeth's hand too now. "I assume you're Mrs. Bexley?"

"Yes," Elizabeth said.

He nodded, folded the manicured fingers, and stood as if in a reception line at a church. And, in a moment, as though the whole thing were choreographed, a man in a sea-green surgical blouse approached through the glass doors. He was round, low-shouldered, balding, the hair above his ears deeply waved, gray, wirelike.

"This is Mrs. Bexley," said Mr. Walker. Then he looked at Vincent. "And—I didn't get your name, Father."

"Monsignor Shepherd."

The balding man shook Vincent's hand. "Did you know the deceased, Father?"

"Yes."

"Have you made any arrangements?"

"He was a veteran," Elizabeth said. "A Bronze Star of Korea."

"She's made the arrangements with me," said Walker.

"There'll be some forms to fill out," the balding man said to Vincent. "Can you identify the deceased?"

"Where is my husband," Elizabeth said. There was no emotion at all in her voice.

"Ma'am," said the balding man, "we don't need you to—

you don't have to do anything here if you don't want to. I'd say that in your condition you probably shouldn't."

"I want to see my husband."

The man looked at Vincent. "Things being what they are."

"Please," Elizabeth said.

The man half shrugged, shook his head. "All right," he sighed. "Follow me."

Again there was the sound of their shoes in the corridor. The balding man led them almost to its other end, reaching into his pockets to bring out some keys on a chain. Vincent experienced an eerie moment of feeling Bexley as part of the material of the building, all the inanimate bricks and joists and lintels, the tiles and the stone under his feet. The balding man opened a door to the right, took them down another corridor to a stairwell and down. At the bottom of the stairs, through a metal door, they entered a large gray room. But then, Vincent saw, it was not so large as it was empty—metal slabs, like bunk beds, lined the left wall, and to the right there were two rows of numbered metal panels.

"Here," the balding man said.

He unlocked one panel near the back wall and pulled its ring-handle. It opened out, like an enormous file drawer, showing the shape of a body under what looked like rubber. Vincent felt his heart go, held on; it was freezing cold under his eyes. He saw gooseflesh on the balding man's arms. The room was refrigerator cold. He hadn't noticed. Then, absurdly, he remembered that he had noticed, had marked the difference as soon as he had entered; but Elizabeth's quiet calm, the knowledge of Duck Bexley's body in nearness, the emptiness, the depthless silence of the place, had taken hold of him, had purged somehow his sense of himself, as if he were no longer Vincent Shepherd, with Vincent Shepherd's eyes and ears, but an extremely slow-moving and astounded other, who only now realized the cold, who only now understood that the rubber something was zippered shut. Elizabeth's hand trembled over what would be the chest. Vincent reached out and took her hand.

The balding man opened the zipper.

An ear, hair; and Elizabeth said, "Yes."

Then the rubber was back away from the face. Elizabeth's grip on Vincent's hand tightened almost imperceptibly.

"Yes," she said again—a breathless whisper, a sigh, like a sleep sound. Her husband's face was composed, though more angular. There was a small cut above the eye, and some blue swelling around the mouth. The eyes were so emphatically shut that Vincent's eyes recoiled, traveled down the face to the neck. The balding man closed the zipper with quick, cold efficiency. Vincent could not be sure if what he had seen in the neck was a wound; it might have been a mole.

"Oh," Elizabeth said. "Oh."

In the corridor again, walking behind the balding man toward the yellow door, she began to moan. Her voice traveled along the walls and came back. Vincent had marveled at her calm, and now he marveled at the full force of her grief. The cries went out of her and became one long cry, and then she doubled over, arms under her abdomen, coughing and spitting and choking. There was nothing in her stomach to come up and so she only made a little pool of spittle on the floor. Vincent and the balding man stood on either side of her, holding her up, and then it passed, suddenly as it had come. They helped her to the room, where she lay down on the couch. The balding man took her pulse.

"Keep still," he said. "Rest awhile."

"I'm all right now," Elizabeth said.

"Rest. There's no hurry."

Mr. Walker, who had been sitting patiently on the couch when they brought Elizabeth in, stood now at Vincent's side, and spoke in his ear. Vincent breathed the odor of tobacco. "I'll go ahead and transfer the remains to Demera. I suppose you know she doesn't want prayers said over him."

"Yes," Vincent said.

"Lie still," the balding man was saying. "Lie very still. There we are."

3

That night Vincent lay in bed and thought a bird sang at his window. It was not a pleasant sound, and when he pulled himself out of the bed, faltering to the window, he seemed to discover that the sound had been inside his head. There was a humming in his ear now. He stood with the tips of his fingers on the cold glass and had a quick sensation of falling, caught himself up, reaching for the white shape of the bed. Then he waited. In one pane of the window the moon looked at him, bright as a streetlamp and bigger than he could ever have imagined it to be. He could see its pitted surface, the valleys and mountains shaped by a faint bruise. There were motes of white, blue, green; luminous clouds drifted just under it. And the bird, whatever it was, sang again. He was inexplicably angry at the bird, searched for it in a landscape of shadowless moonlight. There was nothing but field, tall grass, a lone tree far off. The social hall and the church were gone, and, seeing this, he had a moment of panic: what building was this? What window? He opened it—it went up at the touch of his hand—and floated out, falling again, arms outspread like wings.

And woke up, his heart beating in his own earlobe against the pillow. He turned in the bed, put his head under the blanket, cradling the soft cool underside of the pillow, and his breathing made a little cave of warmth. In the first tactile moments, assured that he had dreamed the bird and the window and his tumbling downward, he thought he might never move again; it was as if he had the power to make such a decision; he felt young, relieved, free. And then, a little too suddenly, he was driven lightward, unable to breathe. The window was bright, so he got out of bed and walked into the hallway, where he came face to face with Elizabeth. He knew she was supposed to be at Torgeson's, but he said nothing about this. He watched her smile, and then she said she knew he had done the best thing. He answered her—a formless string of words that seemed to make a sort of ultimate sense—and then apologized for having slept so late.

"Did you kill Duck?" she asked.

"Yes," he answered.

"He's dead?" she asked.

"Yes," he said.

"Will you love me like you loved Janet Miller?"

"Janet Miller?"

She leaned down, and brought up a baby.

And he woke again.

His heart was beating so fast, he was afraid to move. Then he did move, almost without having decided to. He knelt by the bed, his hands knotted over the rumpled sheet. He stayed like that for perhaps ten minutes, shivering a little and feeling his mind block off what he had dreamed.

"Lord," he said at last, "I throw myself at your feet."

The words, as usual, went off into a space, as if a stranger had spoken them and a stranger had heard them. He got up, his bones protesting like dry wood, and went to the window and opened it, standing in that icy space, breathing deeply and slowly. The sky was thick, white, snowing. It seemed to have broken up, the pieces tumbling down in a dead quiet.

Duck Bexley's body was now at the funeral home, Walker & Edison, in Demera, and today the children would see their father for the last time. Elizabeth had arranged to have the body taken by train to Treetop, so her husband could lie next to Alphonse Bexley. And she would, in spite of her condition, travel with it, and see it put into the ground. And then no one, least of all Vincent, knew what would happen. Torgeson, last night, had said he supposed Elizabeth would stay in Demera until the baby was born. At any rate Vincent could see easily enough that this was what Torgeson hoped would happen.

Now, as the snow brushed the sill of the window, Vincent saw a car come into the lot below. It was a white car, but its underside was dirty, and by contrast the snow beneath it seemed white as the idea of white, the principle of whiteness.

He closed the window and threw a robe on and went down to let them in.

They had outside air all over them, a dust of snow on their hats and shoulders. They talked about how it was really coming down out there, brushing themselves with their gloved hands. They were very polite, introduced themselves— Bedsole and Moore, State Police—and apologized for the hour and the nature of their visit.

"What is the nature of your visit?" Vincent asked.

"Well," said Bedsole, smiling, "it's unannounced, for one thing."

Vincent put some water on for tea, and then went upstairs, shaved, and dressed. When he returned, they had already poured the tea, and sat comfortably in the living room in identical cross-legged poses, one on the couch, the other in Vincent's chair. Moore spoke for a moment about being Catholic, as if some honor accrued to him from Vincent on that account. He had bright red hair and a way of smacking his lips as he spoke; he seemed supremely satisfied with the sensation of speech, or with the fact that he had lips. He had an oval face, a soft chin, large brown freckles at his hairline, which was receding. Vincent paid attention to every detail of his face.

"You look a little pale, Father," he said, while Vincent watched the lips.

"I'm upset—a little upset. I had a bad night."

Bedsole, who was short, muscular, dark, his clothes about to burst with him, had the carriage and mannerisms of an athlete, but his voice was almost female as he spoke: "Must get lonesome here."

"Yes," Vincent said. "Quite so now, anyway." Something like relief sailed back to him from the sound of what he had heard himself say; it was gone before he could grasp it.

Bedsole said, "Now, Father, about this Bexley thing."

"Yes."

"Mrs. Trevinos's son is claiming that she was robbed as well as murdered. He claims she kept a lot of money around the house and on her person."

"I wouldn't know," said Vincent. "I'd heard that, of course."

"From who?"

"A number of people."

"Bexley?"

"I don't recall."

"You know they found very little money on him," Moore said.

"Yes."

"The old lady's son thinks Bexley might've hid the money."

"I just—" Vincent began.

"How well do you know the Bexleys, Father?"

"I don't know," Vincent said. "I haven't known them long."

"How long," said Bedsole.

"Since October."

"All right. Let me ask you this: Do you think, from what you *do* know about them, that they'd—that her and the children—that she might be the type of woman who would keep stolen money, say, that maybe her husband might've given to her after he killed Mrs. Trevinos?"

"You can't be serious," Vincent said.

"The son—Mrs. Trevinos's boy, Father, he wants to have her—Mrs. Bexley—"

"He wants us to question her," Moore said.

"That's right," said Bedsole. "You see, there was something a little strange about the way Bexley died."

"How so," Vincent asked.

"Well," said Moore, "he'd been in this fight—you knew about that?"

"Yes."

"Well, the police got there and he'd had this guy down on the floor and was holding a broken bottle down close to his neck. But he hadn't touched him with it yet. He was just holding it an inch or so away from the guy's neck. And the police put a gun on him, you know, and it looked like everything would be all right—just a couple of guys bumped up in a bar on a Saturday night. Except that Bexley started cutting on the man right there under the gun. And so then, of course, they shot him. But the funny thing was, the whole thing seemed staged. Bexley came in from the street, picked the fight, and then just sort of managed the whole thing."

"Like a suicide or something," said Bedsole.

"It's just"—Moore went on—"it's just something isn't right—I mean it doesn't fit, you know?"

"I'm sorry," said Vincent. "You're going to have to explain what you mean."

"It's like he led everybody away from here."

"We think he could've either hid the money," Bedsole said, "or given it to her. He had time to do that, see."

"We know how delicate the situation is with her now, Father. But we have to look into it."

"The old lady's son is sort of forcing the issue," said Bedsole.

"It's absurd," Vincent said, standing. "Why would he want to kill himself if he'd had her money."

"The whole thing's odd, see. So we can't really figure he was thinking very logically. We have to look into every possibility."

"Well, it's not possible that Elizabeth Bexley has any of it. I mean that's just the most ridiculous idea I ever heard."

"Father," Moore said, "did you ever have a conversation with Bexley about the old woman? Specifically about her money?"

"No," Vincent said quickly. He sat down again. He had remembered, as he spoke, the way Bexley had talked at Thanksgiving dinner.

"Are you keeping something back?" Bedsole asked.

"Mr. Moore, could you ask the questions, please?"

Moore's face was deadpan. "Answer Mr. Bedsole's question, Father."

"All right. No, I am not holding anything back."

"We're asking you because we're hoping we're not going to have to ask her."

"Well," Moore said, reaching into his pocket, "we have a search warrant—for the hall. Everything's still over there, right?"

"You've been to Torgeson's?" Vincent asked.

"We've talked to him. Of course. She didn't have any inkling of what we were doing, I assure you. We're not heavies, Father. We wouldn't do anything to hurt her needlessly."

"So you talked to Torgeson—"

"Bexley worked for him, Father."

"And now you've come to search my social hall."

"That's right."

"You hit it right on the head," said Bedsole.

"And you think you'll find money."

"We don't know what we'll find. We probably won't find anything. It's just something we have to do."

"You don't even know for sure that Duck Bexley killed the old woman."

"Well then, nothing figures, does it?"

"No," Vincent said. "Nothing figures."

"Why does this—why are you taking this so personally?"

"I don't know. Enough is enough—they have been through enough. To have what few things they have searched. It is excessive."

"We don't like it," Moore said, "any more than you do."

In the hall, near the end of what seemed a clumsy search, they found Vincent's chalice. Bedsole brought it out of the pillowcase, held it up to the light. It had been polished and polished. Inside, rolled tightly and tied in a rubber band, were a lot of pieces of notepaper with drawings covering every space. Horses straining to leap off the page, drawn with the predictably heavy pencil-point.

"My chalice," Vincent said with surprise.

"You didn't know it was here?" Bedsole asked.

Vincent was silent. He had an abrupt sense of himself as a defender of the debris. Both men were looking at him, and he looked back as calmly as he could. Moore took the chalice from Bedsole and held it out to him.

"Worth a lot of money, isn't it, Father?"

"Looks to me like silver," Bedsole said.

"It is," said Vincent.

"You didn't know it was here."

"No, I didn't."

"Had you missed it?" Moore asked. Bedsole had turned, and was lifting the stand-up lamp to look under its base.

"I thought they'd taken it with them to Torgeson's," Vincent said. "It was a gift. I gave it to the boy, Harvey. The one who can't talk."

"Can't talk."

"Yes," Vincent said, more confident, "the oldest one. He can make sounds but he can't talk."

"The kid's an artist," Bedsole said. He had found another packet of drawings. "Funny how he hides them."

"He's very sensitive about it," said Vincent.

"Guess so."

"Elizabeth—the Bexleys were very careful of him. Elizabeth, where the art is concerned, and Duck, where his inability to speak is concerned. I think Duck had even learned to be proud of him, though you could see how painful it was for him. And of course Harvey—well, this has all been hardest on him in some ways. He and his father were very close. Really very close."

Moore smiled. "Thought you didn't know these people very well, Father."

Vincent heard himself say, "I love them. I love them all."

"I can see you do."

"All of them," Vincent repeated, consciously this time. "I loved them all."

But the two men had completed their search. They seemed to have lost interest quite suddenly, as if some tiny alarm had gone off in their heads.

"Well, unless he buried it, I guess he didn't have it," Bedsole said.

Moore took Vincent's hand. He still held the chalice. "I'm sorry we had to do this, Father." He gave Vincent the chalice.

"Coming with us?" Bedsole asked.

"No," Vincent said. "Unless you have other questions."

"We're satisfied. Of course we'll have to watch what she does for a while, just as a matter of course—as long as this kid insists that his mother was robbed. I'll tell you, I think Bexley might've tried to rob her, and maybe killed her when he couldn't get anything."

"I don't think he killed her," Vincent said.

"We'll probably never know, Father."

"You're staying here?" Bedsole asked. He was at the door, and Moore had walked over to join him.

"I want to pray a little," said Vincent.

"Sure," Moore said. "Well—sorry again."

Vincent watched the door close on them. Then, in the quiet, he held the chalice against his chest, looking at the unmade beds, the piled clothes, the odd pieces of paper, the scattered toys, and the boxes of unused dishes. He stood there for a long time, gazing at these things, as if he must commit them all to memory. Then he put the chalice down among the childish debris of Harvey's cedar box, and made the lonely trek back to the hall.

4

All of Virginia was buried under the snow. People were sealed off in their little islands of light and warmth: cars and fences were buried, trees drooped and cracked; wires flew in the wind, great clouds of snow swirling everywhere like a manifestation of the flight of electrons in air. It had snowed all day and all night, steadily, relentlessly, and Vincent spent most of that time in his room, prey to his solitude and his foul dream of the night before. Hour upon hour he spent at the window, watching the steady fall; or stared at the telephone, which would not ring now, was dead now under the weight of the storm. Sometime after midnight the lights went out, and he managed to sleep a little, but by early morning he had come down to sit at the kitchen table, hands folded in his lap, trying to work up enough energy to make himself some tea. Torgeson arrived shortly after first light. He had walked across the field, and there was snow all over him; his face looked sunburned, healthy, flushed with some excitement he could not hold in. But it was just the cold. Torgeson stood in a pool of melting snow and said, "Twenty-seven inches—and that was around midnight. God knows what it is now."

"My power is out," said Vincent. "The phone's dead."

"Everything's shut down—the roads, everything. Worst storm I've ever seen."

Vincent offered him some tea.

"It's cold in here," Torgeson said. "Aren't you cold?"

"No."

"Well, come on, I came to get you—there's no telling how long the power will be out, and you don't want to depend on a gas stove for warmth."

"I had a bad night."

"I can imagine. Come on, we have the fireplace and plenty of wood."

Vincent had spent the night in his clothes, and now he was confused. He stood in the middle of the kitchen, trying to think what he might need. "I was going to make some tea," he said.

"I have tea. Let's get going before it gets much worse."

Vincent put his coat on, then had to look for his shoes. He went into the living room and Torgeson followed. "I don't have any boots."

"What you have will have to do."

Presently Torgeson said, "You know I had a visit from the police yesterday."

"Yes," said Vincent, tying his shoes. "They stopped here too. Searched the social hall."

"As if she didn't have enough. Her husband laying on a slab not five miles away."

"How is she?"

"Not good. She walked around a lot last night."

"The children?"

"Harvey's taking it pretty bad."

As they were going down the snow-lump that had been the stoop, Torgeson took Vincent's arm and said, "I have to tell somebody, Father—" He stopped. They both stopped. A grainy dust of snow still dropped around them.

"I can't help thinking this whole thing's my fault." Torgeson's voice shook. "If I hadn't—"

"If you hadn't," Vincent said. "If I hadn't. If he hadn't. Nobody knew, Torgeson. Nobody knew. It just—took place."

"Every time I look at those kids."

"Just please shut up, will you."

They went out toward the field, the snow coming heavier, steadily heavier, a long slant out of the west, like a wet wall. They climbed a sweeping drift, stepped over the fence, and crossed the undulant whiteness, their feet sinking through it until it seemed to suck at their thighs—a live thing that wanted to digest them. Vincent had to stop two or three times to rest, standing with his hands on his knees, his face down at the broken surface already traversed by Torgeson, who went on ahead a few yards. The field rose gently to a crest, and through a chink in the sky along its edge, the sun shone through a solid white curtain. Vincent could not catch his breath.

"Keep moving," Torgeson called to him.

"I—I can't—"

They walked on, reached the crest. Beyond was another, smaller one. "There's a little creek at the bottom of the hill," Torgeson said.

"Oh, God."

"It's just a trickle, but you have to watch for it."

And they both saw, in that instant, a figure coming toward them from the smaller hill, running, falling, rising with snow adhering to it. Vincent saw that it was a woman.

"Marie," said Torgeson. Then he shouted. "Marie?!"

She stopped and waved frantically. She was only yards away, but they could not hear her.

"Goddamn," said Torgeson. "Something's wrong."

"Go on," Vincent said. "Go on."

"Don't trust the ice over the creek." Torgeson was struggling to run, plowing through, falling, rising again, flailing to the bottom of the hill, where he stopped, gathered himself, and leaped a small space. Marie kept waving wildly, and then she was screaming.

He sat down for a moment at the bottom of the hill, feeling his heartbeat at the back of his neck and in his temples. The snow whipped at him in gusts, and he knew he must rise. But he was so cold—his feet had been soaked in the first minutes—and with his arms up, hugging his knees, he felt some warmth around his upper body. Finally, with an effort that fairly exhausted what reserves he had left for the second hill, he stood, made the last few feet in a sliding descent to the creek, which was only a scar in the drifting snow. He took a step, thinking of the edge: *where is the edge.* He felt himself start to sink, and so he tried, too late, to leap. One foot went through the ice into burning cold, and the other came down on something hard and round. His legs slipped painfully apart, and he fell hard, hearing something crack in his knee. But there was no pain. There was a slow, downward floating, something running under him, letting him down, cracking, a brittle sound; his head broke through a thin membrane and lay in a floating of his own hair.

"Torgeson," he said, gasping. "I fell in the water."

Now there was pain in the knee. He brought himself to a sitting position, rolled in the water, dragging himself up onto the snow and lying over on his back again. He kept his head up, supporting himself on his elbows, and looked at the little dark wound in the creek where he had fallen. The water was black and fast, roiling. Farther down, white shadows in a white rush, were some pines. He thought he saw a rabbit— a parcel of smoky fur under one of the pines. The presence of the animal—and then its absence—terrified him.

"Torgeson," he shouted.

But then he didn't know if he had managed to shout. As he lay back, the pain in his knee brought something up from his throat, and he tried to spit it out. Then he saw a shadow, two shadows, shapes made out of the swirling flakes. Everything dissolved, or he had imagined it. He began to be aware of a weight on his chest.

When he opened his eyes, he saw the hurt leg held out, realized that he was moving—being half carried. He lifted his head, saw the house, a blur of angles. Torgeson labored under his left arm, held him tight around the middle; Harvey plodded along on the other side, supporting the injured leg.

"Harvey," Vincent said, "I found the chalice. You can have it. You can have the chalice." Then he could not be sure he had actually spoken.

The lines of the house became clear as they neared it. There was a door, its miniature ledges and panels daubed with triangular patches of the snow. The door opened. Marie stood there with a towel. He said, "Marie." And then he closed his eyes again.

"No change?" Torgeson said as the door closed behind them.

"No. Priscilla's with her."

"The pains?"

"About ten minutes apart."

They were moving into the living room. Vincent could feel sleep, but he opened his eyes again. His feet were already stinging.

"You try the phone again?" Torgeson asked.

"Still dead."

They lay him down on the sofa. Marie wiped his face with the towel, and then she got his coat off and put the towel around his head.

"My knee," he said.

"Make some tea," said Torgeson.

"I don't want it," Vincent said.

"Whiskey?"

"Yes, whiskey."

"Coming up," Marie said.

"I'm cold," Vincent said.

"We'll fix you up."

"My knee—I think it's broken."

"We'll look at it—just keep still."

"Never should've left the rectory."

"It would've been all right if I hadn't had to leave you there in the snow."

Vincent lay breathing for a moment. Marie brought him a glass of whiskey, and then went upstairs.

"Elizabeth's having the baby," Torgeson said. "You all right now? I've got to get back up there."

"Go," said Vincent. "Go."

"I'll send Marie down to get you some dry clothes and all the rest. Just lay still."

"Where are the children?"

"Harvey's keeping them in the kitchen, by the stove."

"I didn't see them."

"Drink the whiskey and don't move," Torgeson said.

Vincent took a large gulp, set the glass down, and in a moment he had drifted off to sleep. It was a dreamless sleep, profound and still, and then Marie was kneeling by his face, saying his name.

"Don't go to sleep," she said. "You have to get into some dry clothes, Father."

The pleasant accent, the odor of her perfume or her bath soap or her cologne or whatever it was, made him think of summer. He felt his knee. The pain had lessened a little, and so he thought he must have slept for a long time.

"How long have I been asleep?"

"Maybe two minutes."

He looked for the whiskey.

"Now," she said, "we have to look at this knee."

"It doesn't hurt as much."

She forced the pant leg up, carefully, slowly.

"Bruised pretty bad."

"Is it broken? Can you tell?"

"I can't tell, but it don't look like it."

"It doesn't hurt as much."

"Can you stand up?"

"Let me have the whiskey."

She brought the glass to his lips. "Listen, I want to apologize for what happened—for when I met you before."

Vincent sipped the whiskey. It warmed him now. He shook his head. "Don't trouble yourself with that."

"Well, that's kind of you."

"Is Elizabeth—the baby—"

"Still no change. Looks like this one might take a while."

Vincent was silent. He took another sip of the whiskey.

"Those poor kids are in there scared out of their minds, Father. What with all that's happened to them this week."

"This year."

"Sure is sad."

Presently she said, "Can you move your leg?"

Vincent tried. It hurt, but he could move it. He brought it around and sat up, let both feet touch the floor. "Have you been staying here?"

"Since they moved in."

He nodded, took the towel from around his neck.

"And—some weekends before then."

He did not respond to this. "Do they need any help up there?"

"It's pretty quiet now." She took the glass from him and gently lay it on the table next to the sofa. She wore slacks, and he could see a dark place just below the knee, as if the cloth there were dyed black. Beyond the curve of her shoulder, the faint shapes of the fish in the aquarium bumped the sides.

"I'll get you a change of clothes," she said. "Sit still."

But he could not sit still. He got up, limped into the kitchen. There he found Harvey and the twins and Sandra June, all huddled around the table.

"It'll be all right," he said. "It'll be all right."

Sandra June whimpered. The others were quite still.

"Don't be afraid," Vincent said.

5

The day passed with the occasional noise of the children; Marie fed them and, for the most part, kept them occupied. Vincent, because he was hobbled by the knee, was confined to the living room, but he managed to tend the fire, and during lunch he showed Harvey the fish in the tank, leaning against the wall with one foot resting on the other to keep the weight off his knee, and then lying on the sofa and watching the boy draw the fish.

"That looks lifelike," he said over and over. "That looks lifelike."

There was no sound from the upstairs room.

Twice Priscilla came down to fill hot-water bags, this to warm the bed her mother lay in. Torgeson did not even come down to eat. Vincent lay on the sofa and his knee ached, and he thought about the baby coming, each moment the possible one, the one that would give him the crying sound. But the hours passed and then it was dark; the children had been put to bed, and Marie sat across from him with a magazine in her lap, desultorily turning the pages, sniffing from time to time and running her hand over her nose, from the tip of her fingers to the palm, upward—a childlike motion that made him want to call her by her name.

"Marie," he said.

"Hunh?"

"Why is it so quiet up there."

"She's resting."

"Torgeson?"

"Victor's watching her—she's dilated, but nothing's happening. She's not in any real pain yet."

"Have you ever had a child?" he asked.

"Lord, no."

"Do you want to have children?"

"I don't know—maybe."

"Are you and—Victor—"

"Oh," she said, making that motion to wipe her nose, the tip of the finger to the palm, "we're just—friends. Good friends."

In a moment she said, "Go to sleep, Father. I'll tend the fire."

He wanted to ask what time it was but then, lying back, the ache in his knee letting up just enough, he began to get sleepy. He closed his eyes and listened to the crackling of the fire, and to the pages of the magazine as she turned them.

"You're a very nice girl," he said, and she thanked him.

It was now past one o'clock in the morning. Torgeson had come downstairs and waked Vincent, and had helped him into the kitchen, where he poured whiskey for them both. The electricity had been restored, so they had light and heat. The house was quiet. Elizabeth's contractions had let up enough for her to sleep; she was resting comfortably, as Torgeson put it. The children, save Priscilla, who slept in a chair by her mother's bed in the guest room, were all in his bed, under piles of blankets and a thick quilt his wife had left behind. Marie lay by the dying fire, and Torgeson would join her there. Vincent would have the sofa. If the electricity held out, everything would be all right.

"Why is it taking her so long to have the baby?" Vincent asked.

"Just is," said Torgeson.

They sat at the table. Torgeson's barren kitchen, with its paler places on the walls where utensils and pictures had hung, and its slightly gritty floor, off-white linoleum stained by wet boots and spilled food. The pantry door was blocked by a wrought-iron aquarium stand, and beyond this, on what looked like a washing machine barrel, was the empty aquarium itself, the sides thinly coated with algae. It was a large room, with a high ceiling and a single, bright light in a dish-like fixture. They drank the whiskey neat, sipping politely.

"Last night," Vincent said, "was one of the longest nights of my life."

"Seems strange to hear you say that," said Torgeson. Then, with what might have been a touch of irony, he said, "Father."

"Don't call me that."

"What should I call you?"

"Call me Vincent, why don't you. It's my name."

"Your given name?"

"Yes."

"All right. Vincent."

They drank. Vincent had felt light-headed with the first drink, though he had drunk, without any noticeable effect, most of the glass he had been given when he had first come. Now he was a little woozy, but he thought this must partly be from just having awakened.

"Why did you wake me up?" he asked.

"I didn't feel like talking to Marie."

"Why?"

"Just didn't. She can be a strain to talk to sometimes."

"She's a very nice girl."

"Vincent, she's anything but a very nice girl."

"Shhh." Vincent put his index finger over his mouth. "She'll hear you."

"She's asleep."

"I don't understand you," Vincent said. Then he said, "How old is she?"

"She's twenty-five," said Torgeson, drinking. He swallowed. "Or she'll be twenty-five."

"Where did you meet her?"

"Used to work with her—before I made my money."

Another moment passed.

"I'm getting drunk," Torgeson said, pouring himself another drink. "Never took much for me."

"She's so young."

"Who?"

"Marie. She's just a child."

"Don't let her fool you—she knows more than either of us. She's a University of the South graduate in English."

"What's she doing here?"

"Shit," said Torgeson. He drained his glass, poured some more. Vincent did the same.

"I don't mean that about you, Torgeson."

"Look, ever since I've known you, you've been calling me that. The name is *Victor* Torgeson. Victor. And if you really want to know why Marie is here, it's because I've got the money to keep her. She likes to live good."

Vincent drained his glass.

"You want more?" Torgeson asked.

"No."

They were quiet again. Torgeson drank, gulping now.

"You better not get drunk," Vincent said. "She might have that baby tonight."

"I'm already drunk."

After a moment Vincent said, "Torgeson—Victor—I'm thinking of leaving the priesthood."

Torgeson merely looked at him.

"You hear?"

"Yes."

"What do you think?"

"I don't know. What am I supposed to think?"

"Am I embarrassing you?"

"Look, Father—"

"Don't call me Father."

"Vincent—" Torgeson took a long drink, but tightened the cap on the bottle this time. "Vinnie," he said smiling, "I always had the damnedest and most extreme sexual appetite."

"Is that so."

"It drove my wife away."

Vincent took the last of his drink.

"Whores have always been a regular thing, Vinnie."

"Vincent."

"Yeah. Vincent."

Presently Torgeson said, "You know, Vinnie, I always thought you were a little stuffy."

"I probably was, Torgeson."

"Victor."

"Victor."

"Where did you grow up, Vincent?"

"Right around here—Point Royal."

"I grew up in Richmond."

"Never been there."

"Chasden River area."

Vincent said, "Never heard of it."

"Near Petersburg, actually."

"You have any brothers or sisters?" Vincent asked.

"Not one."

"Me either. I had a brother, but he died as an infant. I never knew him."

"Were your parents religious people?"

"Not especially—my mother was, I guess."

"My parents were strict Lutherans."

Vincent did not answer.

"My wife was strict Catholic."

"Yes, you told me."

"You want to know why I kicked the Bexleys out of the other house?" Torgeson asked. The question surprised Vincent, who could only look at the other man and wait. "I needed a place for Marie to stay. I wanted her handy, but I didn't want to live with her."

Vincent was silent.

Torgeson whispered, "I got them to clean the place up, and I was looking for a way out—a way to get them out. And you know, it all just—well you know it all just happened. Bexley didn't look like the type to stay very long."

Vincent tried to think of one word.

"Then I got to feeling guilty." Torgeson laughed, almost crazily. "Imagine what I'm feeling *now*."

"Don't say any more," Vincent said. "Just—keep quiet."

"Never had any idea it would end up—"

"Just please," Vincent said, "shut up."

"Don't get righteous on me, Father—you did nothing but try to get rid of them from the first minute you saw them."

They sat staring at each other. Then Vincent got up, holding on to the table and the back of his chair. The knee throbbed.

"Look," Torgeson said. "Wait."

Vincent paused. The other man was standing too now, and he held the back of *his* chair.

"Look, I'm sorry—you can't imagine how sorry I am."

"You're a most dangerous man," said Vincent. "You play with people's lives."

"I told you, I didn't know any of this would happen."

"You played with my life and you played with their lives—and her life . . . that—that girl in there."

Torgeson was quiet.

"Good night," Vincent said.

"I've tried to make up for it," Torgeson said.

"I'm tired," said Vincent. "I don't want to talk about it anymore." He tried to move to the door, but the knee buckled. Torgeson stepped quickly to his side and held him up.

"Thank you," Vincent said.

Because they had been drinking, the walk into the living room was clumsy, their weight tottering, their bodies bumping with each step. Vincent lay down on the sofa again, while Torgeson stoked the fire. They did not speak again.

6

Just before dawn Priscilla came down to wake Torgeson. Vincent saw her shape in the low embers of the fire.

"Priscilla?" he said.

The shape moved. "It won't come," Priscilla said. Then Torgeson was sitting up, moaning.

"It's hurting her," said Priscilla.

"Jesus," Torgeson said. "I'm sorry." He stood, running both hands through his hair. "Did you have a hard time waking me?"

"It won't come and she's hurting."

"Let me help," Vincent said.

"No," Torgeson said. "Marie can help."

Priscilla had left them, was climbing the stairs. Torgeson had knelt to wake Marie, who gasped, startled.

"Torgeson, I don't want to lay here and listen anymore," Vincent said.

"Mr. Torgeson," Priscilla called from the room.

"There must be something I can do," Vincent said, and tried to stand. The knee was stiff and he fell back. Marie took his wrist, but he gently removed her hand.

"I'm all right."

The second time, though it hurt, the knee held, supported him, and he went slowly to the stairs, Torgeson and the girl having gone ahead of him. When he reached the stairs, he had the rail to hold on to, and he made his way upward, hearing them in the hall, and hearing, too, the low, guttural murmuring he knew was Elizabeth. He got to the top, looked down the hall opposite the loft, saw the door ajar, a long stripe of white light. Again he heard the sound. Then he heard Marie's voice. He made his way to the door, pushed it, the lightest, most tentative touch, and stood leaning on the jamb. It was a small room: two chests of drawers, a desk and chair, a lamp on the near wall. And the bed, Marie and Priscilla on one side, Priscilla patting her mother's forehead with a damp cloth, while Marie stood by, looking at her watch. Elizabeth lay on her side, facing them, and Torgeson knelt behind her on the bed, bending her hips, or massaging them. It was not right. Vincent thought about how it wasn't right. None of it: the odor of the room, the sweat on their faces, the grotesqueness of their ministerings to the grotesque figure in the bed; it was like a death; it was like so many death rooms he had seen. Torgeson now stepped back, one foot down on the floor with the toes under the falling bedspread, his hands down, hair dangling; as he pulled back and stood up, Elizabeth rolled over, a sudden, too agile motion, and began to massage, with her fingertips, the frightening bulge of her body, staring wildly at the ceiling as if there were a face in the light fixture. Her lips were white as the sheets, and they came apart suddenly, letting out a sound so thin, it seemed to reach the priest like an air current; it registered on his cheek-bones rather than his ears. Torgeson had the sheets back, the thin legs wide, and Vincent saw the red middle, opening, the center and the round head, bloody as a wound. "Dammit," Torgeson said. "Let go—come on." He was holding his hands out to the place, Elizabeth bridging, back-lifting in the bed, and then sighing, a long "Ah."

"It's close now," said Torgeson. "Close."

Vincent looked away, felt himself wrenching his eyes away, saw a cut smaller than a printed letter in the lampshade; everything was registering on him, everything hooking up like wires. It was wrong, he thought. Something was terribly wrong, and now Elizabeth would die too.

"Okay, now," Torgeson said. "Push—like you're going to the bathroom—push. Push."

Vincent made his way to the bed, to the other side of Marie and Priscilla, who held Elizabeth up a little, their arms down under her; he had just leaned down to help lift, his hand touching the hard, flexed shoulder, when the whole thing collapsed, Elizabeth falling back, Marie and Priscilla patting and massaging, Torgeson kneeling there, saying, "Push it next time, push it out." He was sponging blood with part of the sheet. "You got to get it out this time or it—" He didn't go on. Elizabeth gasped and breathed, and then she began to build up a scream. Vincent put wet hands in under her shoulders, helped lift her, and again Torgeson was shouting, "Push it, push it now. Push!" And there was a shuddering, sudden spasm at the end of the moment, as if the room had shaken, Elizabeth's arms dropping, a prodigious sigh tumbling out of her, and Torgeson let fall on her bare, veined belly a violet doll, testicled and profoundly crooked and still—bright blood striping it. As Vincent staggered out of the room, he saw Torgeson put one long finger into the tiny slack mouth, the rubbery flesh of the cheeks trembling. He stood at the door again, leaning out into the hall, which tilted, changed shape.

"Come on," he heard Torgeson say. "Come on you little—breathe, damn you!"

He made it to the stairs and down, through that hallway, hands on the wall, to the kitchen and the whiskey. He took a long gulp from the bottle, and then carried it into the living room, where he took another gulp, set it down, and made his way to the front door. It was full light now, the sun blinding low across the drifted snow, leaving little hulls of shadow in the footprints of some animal that had crossed the field and come to stand near the house, as if to keep watch, and apparently wandered off in much the same direction from which it had come. There was a dropping sound, and he realized that here, in the lee of the porch out of the wind, it was warm; the sun had already begun to melt the little ledges of snow along the drainspout, the clearest water, water ignited by sunlight, dropping at his feet. He lost himself in the sound of it, and then he was touched, lightly, in the middle of his back.

It was Harvey.

"Harvey," he said.

The mute boy cried into his chest. Vincent held him for a while, then walked him into the living room to look at the fish. The fish darted and swam as always, though one, in the back corner, lay over on its side just below the waterline. The water was green and unhealthy-looking. Harvey pointed half-heartedly to the one fish.

"Yes," Vincent said. "That one isn't moving, is he?"

The boy seemed unsatisfied.

Vincent rolled his sleeve up and reached into the water. "Let's see," he said, prodding the fish, knocking it downward and waiting for it to float back up to his fingers. "If it's alive—let's see. If it's alive, and I irritate it enough, it'll move." He prodded the fish once more and it fluttered away, only to lie still at the bottom. He had been hearing a soft murmur he knew now was Elizabeth, and now he heard the thin small first infant cry.

"I'm going to take care of you, boy," Vincent said. "I swear to God."

Harvey was looking back at the stairs.

"I'm going to take care of you all."

Behind him—a shouting, a noise, a confusion of nearly singing voices—the other children were coming down.

VOICES OF THE SOUTH

Hamilton Basso
  The View from Pompey's Head
Richard Bausch
  Real Presence
  Take Me Back
Doris Betts
  The Astronomer and Other Stories
  The Gentle Insurrection
Sheila Bosworth
  Almost Innocent
  Slow Poison
David Bottoms
  Easter Weekend
Erskine Caldwell
  Poor Fool
Fred Chappell
  The Gaudy Place
  The Inkling
  It Is Time, Lord
Kelly Cherry
  Augusta Played
Vicki Covington
  Bird of Paradise
Ellen Douglas
  A Family's Affairs
  A Lifetime Burning
  The Rock Cried Out
Percival Everett
  Suder
Peter Feibleman
  The Daughters of Necessity
  A Place Without Twilight
George Garrett
  Do, Lord, Remember Me
  An Evening Performance
Marianne Gingher
  Bobby Rex's Greatest Hit
Shirley Ann Grau
  The House on Coliseum Street
  The Keepers of the House
Barry Hannah
  The Tennis Handsome

Donald Hays
  The Dixie Association
William Humphrey
  Home from the Hill
  The Ordways
Mac Hyman
  No Time For Sergeants
Madison Jones
  A Cry of Absence
Nancy Lemann
  Lives of the Saints
  Sportman's Paradise
Willie Morris
  The Last of the Southern Girls
Louis D. Rubin, Jr.
  The Golden Weather
Evelyn Scott
  The Wave
Lee Smith
  The Last Day the Dogbushes Bloomed
Elizabeth Spencer
  The Salt Line
  The Voice at the Back Door
Max Steele
  Debby
Walter Sullivan
  The Long, Long Love
Allen Tate
  The Fathers
Peter Taylor
  The Widows of Thornton
Robert Penn Warren
  Band of Angels
  Brother to Dragons
  World Enough and Time
Walter White
  Flight
Joan Williams
  The Morning and the Evening
  The Wintering
Thomas Wolfe
  The Web and the Rock